A TAN
AND
SANDY
SILENCE

BY JOHN D. MACDONALD

The Brass Cupcake
Murder for the Bride
Judge Me Not
Wine for the Dreamers
Ballroom of the Skies
The Damned
Dead Low Tide
The Neon Jungle
Cancel All Our Vows
All These Condemned
Area of Suspicion
Contrary Pleasure
A Bullet for Cinderella
Cry Hard, Cry Fast
You Live Once
April Evil
Border Town Girl
Murder in the Wind
Death Trap
The Price of Murder
The Empty Trap
A Man of Affairs
The Deceivers
Clemmie
Cape Fear (The Executioners)
Soft Touch
Deadly Welcome

Please Write for Details
The Crossroads
The Beach Girls
Slam the Big Door
The End of the Night
The Only Girl in the Game
Where Is Janice Gantry?
One Monday We Killed Them All
A Key to the Suite
A Flash of Green
The Girl, the Gold Watch
   & Everything
On the Run
The Drowner
The House Guest
End of the Tiger and Other Stories
The Last One Left
S*E*V*E*N
Condominium
Other Times, Other Worlds
Nothing Can Go Wrong
The Good Old Stuff
One More Sunday
More Good Old Stuff
Barrier Island
A Friendship: The Letters of Dan Rowan
   and John D. MacDonald, 1967-1974

THE TRAVIS MCGEE SERIES

The Deep Blue Good-by
Nightmare in Pink
A Purple Place for Dying
The Quick Red Fox
A Deadly Shade of Gold
Bright Orange for the Shroud
Darker Than Amber
One Fearful Yellow Eye
Pale Gray for Guilt
The Girl in the Plain
   Brown Wrapper
Dress Her in Indigo

The Long Lavender Look
A Tan and Sandy Silence
The Scarlet Ruse
The Turquoise Lament
The Dreadful Lemon Sky
The Empty Copper Sea
The Green Ripper
Free Fall in Crimson
Cinnamon Skin
The Lonely Silver Rain

The Official Travis McGee Quizbook

"It will be for his crisply written, smoothly plotted mysteries that MacDonald will be remembered." —*USA Today*

"MacDonald had the marvelous ability to create attention-getting characters who doubled as social critics. In MacDonald novels, it is the rule rather than the exception to find, in the midst of violence and mayhem, a sentence, a paragraph, or several pages of rumination on love, morality, religion, architecture, politics, business, the general state of the world or of Florida."

—*Sarasota Herald-Tribune*

Praise for the Travis McGee series

"There's only one thing as good as reading a John D. MacDonald novel: reading it again. MacDonald was a writer way ahead of his time, and his Travis McGee books are as entertaining, insightful, and suspenseful today as the moment I first read them. He is the all-time master of the American mystery novel." —JOHN SAUL

"One of the great sagas in American fiction."

—ROBERT B. PARKER

"In McGee mysteries and other novels as well, MacDonald's voice was one of a social historian." —*Los Angeles Times*

A TAN AND SANDY SILENCE

A *Travis McGee* NOVEL

John D. MacDonald

RANDOM HOUSE TRADE PAPERBACKS

NEW YORK

2013 Random House Trade Paperback Edition

Copyright © 1971 by John D. MacDonald Publishing, Inc.
Copyright renewed 2000 by Maynard MacDonald
Introduction copyright © 2013 by Lee Child
Excerpt from *The Scarlet Ruse* by John D. MacDonald copyright © 1973 by
John D. MacDonald Publishing, Inc. and copyright renewed 2001 by
Maynard MacDonald

Published in the United States by Random House Trade Paperbacks, an imprint of
The Random House Publishing Group, a division of Random House, Inc., New York.

RANDOM HOUSE TRADE PAPERBACKS and colophon are trademarks of
Random House, Inc.

Originally published in mass market in the United States by Fawcett,
a division of Random House, Inc., New York, in 1972.

The lines from "A Year's Changes" by Jim Harrison, which appeared in the collection
titled *Locations,* published by W. W. Norton & Company, are reprinted courtesy of the
author. Copyright 1968 by Jim Harrison.

ISBN 978-0-8129-8403-3
eBook ISBN 978-0-307-82674-9

Printed in the United States of America

www.atrandom.com

Book design by Christopher M. Zucker

Introduction

Lee Child

SUSPENSE FICTION trades on surprising and unexpected twists. Like this one: A boy named John Dann MacDonald was born in 1916 in Sharon, Pennsylvania, into the kind of quiet and comfortable middle-class prosperity that became common in America forty or fifty years later but which was still relatively rare early in the century. Sharon was a satellite town near Pittsburgh, dominated by precision metalworking, and John's father was a mild-mannered and upstanding citizen with secure and prestigious salaried employment as a senior financial executive with a local manufacturer. Young John was called Jack as a child, and wore sailor suits, and grew up in a substantial suburban house on a tree-lined block. He read books, played with his dog, and teased his little sister and his cousin. When he was eighteen, his father funded a long European grand tour for him, advising him by letter "to make the best of it . . . to eat and function regularly . . . to be sure and attend a religious service at least once on each Sunday . . . to keep a record of your expenditures as a training for your college days."

Safely returned, young Jack went on to two decent East Coast schools, and married a fellow student, and went to Harvard for an MBA, and volunteered for the army in 1940, and finished World War II as a lieutenant colonel, after thoroughly satisfactory service as a serious, earnest, bespectacled, rear-echelon staff officer.

So what does such a fellow do next? Does he join General Motors? IBM? Work for the Pentagon?

In John D. MacDonald's case, he becomes an impoverished writer of pulp fiction.

During his first four postwar months, he lost twenty pounds by sitting at a table and hammering out 800,000 unsold words. Then in his fifth month he sold a story for twenty-five bucks. Then another for forty bucks, and eventually more than five hundred. Sometimes entire issues of pulp magazines were all his own work, disguised under dozens of different pen names. Then in 1950 he watched the contemporary boom in paperback novels and jumped in with his first full-length work, which was followed by sixty-six more, including some really seminal crime fiction and one of history's greatest suspense series.

Why? Why did a middle-class Harvard MBA with extensive corporate connections and a gold-plated recommendation from the army turn his back on everything apparently predestined, to sit at a battered table and type, with an anxious wife at his side? No one knows. He never explained. It's a mystery.

But we can speculate. Perhaps he never wanted a quiet

and comfortable middle-class life. Perhaps, after finding himself amid the chaos of war, he felt able to liberate himself from the crushing filial expectations he had previously followed so obediently. As an eighteen-year-old, it's hard to say no to the father who just paid for a trip to Europe. Eleven years later, as a lieutenant colonel, it's easier.

And we know from what he wrote that he felt he had something to say to the world. His early stuff was whatever put food on that battered table—detective stories, westerns, adventure stories, sports stories, and even some science fiction—but soon enough his long-form fiction began to develop some enduring and intertwined themes. From *A Deadly Shade of Gold,* a Travis McGee title: "The only thing in the world worth a damn is the strange, touching, pathetic, awesome nobility of the individual human spirit." From the stand-alone thriller *Where Is Janice Gantry?:* "Somebody has to be tireless, or the fast-buck operators would asphalt the entire coast, fill every bay, and slay every living thing incapable of carrying a wallet."

These two angles show up everywhere in his novels: the need to—maybe reluctantly, possibly even grumpily—stand up and be counted on behalf of the weak, helpless, and downtrodden, which included people, animals, and what we now call *the environment*—which was in itself a very early and very prescient concern: *Janice Gantry,* for instance, predated Rachel Carson's groundbreaking *Silent Spring* by a whole year.

But the good knight's armor was always tarnished and rusted. The fight was never easy and, one feels, never actually winnable. But it had to be waged. This strange, weary blend of nobility and cynicism is MacDonald's signature emotion. Where did it come from? Not, presumably, the leafy block where he was raised in quiet and comfort. The war must have changed him, like it changed a generation and the world.

Probably the best of his nonseries novels is *The Executioners,* which became *Cape Fear* as a movie (twice). It's an acute psychological study of base instinct, terror, mistakes, and raw emotion. It's about a man—possibly a man like MacDonald's father, or like MacDonald himself—who moves out of his quiet and comfort into more primeval terrain. And those twin poles are the theme of the sensationally good Travis McGee series, which is a canon equaled for enduring quality and maturity by very little else. McGee is a quiet man, internally bewildered by and raging at what passes for modern progress, externally happy merely to be varnishing the decks of his houseboat and polishing its brass, but always ready to saddle up and ride off in the service of those who need and deserve his help. Again, not the product of the privileged youth enjoyed by the salaried executive's son.

So where did McGee and MacDonald's other heroes come from? Why Florida? Why the jaundiced concerns? We will never know. But maybe we can work it out, by mining the millions of words written with such haste and urgency and passion between 1945 and 1986.

LEE CHILD
New York
2012

In northern Manitoba
a man saw a great bald eagle—
hanging from its neck,
teeth locked in skin and feathers,
the bleached skull of a weasel.

BY JIM HARRISON
(From "A Year's Changes")

A TAN AND SANDY SILENCE

One

ON THE MOST BEAUTIFUL DAY any April could be asked to come up with, I was kneeling in eight inches of oily water in the cramped bilge of Meyer's squatty little cabin cruiser, the *John Maynard Keynes,* taking his automatic bilge pump apart for the third time in an hour.

The socket wrench slipped, and I skinned yet another knuckle. Meyer stood blocking out a sizable piece of the deep blue sky. He stared down into the bilge and said, "Very inventive and very fluent. Nice mental images, Travis. Imagine one frail little bilge pump performing such an extraordinary act upon itself! But you began to repeat yourself toward the end."

"Would you like to crawl down in here and—"

He backed up a hasty half step. "I couldn't deprive you of the pleasure. You said you could fix it. Go ahead."

I got it apart again. I spun the little impeller blade and

suddenly realized that maybe it turned too freely. Found the set screw would take a full turn. Tightened it back down onto the shaft. Reassembled the crummy little monster, bolted it down underwater, heaved myself up out of the water, sat on the edge of the hatch, and had Meyer flip the switch. It started to make a nice steady wheeeeeeng, gouting dirty bilge water into the Bahia Mar yacht basin.

Meyer started to applaud, and I told him to save it until we found out if the adorable thing would turn itself the hell off like it says in the fine print. It took a good ten minutes to pump the water out. Then it went weeeeeeng-guggle-chud. Silence.

"Now cheer," I said.

"Hooray," he said mildly. "Thank you very much and hooray." I looked at him with exasperation and affection. My mild and bulky friend with the wise little blue eyes, bright and bemused, and with the bear hair, thatch black, curling out of the throat of his blue knit shirt.

"Another half inch of rain last night," I told him, "and you could have gone down like a stone."

He had stepped out of his bunk in the dark after the rain stopped and into ankle deep water. He had sloshed over to my houseboat, the *Busted Flush,* and told me he had a small problem. At three in the morning we had toted my auxiliary pump over and set it on the dock and dropped the intake hose into his bilge. His home and refuge was very low in the water, the mooring lines taut enough to hum when plucked. By first light the *Keynes* was floating high again, and we could turn the pump off and carry it back. Now the repaired automatic bilge pump had taken out the last of the water, but he was going to live in dampness for quite a while.

"Perils of the sea," he said.

I stepped up onto the dock and squatted and began to rinse the grease and bilge water off my hands under the hose faucet. Meyer shaded his eyes and looked toward the *Flush*. "You've got a visitor, Travis. Isn't that what's-his-name?"

I stood up and stared. "It sure is. Good old what's-his-name. Harry Broll. Do you think that son of a bitch has come to try me again?"

"After the showing last time . . . Was it two years ago?"

"At least."

"I think he's at least bright enough not to try again."

"Not the same way. But he did catch me with one very nice left. True, he broke his hand, but it was one to remember."

"Want company?"

"No thanks."

Harry turned and saw me when I was about fifty feet away. He was big, and he had gotten bigger since I'd seen him last. More gut and more jowls. Not becoming. He wore a pale beige suit, a yellow shirt, and he had a chocolate-colored neckerchief with an ornate, gold slip ring.

He raised his hands in the most primitive gesture of reassurance. Palms out. Sickly smile to go with it. As I came up to him he said, "Hi, McGee." He put his hand out. I looked at it until he pulled it back. He tried to laugh. "Jesus, are you still sore?"

"I'm not sore, Harry. Why should we shake hands?"

"Look. I want to talk to you. Are you busy or anything?"

"What about?"

"About Mary. I know you've got no reason in the world to do me any favors. But this concerns . . . Mary's well-being."

"Is something wrong with her?"

"I don't know. I don't really know."

I studied him. He seemed concerned and upset. He had the pallor of desk work. His black hair had receded since I had seen him last. He said, "I couldn't think of anybody else to come to. I can say please if it'll help. Please?"

"Come on aboard."

"Thanks. Thanks a lot."

We went into the lounge. I had on an old pair of denim shorts and nothing else. The air-conditioning cooled the sweat on my shoulders and chest. He looked around, nodding and beaming, and said, "Nice. Real nice. A nice way to live, huh?"

"Want a drink?"

"Bourbon, if you've got it."

"Got it."

"On the rocks."

I put out the bottle and the glass and said, glancing down at my soiled hands, "Ice is in the bin there. Help yourself while I clean up, Broll."

"Thanks. You sure keep yourself in shape, McGee. Wish I had the time. I guess I better make sure I have the time one of these days."

I shrugged and went forward, dropped the shorts into the hamper and stepped into the oversized shower, thinking about Mary and wondering about her as I sudsed and scrubbed away the rest of the grime from the repair job.

Miss Mary Dillon when I had known her. Then abruptly—maybe too abruptly—Mrs. Harry Broll. When I put my watch back on I saw that it was nearly four o'clock. Meyer and I were invited for drinks at six aboard the *Jilly III*. I put on fresh slacks, an oyster-white sailcloth sports shirt, my ancient Mexican sandals. On the way back to the lounge I stopped in the galley and put some Plymouth on the rocks.

He was sitting on the yellow couch, and he had lit a small cigar with a white plastic mouthpiece. "It must really be something, being able to just take off any time you feel like it."

I slouched into a chair facing him, took a swallow of my drink, and put it on the coffee table. "You've got a problem, Harry?"

"About that time I made such a damn fool of myself . . ."

"Forget it."

"No. Please. Let me say something about that. Like they say, the first year of marriage is the hardest, right?"

"So they say."

"Well, I knew you and Mary were old friends. I couldn't help knowing that, right? I mean, you and Meyer came to the wedding and all. I wondered how good friends you had been. I couldn't help wondering, but I didn't want to really know. Do you understand?"

"Sure."

"The way it happened, we got into a hassle. It was the first real one we'd had. People shouldn't drink and fight when they're married. They say things they don't want to say. I started saying some pretty ugly things about her and you. You know Mary. She's got a lot of spirit. She took it and took it, and finally she let me have it right between the

eyes. I deserved it. She blazed right up at me. She said she'd
been cruising with you alone aboard this houseboat, down
through the Keys and up the west coast to Tampa Bay, and
she'd lived aboard for a month and cooked your food and
washed your clothes and slept in your bed, and you were
kind and decent and gentle and twice the man I am. So that
Sunday afternoon I slammed out of the house and got in the
car and came over here to beat on you. I could always handle myself pretty good. I wasn't drunk enough for that to be
any excuse. Jesus, I never hit so many arms and elbows and
shoulders in my life."

"And the top of my head."

"That's what popped the knuckles. Look. This knuckle is
still sort of sunk in. How many times did you hit me? Do
you know?"

"Sure I know. Twice."

"Twice," he said dolefully. "Oh, shit."

"I waited until you ran out of steam, Harry. I waited
until you got arm weary."

He looked at me in an appraising way. "I wish I'd done
more good."

"I had a pair of sore arms. You bruised me up, Harry.
And a three-day headache."

"I guess I had to get it out of my system. Do you understand it's still pretty hard for me to come to you to ask for
anything?"

"I suppose it might be."

"Mary kept telling me to grow up. Okay. I'm trying to
grow up. I'm trying to be a mature, rational human being.
Like they say, I've been examining my priorities and my
options."

"Good for you. But where do I fit in?"

"Here's what I want you to tell Mary."

"But I—"

"Give me a chance. Okay? Tell her that as soon as the SeaGate project is all set up, I think we ought to get away, just the two of us. A cruise or fly over to Spain, whatever. And tell her that the Canadian girl didn't mean a damn thing to me, that I didn't bring her back down here or ask her down, that she came on her own. And tell her to please get in touch with me so we can talk."

"Hold it! I don't know where Mary is."

His face turned red. "Don't give me such crap. You willing to let me search this houseboat?"

"She isn't here, you damn fool."

"I'll find something of hers. Clothes, lipstick, something."

"Harry. Jesus. Look around all you want."

He settled back in the chair. "Okay. You and Mary knew I'd come here sooner or later. So you haven't been having your fun aboard this boat."

"That's called paranoia, old buddy. When did she leave you?"

"January fifth."

I stared at him in disbelief. "This is the fourteenth day of April. You have a slow reaction time."

"I've been hoping she'd come back or get in touch. Tell her how much I've been hoping. She caught me dead to rights. She went around the house with a face like a stone for nearly two weeks, then when I got home that Tuesday, she'd packed and left. No note, even. I went down the list of her friends and called them. It was humiliating for me."

"I bet."

"Now just one damn minute—"

"What makes you think she'd come to me?"

"I thought about it. I mean, back in January. It seemed like the most likely thing for her to do. I spent a whole weekend hanging around here. You had . . . another friend. So I decided if Mary had come here, she'd found you were busy, gone someplace else."

"She didn't come here, Harry."

"Not right away."

"What is that supposed to mean?"

He leaned forward. "Okay. Where were you at ten o'clock on Friday morning, April second?"

"I haven't the faintest idea."

"You and Mary came off this houseboat at ten that morning, and you went out to the parking lot and got into a white Ford LTD convertible with rental plates. A friend of mine happened to be here and happened to see the two of you get in and drive off. This friend followed you. You went over to the Parkway and turned south toward Miami, and he came back, and he phoned me about it."

"Are you willing to listen a minute? Are you willing to try to listen?"

"All I know is my wife left me and she's sleeping with you, McGee, and I'd like to see you dead."

"The woman I was with is about Mary's height, and her figure is just as good, at least as good as Mary's used to be. Her hair is dark like Mary's. The woman is an old friend. That's her rental convertible, and it's still out there on the lot. With her hair in a scarf and dark glasses, she was all prepared for a trip in an open car. She's here aboard her boat.

Her name is Jillian Brent-Archer. I haven't seen Mary since the wedding. Not once, Broll. And that was better than three years ago."

He looked at me. "You're real cute, McGee. Jesus, you're cute. Most of the damn fools in this world would believe you. Are you going to tell Mary what I told you to tell her, what I've begged you to tell her?"

"How can I, when I don't even know . . ."

And the dumb little weapon came out from under his clothes somewhere, maybe from the waist area, wedged between the belt and the flab. A dumb little automatic pistol in blued steel, half-swallowed in his big, pale, meaty fist. His staring eyes were wet with tears, and his mouth was twisted downward at the corners. The muzzle was making a ragged little circle, and a remote part of my mind identified it as .25 or .32 caliber, there not being all that much difference between a quarter of an inch diameter and a third of an inch. There was a sour laugh back in another compartment of my skull. This could very possibly be the end of it, a long-odds chance of a mortal wound at the hand of a jealous husband wielding something just a little bit better than a cap gun. The ragged circle took in my heart, brain, and certain essential viscera. And I was slouched deep in a chair facing him, just a little too far away to try to kick his wrist. He was going to talk or shoot. I saw his finger getting whiter, so I knew it was shoot.

I shoved with my heels and went over backward in the chair. The weapon made a noise like somebody slapping shingles together. My left heel went numb. I rolled to my right, knocked over a small table, fielded the chunky glass ashtray on the first bounce, rolled up onto my knees, and slung it underhand at his head as he came up out of the depths of the yellow couch. I missed him shamefully, and was caught there too close to him as he aimed at the middle of my face from five feet away and tried to pull the trigger. But the slide was all the way back, the clip empty.

I got slowly up onto very wobbly knees as Harry Broll lowered the gun to his side, relaxed his hand, let it fall. My heel tingled. A slug had grooved the hard leather on the bottom of the heel. The lounge smelled like the Fourth of July.

Harry's big face wrinkled like a slapped baby, and he took a half step toward me, arms half reaching out for comfort and forgiveness, and then he plumped back down on the couch and bellowed once, a walrus on a lonely strand.

My drink was gone, spilling when the table went over. I moved cautiously, checking myself for any area that might feel dead and damp. That is the bullet feel, dead, damp, and strange, before the torn nerves and muscles catch up and begin screaming. No such areas. I made tall careful steps into the galley, made a new drink. I went back in. Harry Broll sat with face in hands, snuffling drearily. The paper had kept me aware of him over the years. Broll plans new condominium complex. Broll given zoning board exception. Broll unveils shopping plaza concept. Chamber lauds Broll.

I sat opposite him again after putting the chair back on its legs. Looking around, I could count five ejected cartridge cases.

"How old are you, Harry?"

He sighed and mumbled it into his hands. "Thirty-five."

"You look fifty."

"Get off my back."

"You're too soft and too heavy. You sweat a lot, and you're short of breath, and your teeth need cleaning."

He lifted his mottled face and stared at me. "Why are you saying these things?"

"Maybe if you hadn't gotten so sloppy, Mary could have given you a second chance. Or maybe it was already a second chance."

"Oh, no. I don't play around. Jesus, I haven't had the time or the energy. This was the first time, I swear."

"You don't play around, and you don't go around killing people."

"You pushed me too far and—"

"You always carry that thing?"

"No, I—"

"You brought it along in case you felt like killing me?"

"Thank God, I missed you. I'm not thinking right lately. Everything would have gone down the drain. Everything."

"It would sort of spoil my day, too."

"You know, when a man takes a good look at himself, he begins to wonder why. You know? I've been pushing myself hard. Drinking too much, smoking too much. Late nights. Conferences. For what? Damned if I know. For the sake of winning? How did that get to seem so important? But you shouldn't have tried to lie to me, McGee."

"Your friend is an idiot. Mary never came near me. She hasn't phoned me or written me. I didn't know she'd left you. Look, I knew her a long time ago. She was at one of those crisis points in her life. She'd never met you, Harry. Never seen you, never heard your name, never knew she'd marry you. We were friends. We took a cruise down through the Keys and up the west coast, and she got things sorted out. We made love. Not for the first two weeks of the cruise. That wasn't the purpose of it. Once all the knots and springs began to loosen up, then it seemed like a natural thing to have happen. It made pleasure. It was a way of saying hello. Nobody was a victim. She was a very sweet lady, and what I remember best is that we laughed a lot."

"I . . . I have to talk to her before the thirtieth."

"Why the deadline?"

"It's a business thing. Some things to sign. To protect my interest in SeaGate. Of course, if I'd shot you, what difference would it make whether I kept my share of SeaGate or not?"

"Will it make a lot of difference when I sign the complaint against you?"

"Complaint?"

"Assault with a deadly weapon. Attempted homicide?"

"You wouldn't!"

"What's to stop me? My undying affection for you?"

He pulled himself together visibly. He wrapped up the emotions and put them on a high shelf. I could almost see the nimble brain of the entrepreneur take over. "We'll both have versions of what happened here, McGee. I'm essentially a salesman. I think I can sell my version far easier than you can sell yours."

"What's your version?"

"I'll let that come as a surprise to you."

I could think of several variations that could leave him looking pretty good. And, of course, there was the usual problem of believability. Does one believe Harry Broll, pillar of the business community, or a certain Travis McGee, who seems to have no visible means of support, gentlemen?

"A man as shrewd as you, Harry, should realize that the guy who gave you the bad information made an honest mistake."

"I know Mary. She'd get in touch with you."

"Would that she had."

"What?"

"A troubled friend is a friend in trouble. I'm right here. She could have come around, but she didn't."

"She made you promise not to tell where she is."

I shook my head. "Broll, come with me. I will show you that rental convertible, and I will show you the lady who rented it and who went to Miami with me and came back with me."

"It's a nice try. You've got a lot of friends. They'd all lie for you. Every one. Think it over. Tell her what I said. She has to get in touch with me."

We stood up. I picked up his little automatic, released the catch and eased the slide forward and handed it to him. He took it and looked at it, bounced it on his big hand, and slipped it into his side pocket. "I better get rid of it," he said.

"If you think you might get any more quaint ideas, you better."

"I was going to scare you. That's all."

I looked him over. "Harry. You did."

"Tell her to call the office. I'm not living at home. It was too empty there."

"If after all these years I should happen to see your wife, I'll tell her."

Two

MEYER CAME ABOARD the *Busted Flush* at twenty minutes to six, five minutes after Harry Broll left. He was dressed for the small festival at six o'clock aboard Jillian's great big motor-sailer trimaran. He wore pants in a carnival awning pattern and a pink shirt that matched one of the myriad stripes in the awning.

"Goodness gracious," I said.

He put a hand on a bulky hip and made a slow 360-degree turn. "Plumage," he said. "And have you noticed it's spring?"

"If you'd carry a camera around your neck and walk fifty feet ahead of me, nobody would know we were together."

"Faw," he said. "And tush." He went toward the bottle department, saying, "About Mr. Harry Broll . . . ?"

"Who? Oh, yes. Of course. Mr. Broll."

"McGee, don't try me, please."

"You are supposed to walk in here, and instead of giving me a fashion show, you are supposed to snuff the air, look about with darting glances. Then you are supposed to find those six cartridge cases in that ashtray and snuff at them. Then you prowl around and find where all six hit, including the one that's hard to find. It hit right smack in the middle of my model 18 Marantz and killed it as dead as Harry tried to kill me."

Meyer backed to the nearest chair and lowered himself into it. "Six shots?"

"Six."

"With serious intent?"

"Damn well told."

I explained the situation. Meyer listened, looking very troubled.

"Don't sit there looking like an old beagle," I told him. "Harry won't be back."

"Maybe somebody else will."

"What is that supposed to mean?"

"Travis, are you just a littler slower than you were a few years ago? Half a step, maybe?"

"I don't know. Probably."

"Why should you get slower and get careless at the same time?"

"Careless?"

"Don't try to kid yourself. You would have stumbled against him or spilled something on him and brushed it off. You would have checked him out and located the gun and taken it away from him."

"This was just old Harry Broll."

"And you are just old T. McGee, trying to pretend you

don't know what I'm saying. You could be on the floor with a leaking hole in your skull."

"I can't go around acting as if everybody was going to—"

"You used to. And you are alive. What has given you this illusion of immortality of late?"

"Lay off, Meyer."

"Staleness? People are very good at things they are very interested in. If you lose interest, you are dead. If a Harry Broll can damn near kill you, Travis, what about somebody with a more professional attitude and background?"

"Wouldn't I be more alert?"

"Don't some of them look and act as innocuous as Harry Broll?"

"What are you getting at?"

"If you just go through the motions, Travis, maybe it's time to give the whole thing up. What good is a way of life if it turns out to be fatal?"

"Are you going to support me?"

"Not a chance. Anyway, isn't Jillian first in line?"

"Come on!"

"There are worse ways to live."

"Several hundred thousand worse ways, Meyer, but just because Harry Broll. . . . Consider this. Six shots in a very confined space. What's the matter with my reaction time?"

"The trouble is that they were fired at all. He came here once to try to beat your face flat. So two years later he comes around again, and you invite him in to try his luck with a gun. What are you going to dodge next time? A satchel charge?"

"I have to depend on instinct. I did not sense any kind of murderous intent on his—"

"Then your instincts are stale. Listen. I don't want to lose a friend. Go where I can visit once in a while. Exchange Christmas cards. Better than putting a pebble on your gravestone."

"Just because—"

"Don't talk. Think a little. And we should be going."

I shrugged and sighed. When he gets into one of those moods, there is nothing one can do with him. He smells doom. I buttoned up the *Flush,* making certain my little security devices were in operation. The sun was low enough to make a yellow-orange glow across all the white gleam and brightwork of a vulgar multimillion dollars' worth of seagoing toys. Hundreds of millions, in truth. As we walked over I saw the sixty-plus feet of a big new Bertram, grumbling, bubbling, sliding elegantly into a slip. Six thousand dollars a foot. It doesn't take too many of those, too many Matthews, Burgers, Trumpys, Huckins, Rybovitches, and Strikers, to make a row of zeros to stun the mind.

I stopped and leaned my crossed arms atop a cement piling and looked down at a rainbow sheen of oil on twilight waters.

"What's the matter now?" asked Meyer.

"Harry is right, you know."

"To try to kill you?"

"Very funny. He's right about Mary getting in touch. I get the feeling she would. Emotional logic. The last time her world ruptured, I helped her walk it off, talk it off, think it off."

"So maybe she had enough and said the hell with it."

"She is one stubborn lady. Harry is no prize. She married him a little too fast. But she would really bust a gut to make the marriage work. She wouldn't quit. She wouldn't run."

"Unless he did something that she just couldn't take. Maybe it got to her gag reflex. Wouldn't she run then?"

"Yes. I guess so. And maybe she's a stronger person than she was back when I knew her. All Harry said was that he had gotten mixed up with some Canadian girl, a first offense. I know that wouldn't make Mary give any ringing cheers. But I think she's human enough to know it wouldn't be the end of the world or the marriage. Well, he has to locate her before the end of April, or he has big business problems."

"Hmm?"

"Something about signing something so he can keep his interest in SeaGate, whatever the hell that is."

"It's a planned community up in the northeast corner of Martin County, above Hobe Sound where there's no A-1-A running along the beach. It's a syndicate thing, way too big for anybody like Broll to swing by himself."

"How do you know all that stuff?"

"There was a feature story about planned communities in the *Wall Street Journal* a month ago. The local papers have had articles about it for over a year. I believe *Newsweek* had a—"

"Truce. Could a guy like Broll do well in a deal like that?"

"Depends. The ownership structure would be the important consideration."

"Could you find out where he fits and how, and why Mary would have to sign something?"

"I imagine I could. But why?"

"Harry's nerves are bad. He looks bad. He has a money

orientation. If he misses out on large money because Mary runs and hides and won't sign, it somehow doesn't sound like Mary. It would be a cheap shot and a dumb shot. She isn't dumb. Whether she stays with him or leaves him, it would be better for him to have money. She's been gone for two months. If he was so certain she'd run to me, where has he been for two months? Time is running out in two weeks. So he comes around with shaking hands and a sweaty shirt and a couple of places he missed while shaving. Time is running out not on the marriage, on the money. It makes me wonder."

"I'll look into it," he said as we walked.

End of discussion. We had arrived at the area where they park the showboats, the ones too big to bring around inside, and thus have to leave them on the river, not far from the fuel pumps, where two out of every three Power Squadron types who cruise by can whap them against the cement with their curling wash. The *Jilly III* is a custom motor-sailer trimaran out of St. Kitts, owned by Jillian, the widow of Sir Henry Brent-Archer. It is seventy feet long with a beam that has to be close to fifty feet. It rides a bad sea with all the stability of a brick church. Minimal superstructure to emphasize an expanse of teak deck as big as a tennis court, with more than half of it shaded by the big colorful awning tarp her crew of three always strings up as soon as they are at dockside.

The bar table was positioned, draped in white damask. A piano tape was playing show tunes with muted discretion over the stereo system I'd helped her buy the last time she was in Lauderdale. There were a dozen guests assembled, three conversational groups of elegant folk sipping the very best booze from the most expensive glasses. Jilly saw us approaching the little gangplank and came a-striding, beaming, to welcome us aboard.

A lady of unguessable years, who made damned well certain she gave you no clues at all. If she turned up as a Jane Doe, DOA, traffic, a hasty coroner could not be blamed for penciling in the apparent age as plus or minus twenty-seven. Tall, slender brunette of such careful and elegant grooming, such exquisitely capped teeth, it seemed safe to assume she was in some area of entertainment. But she had such a much better tan and better physical condition than most show business people, one might safely guess her to be, perhaps, a model for beachwear? A lead in a commercial water ballet?

But a coroner less hasty, more sophisticated, who searched the scalp and elsewhere for the faintest of traces left by superb Swiss surgeons, who slipped the tinted plastic lenses off and studied the eyes closely as well as the backs of the hands, base of the throat, ankles, wrists. . . . He might add a quotient of years in direct ratio to his quality of observation and his experience.

Jilly had a lively and animated face peering out from the careless spill of black hair, all bright questing eyes, black brows, big nose, broad and generous mouth. Ever since I had known Jilly, her voice had cracked like that of a boy in early adolescence, changing from the piercing, songbird clarity of the Irish upperclass countryside to a burring baritone honk and back again. It was so effective it seemed contrived. But a small sailboat had foundered one night in a bad sea, and she had clung to a channel buoy, permanently spraining her vocal cords shouting at the boat traffic until finally she was heard and she and her injured friend were rescued.

"Meyer!" she cried. "My *word,* darling! You're of a surpassing radiance. Travis dear, what happened to him? Did he molt or something?" She linked her arms through ours and croaked, "Come on, dears. Meet the ones you don't know and get smashed soon as you can because I am gallons ahead of you."

The introductions were made. Jillian slipped away to greet more guests. We drank. The sun went down. The night breeze was gentle but cool, and ladies put their wraps back on. The party lights strung from the rigging were properly dim, flatteringly orange. The buffet materialized, as if the table had risen up out of the teak. The music tape was more lively, the volume louder than before.

I found myself inadvertently paired with a smallish, withered Englishwoman with a shrunken face the color of weak tea and hair dyed the color of raspberry ice. A Mrs. Ogleby. I had seen Meyer talking to her towering and cadaverous husband, pumping him about the latest Common Market difficulties. We carried our buffet plates forward where she could sit on a narrow shelflike bench built out from the bow where the rail was solid. I sat crosslegged on the deck with my plate atop the massive bow cleat.

"I understand that you are one of dear Jillian's very favorite Americans, Mr. McGee."

She managed to load the comment with sweetly venomous insinuation. I beamed up at her. "And she's one of my favorite foreigners."

"Really! How terribly nice for her. Actually, Geoffrey

and I were old friends of poor Sir Henry long before he married Jillian."

"Then Jillian isn't one of your favorite people, eh?"

She clinked her fork against the plate and leaned forward and peered down at me. "Whatever gave you such an odd idea? She is *very* dear. Very dear to both of us."

"I knew Sir Henry, too."

"Really! I wouldn't have thought you would have known him."

"I was a houseguest at St. Kitts for a few weeks."

"But that would have been after he was quite ill, I take it." Her smile was thin and knowing in the light of the nearby party lantern. A truly poisonous little woman.

"No. As a matter of fact, Mrs. Ogleby, Henry and I swam our three miles every morning, went riding or sailing every afternoon, and played chess every evening."

She paused and regrouped. "Before he became ill, Sir Henry had really fantastic energies. How strange we all thought it that he would marry someone that young, after being a widower so long. It seemed odd. But, of course, that was so awfully long ago it is rather difficult to think of Jillian as—"

"Just think of me, dears, no matter how difficult it may be," said Jilly. "Hmmm. What is this you have, Lenore? I didn't see it at all. May I? Mmmm. Shrimp, and what a deliciously fiery sauce! Difficult to think of me as what, Lenore darling?"

When Mrs. Ogleby hesitated, I said, "She was about to pinpoint the date when you and Sir Henry were married."

"Were you, dear? It slips my mind, you know. Was it just before or just after that fuss with the Spanish Armada?"

"Don't be absurd! I was only—"

"You were only being Lenore, which is part of the trouble, isn't it? Travis, I was married to Henry long long ago. Matter of fact, I was but three years old at the time, and most of the people in the church thought it was some sort of delayed christening. There was talk that it was an unwholesome relationship, but by the time I was fourteen— eleven years later—I looked twenty, and everyone said that it had probably been all for the best. And it was, of course. Lenore, you seem to be finished. Dear, come with me and show me just where you found the shrimp, will you please?"

"But if there is any left, it should be quite obvi—"

"Lenore!"

"Quite. Of course. I shall be happy to show you, my dear Jillian."

"I knew it would make you happy to have a chance to be nice to me, Lenore."

Off they went. Old friends, smiling and chattering.

Twenty minutes later as I was moving away from the bar with some Wild Turkey straight, instead of brandy, Jilly intercepted me and moved me into relative shadow.

"Travis, if you are a truly thoughtful and understanding man, you have your toothbrush hidden away on your person."

"I had the idea the party girl would need her eight hours."

"Have a little mercy, dear. There's but one way to settle down from this sort of bash. You shall divert me."

"I can leave and then come back. You know. Like a house call."

"Is its tender little romantical pride bruised because the party girl thinks lovemaking is therapeutic? To say nothing

of being a hell of a lot of fun. Just stay on, dear. Stay by me.
Smile like a tomcat with a little yellow feather caught in his
whiskers, and soon now we can smile them off and sing out
our merry farewells."

"Giving Lenore more food for thought?"

"Thought? Christ, that poisonous bitch doesn't think.
She slanders, because she has her own terrible hunger she
can't ease in any way. She burns in fire, my darling, and
hates and hates and hates. Poor thing. Brace yourself, pet. I
want you horribly."

Three

I DRIFTED IN AND OUT of a placid and amiable doze. Water slapped the triple hulls, whispering lies about how big the seas could really get. I cocked an eye at an upward angle at the battery digital clock fastened to the bulkhead over Jillian's bed. Watched 4:06 turning magically to 4:07. There was a single light on in her stateroom, a rose-colored globe of frosty glass, big as a cantaloupe, standing next to its twin reflection in the dressing table mirror.

It was warm in her stateroom, not unpleasantly so, just enough to leave a humid dew, rosy highlights on our entangled flesh, sprawled and spent, atop a wrinkled dampness of custom sheets in a pattern of green vines with yellow leaves against white.

Jilly lay oddly positioned, her upper torso diagonally across my chest, face in a pillow, cheek against my right shoulder, her slack right arm hooked around my neck. Her long tanned legs were sprawled down there, off to my left. My right arm was pinned, but my left arm was free, my hand resting on the small of her back.

I traced the velvet geographies of that small concave area of the country of Jilly and then made a coin-sized circle of fingernails and thumbnail and made a slow circling motion against her there, a circle as big as a teacup. In time the pattern of her breathing changed. She shifted. She exhaled through slack rubbery lips, making a sound like a small horse.

"Is someone mentioning my name?" she said in a sleepy voice.

"Pure telepathy."

She raised her head, clawed her hair out of the way, and peered up at the clock. "Gawd! What year is it? Don't tell me."

She heaved herself up, tugging her arm out from under my neck. She sat up and combed her hair back with the fingers of both hands, yawning widely as she did so. She shook and snapped her head back, settled her hair, then curled her limber legs under her and smiled down at me. "Been awake long, Travis?"

"Off and on."

"Thinking? About what?"

I hitched myself higher on the pillows. "Random things. This and that."

"Tell me about them."

"Let me think back. Oh, I was wondering how it's possible to make this bed up. It's shaped to fit perfectly into the curves of this middle hull right up at the bow and—"

"There are little lever things on the legs down there, and when you push them down, then you can roll the bed back and make it up. You certainly think about fascinating things."

"Then I heard a motor go on, and I was wondering if it was a bilge pump or a refrigeration compressor or—"

"You are trying to be tiresome. Didn't you think about what I asked you?"

"Maybe I did. A little bit. Like wondering why it has to be me."

"If one could know why a person settles upon a particular person, one would know one of the mysteries, wouldn't one? I think it was because of four years ago. I think it started then."

A friend of a friend had put Sir Henry Brent-Archer in touch with me. A problem of simple extortion. I had gone down to the British Virgins and spent three weeks at their spacious and lovely home and found exactly the right way to pry the two-legged lamprey loose, file its sharp teeth off, and send it unhappily on its way. And during the three weeks I had become ever more sensuously aware of Sir Henry's handsome and lively wife. She made sure of that awareness.

"Because I kept it from starting?"

"Was I all that distasteful to you, my darling?"

"Not you. The situation. I liked Sir Henry. In spite of the fact I was working for him on a special problem, I was still a guest in his home. In a man's home you live by his code. It does not have to be typed out and glued to the guest suite door. He did not want me to kick his dogs, overwork his horses, bribe his servants, read his diary, filch his silverware, borrow his toothbrush, or lay his wife. I accepted the obligation when I moved in."

She snickered. "Would you believe that was the only time in the years I was his wife that I ever tried to be naughty?"

"There's no reason not to believe it."

"I was very grateful to Sir Henry. He came along at just the right time in my life. My whole dreadful family was sliding into the pit, and through him I could save them, so I snatched him up quickly. I liked him well enough for half the marriage, liked him a great deal for the rest of it, and started loving him after he was buried. Anyway, on that stupid night I lay and listened to my heart going bump, bump, bump. Then I got up and drenched myself with that lovely scent and put on the little froth of nightgown and crept through the night like a thief and slipped into your bed. And suddenly got lifted out bodily, carried to the door, given a great whack across my bare behind, and shoved out into the hall. I did not know whether to laugh or cry. I did both."

"It was closer than you'll ever know, Jilly."

"So it's you, dear man. The chosen. Relax and enjoy it. Why not? Am I trying to nail you down permanently? Of course, but through your own choice and decision. I give you full disclosure, dear. I have something over eight hundred thousand pounds, carefully managed by nice little Swiss elves. The income is about a hundred and fifty thousand of your dollars a year, and taxes take hardly any. There is the lovely house with the beach, the bay, and the view, and the boats and cars and horses. I am not exactly a junior miss, but I work very hard at myself, and I come from healthy stock. I suspect I shall go on about the same for years and years and years and suddenly one morning wake up as a shriveled, cackling little old witch. All I ask of you is that you come back home with me, darling. Be my house-guest. Be my love. We laugh at the same things. We enjoy the same things. Last trip and this trip we've certainly estab-lished . . . physical compatibility. Darling, please! We'll travel when you want to and go where you want to go. We'll be with people when you want to, and they will be the people you want to be with. Please!"

"Jilly, you are a dear and lovely lady—"

"But! I know, dammit. But! *Why not?* Do you even *know*?"

I knew but did not want to tell her. You see many such couples around the yacht clubs and bath clubs and tennis clubs of the western world. The man, a little younger or a lot younger than the moneyed widow or divorcee he has either married or is traveling with. The man is usually brown and good at games, dresses youthfully and talks amusingly. But he drinks a little too much. And completely trained and conditioned, he is ever alert for his cues. If his lady unsnaps her purse and frowns down into it, he at once presents his cigarettes, and they are always her brand. If she has her own cigarettes, he can cross twenty feet in a twelfth of a second to snap the unwavering flame to life, properly and conveniently positioned for her. It takes but the small-est sidelong look of query to send him in search of an ash-tray to place close to her elbow. If at sundown she raises her elegant shoulders a half inch, he trots into the house or onto the boat or up to the suite, to bring back her wrap. He knows just how to apply her suntan oil, knows which of her dresses have to be zipped up and snapped for her. He can draw her bath to the precise depth and temperature which please her. He can give her an acceptable massage, brew a decent pot of coffee, take her phone messages accurately, keep her personal checkbook in balance, and remind her when to take her medications. Her litany is: Thank you, dearest. How nice, darling. You are so thoughtful, sweetheart.

It does not happen quickly, of course. It is an easy life. Other choices, once so numerous, disappear. Time is the random wind that blows down the long corridor, slamming all the doors. And finally, of course, it comes down to a very simple equation. Life is endurable when she is contented and difficult when she is displeased. It is a training process. Conditioned response.

"I'm used to the way I live," I told her.

"The way you live," she said. With brooding face she reached and ran gentle fingertips along the deep, gullied scar in my thigh, then leaned, and touched the symmetrical dimple of the entrance wound of a bullet. She hunched closer to me, bent, and kissed the white welt of scar tissue that is nearly hidden by the scruffy, sun-faded hair at my temple. "The way you live, Travis. Trying to trick the tricky ones. Trying to make do with bluff and smiles and strange lies. Filching fresh meat right out of the jaws of the sharks. For how long, dear, before finally the odds go bad and the luck goes bad once and for all?"

"I'm sly."

"Not sly enough. Maybe not quick enough anymore. I think you've been doing it for too long, darling. Too many years of getting things back for silly, careless people who should not have lost them in the first place. One day some dim little chap will come upon you suddenly and take out a gun and shoot you quite dead."

"Are you a witch? Do you so prophesy?"

She fell upon me, hugged me tight. "Ah no, dear. No. You had all the years when that was the thing you had to do. Now the years belong to me. Is it such a sickening fate you can't endure the thought of it?"

"No, Jilly. No, honey. It's just that . . . ."

"Give us a month. No. One week. One insignificant little week. Or else."

"Or else?"

She burrowed a bit, gently closed her teeth onto the upper third of my left ear, then released it. "I have splendid teeth and very strong jaw muscles. If you say no, I shall set my teeth into your ear and do my best to tear it right off your head, darling."

"You just might at that."

"You love to bluff people. Try me."

"No, thank you. One week."

She took a deep breath and let it out. "Lovely! Time in transit doesn't count, of course. Can we leave . . . day after tomorrow?"

"I don't know."

"Why don't you know?"

"I just found out that an old friend might be in trouble. It just seems to me that if she was in trouble, she'd come to me."

Jilly wiggled and thrust away from me and sat up. "She?"

"Frowning makes wrinkles."

"So it does. She?"

"A respectable married lady."

"If she's so respectable, how is it she knows *you*?"

"Before she was married."

"And I suppose you had an affair with her."

"Gee, honey. I'd have to look it up."

I caught her fist about five inches from my eye. "You bahstid," she said.

"Okay. An affair. A mad, wild, glorious liaison which kept us in an absolute frenzy of passion."

Her look was enigmatic. "You are perfectly right, of course, darling. It is none of my business. What's she like? I mean, what physical type?"

"In general, a lot like you, Jilly. Tall, slender brunette. Dark hair, takes a good tan. Long legs, short waisted. She would be . . . twenty-eight or -nine by now. Back when I knew her, she didn't race her motor the way you do. More of a placid, contented person. She really enjoyed cooking and scrubbing and bed-making. She could sleep ten or twelve hours a night."

"You damned well remember every detail, don't you?"

I smiled up into her leaning, earnest face—a small face but strong of feature in the black, bed-snarled dangle of hair. I looked at her limber, brown body in the rose glow of the lamp ten feet away, noting the way the deep tan above and below her breasts decreased in ever more pallid horizontal stripes and shadings down to that final band of pale and pure white which denoted her narrowest bikini top.

"Why are you laughing at me, you dull sod?"

"Not at you, Lady Jillian."

"I am *not* Lady Jillian. That usage is improper. If you are not laughing *at,* then you are laughing *with.* And if you are laughing *with,* why is it that I am not amused?"

"But you are, darling."

She tried to keep her mouth severe but lost the battle, gave a rusty honk of laughter, and flung herself upon me.

"I can't stay angry with you, Travis. You promised me a week. But I'll punish you for that dark-haired lady."

"How?"

"On our way to St. Kitts there will be at least one day or night when we'll spend hour after hour quartering into an ugly, irregular chop."

"I don't get seasick."

"Nor do I, my love. It would spoil it if either of us became ill."

"Spoil what?"

"Dear man, when the chop is effective, one cannot stay on this bed. You are lifted up, and then the bed and the hull drop away from you, and when you are on your way down, the bed comes up and smacks you and boosts you into the air again. It is like trying to post on a very bad horse. When that happens, dear, you and I are going to be right here, making love. We'll see how well you satisfy a lady in midair. I shall have you tottering about, wishing you'd never met Mrs. Whatever."

"Mrs. Broll. Mary Broll. Mary Dillon Broll."

"You think she should have come to you if she's in trouble? Isn't that a little patronizing and arrogant?"

"Possibly."

"What sort of trouble?"

"Marriage trouble. Her husband cheated, and she caught him at it and left him back in January."

"Good Lord, why should she come galloping to you?"

"It's an emotional problem, and when she had one sort of like it years ago, we got together, and she worked her way out of it."

"And fell in love with you?"

"I think that with Mary there would have to be some affection before there could be anything."

"You poor dumb beast. You're *so* obvious."

"What do you mean?"

"You can't for the life of you comprehend why she doesn't come scuttling back to Dr. McGee's free and famous clinic. Your pride is hurt, dear. I suspect she's found some other therapist."

"Even if she had, I think she'd have let me know the marriage had soured. I get the feeling something happened to her."

She yawned and stretched. "Let me make one thing abundantly clear, as one of your grubby little political types says or used to say. Once we have our design for living, if we have any doleful visits from one of your previous patients, my dear, I shall take a broom to them and beat them through the garden gate and down the drive."

"Don't you think you ought to type all these rules up and give me three copies?"

"You're so damned *defensive*! Good Christ, am I some sort of dog's dinner?"

"You are a lively, sexy, lovely, sexy, well-dressed, sexy, amusing, sexy, wealthy, sexy widow lady."

"And some very tidy and considerate men come flocking around. Men with all the social graces and very good at games. Not knuckly, scabrous, lazy, knobbly old ruins like you, McGee."

"So grab one of those tidy and considerate ones."

"Oh, sure. They are lovely men, and they are *so* anxious to please me. There's the money, and it makes them very jumpy and nervous. Their hands get cold and damp. If I frown, they look terrified. Couldn't you be more anxious to please me, dear? Just a little bit?"

"Like this, you mean?"

"Well . . . I didn't exactly mean that. . . . I meant in a more general sense . . . but . . . now that you bring it up. . . . God, I can't remember now what I did mean. . . . I guess I meant this. Yes, darling. This."

The narrow horizontal ports above the custom bed let a cold and milky morning light into the stateroom at the bow of the center hull of the *Jilly III*. As I looked up, 6:31 became 6:32. Jillian's small round rump, her flesh warmer than mine, was thrust with a domestic coziness into my belly. My chin rested against the crown of her head. Her tidy heft had turned my left arm numb. My right hand lay upon the sweet inward curve of her waist.

Worse fates, I thought. A life with Jilly Brent-Archer wouldn't be dull. Maybe it is time for the islands. In spite of all good intentions, all nervous concern, all political bombast, my dirty two-legged species is turning the lovely southeast coast into a sewer. On still days the stinking sky is bourbon brown, and in the sea there are only the dwindling runty fish that can survive in that poisoned brew.

It happens slowly, so you try not to notice it. You tell yourself it happens to be a bad day, that's all. The tides and the winds will scrub it all clean. But not clean enough anymore. One life to live, so pop through the escape hatch, McGee. Try the islands. Damned few people can escape the smudge and sludge, the acids and stenches, the choking and weeping. You have to take care of yourself, man. Nobody else is going to. And this deft morsel, curled sleeping against you, is a first-class ticket for all of the voyage you have left. Suppose you *do* have to do some bowing and scraping and fetching. Will it kill you? Think of what most people have to do for a living. You've been taking your retirement in small installments whenever you could afford it. So here's the rest of it in her lovely sleep. The ultimate social security.

I eased my dead arm out from under her and moved away. She made a sleep-whine of discontent. I covered her with the big colorful sheet, dressed, turned out the rosy light, and made sure the main hatchway locked behind me when I left.

Back aboard the *Flush* I put on swim trunks and a robe to keep me warm in the morning chill. The sun was coming up out of the sea when I walked across the pedestrian bridge over the highway and down onto the public beach. Morning birds were running along the wet sand, pecking and fleeing from the wash of the surf. An old man was jogging slowly by, his face in a clench of agony. A fat girl in a brown dress was looking for shells.

I went in, swam hard, and rested, again and again, using short bursts of total energy. I went back to the *Flush* and had a quart of orange juice, four scrambled eggs along with some rat cheese from Vermont, and a mug of black coffee.

I fell asleep seven and a half inches above my oversized bed in the master stateroom, falling toward the bed, long gone before I landed.

Four

THURSDAY, WHEN I GOT UP a little before noon, the remembered scene with Harry Broll and his little gun seemed unreal. Six loud whacks, not loud enough to attract the curious attention of people on the neighboring craft. The *Flush* had been buttoned up, the air-conditioning on. No slug had gone through glass.

I found where five had hit. At last I spotted the sixth one in the overhead. It had hit tumbling and sideways and had not punched itself all the way out of sight, so by elimination it was the one that had grooved the leather sole of my sandal and numbed my heel.

I had rolled to my right after going over backward in the chair. It gave me the chance to kick a small table over, creating more distraction and confusion, and it also forced him, being right-handed, to bring his arm across his body to aim at me, which is more difficult than extending the arm out to the side. Two into the deck, one into the chair, one into the table, one into the overhead, and one into my stereo amplifier.

So maybe the clip held six, and he had not jacked one into the chamber until he got to the parking lot at the marina. If he'd put one in the chamber and filled the clip all the way, there would have been one left for the middle of my face.

Dead then or a long time in the institutional bed with the drains in place and the pain moving around under the sedatives like a snake under a blanket.

Don't give yourself any credit, Mr. Travis McGee. The fates could have counted to seven just as easily. You had an easy shot at him with the ashtray, but your hand was sweaty and the fingertips slipped. You missed badly.

Meyer could be right. I had depended on instinct. It had been my instinct that Harry Broll had not come to kill me. Then he had done his best, and I had lucked out. So was instinct becoming stale? When it stopped being a precision tool, when it ceased sending accurate messages up from the atavistic, animal level of the brain, I was as vulnerable as if sight or hearing had begun to fail. If soft, sloppy, nervous Harry Broll could almost do me in with a pop gun, my next meeting with professional talent could be mortal.

There was another dimension to it. Once I started doubting my survival instinct, I would lose confidence in my own reactions. A loss of confidence creates hesitations. Hesitation is a fatal disease—for anyone in the salvage business.

There are worse careers than houseguest. Or pet gopher.

Too much solitary introspection started to depress me. I was ready for Geritol and cortisone. I pulled all the plugs and connections on the Marantz and lugged its considerable weight all the way to where I'd parked Miss Agnes, my ancient and amiable old blue Rolls pickup. I drove over to town to Al's Musicade. He is lean, sour, and knowledgeable. He does not say much. He took it out back himself and found bench space in his busy service department. I watched him finger the hole in the front of it. He quickly loosened the twelve Phillips screws that hold the top perforated plate down, lifted it off, found more damage, reached in with two fingers, and lifted out the deformed slug.

"Somebody didn't like the programing?"

"Bad lyrics."

"Week from today?"

"Loaner?"

"Got a Fisher you can use."

We walked out front, and he lifted it off the rack, a used one in apparently good condition. He made a note of the serial number and who was taking it out.

I put the borrowed amplifier on the passenger seat beside me and went looking for Harry Broll's place of business. I had seen it once and had a general idea where to find it. I had to ask at a gas station. It was west of Lauderdale, off Davie Road, over in an industrial park in pine and palmetto country. All of it except the office itself was circled by high hurricane fencing with slanted braces and three strands of barbed wire on top. There was a gate for the rail spur and a truck and equipment gate. I could see a central mix concrete plant, a block plant, big piles of sand, gravel, and crushed stone. I could see warehouses, stacks of lumber, piles of pre-stressed concrete beams, and a vehicle park and repair area. This was a Thursday at one thirty in the afternoon, and I could count only ten cars. Four of those were in front of the office. The office was a long, low concrete-block building painted white with a flat roof. The landscaped grass was burned brown, and they had lost about half the small palm trees planted near the office.

There were too many trucks and pieces of equipment in the park. It looked neat enough but sleepy. BROLL ENTERPRISES, Inc. But some of the big plastic letters had blown off or fallen off. It said:

ROLL E TERP ISES, Inc.

I cruised slowly by. I was tempted to turn around and go back and go in and see if Harry was there and try once more to tell him I'd had no contact whatsoever with Mary for over three years. But he was going to believe what emotions told him to believe.

I wondered how Meyer was doing, using his friends in the banks, brokerage houses, and investment houses to find out just how sweaty Harry Broll might be. The tight-money times and the over-building of condominiums and the pyramiding costs had busted quite a few able fellows lately. Harry probably hadn't come through that bad period without some ugly bruises. I could tell Meyer how idle Broll's place of business looked, if he hadn't found out already.

When I got back to Bahia Mar, Meyer was still missing. I felt restless. I set up the Fisher, hooked up the tape decks, turntables, and the two sets of speakers. It checked out all right. I turned it off and paced. The itch you can't quite reach. Familiar feeling. Like the name you can't quite remember.

I looked up the number for Broll Enterprises and phoned. The girl answered by reciting the number I'd just dialed.

"Maybe you can help me, miss. I'm trying to get a home address for Mrs. Harry Broll."

"In what regard, please."

"Well, this is the Shoe Mart, and it was way back in November we special-ordered a pair of shoes for Mrs. Broll. It took so long she's under no obligation to take them, but they're more a classic than a high-style item, so I figure she probably wants them, but I've been drawing a blank on the home phone number, so I thought maybe they moved or something."

"Will you hold on a moment, please?"

I held. It took her about a minute and a half. "Mr. Broll says that you can deliver them here to the office. Do you know where we are?"

"Sure. Okay. Thanks. It'll probably be tomorrow."

I hung up, and once again, to make sure, I dialed the home phone number for Harry Broll, 21 Blue Heron Lane. "The number you have dialed is not in service at this time."

I scowled at my phone. Come on, McGee. The man is living somewhere. Information has no home number for him. The old home number is on temporary disconnect. The new number of wherever he's living must be unlisted. It probably doesn't matter a damn where he's living. It's the challenge.

Okay. Think a little. Possibly all his mail is directed to the business address. But some things have to be delivered. Booze, medicine, automobiles. Water, electricity . . . cablevision?

The lady had a lovely voice, gentle and musical and intriguingly breathy. "I could track it down more quickly, Mr. Broll, if you could give me your account number."

"I wish I could. I'm sorry, miss. I don't have the bill in front of me. But couldn't you check it by address? The last billing was sent to 21 Blue Heron Lane. If it's too much trouble, I can phone you tomorrow. You see, the bill is at my home, and I'm at the office."

"Just a moment, please. Let me check the cross index."

It took a good five minutes. "Sorry it took me so long," she said.

"It was my fault, not having my account number, miss."

"Broll. Bee-are-oh-el-el. Harry C.?"

"Correct."

"And you said the bill went where?"

"To 21 Blue Heron Lane. That's where I used to live."

"Gee, Mr. Broll, I don't understand it at all. All billing is supposed to be mailed to Post Office box 5150."

"I wonder if I've gotten a bill that belongs to someone else. The amount doesn't seem right either."

"You should be paying $6.24 a month, sir. For the one outlet. You were paying more, of course, for the four outlets at Blue Heron Lane before you ordered the disconnect."

"Excuse me, but does your file show where I am getting the one-outlet service? Do you have the right address?"

"Oh, yes sir. It's 8553 Ocean Boulevard, apartment 61. I've got the installation order number. That *is* right, isn't it?"

"Yes. That's right. But I think the billing is for eleven dollars and something."

"Mr. Broll, please mail the bill back in the regular envelope we send out, but in the left bottom corner would you write *Customer Service, Miss Locklin?*"

"I will do that. I certainly appreciate your kindness and courtesy, Miss Locklin."

"No trouble, really. That's what we're here for."

Four o'clock and still no Meyer, so I went out and coaxed Miss Agnes back to life and went rolling on up Ocean Boulevard. I kept to the far right lane and went slowly because the yearly invasion of Easter bunnies was upon us, was beginning to dwindle, and there was too little time to enjoy them. They had been beaching long enough so that there were very few cases of lobster pink. The tans were nicely established, and the ones who still burned had a brown burn. There are seven lads to every Easter bunny, and the litheness and firmness of the young ladies gamboling on the beach, ambling across the highway, stretching out to take the sun, is something to stupefy the senses. It creates something which is beyond any of the erotic daydreams of traditional lust, even beyond that aesthetic pleasure of looking upon pleasing line and graceful move.

It is possible to stretch a generalized lust, or an aesthetic turn of mind, to encompass a hundred lassies—say five and a half tons of vibrant and youthful and sun-toned flesh clad in about enough fabric to half fill a bushel basket. The erotic imagination or the artistic temperament can assimilate these five and a half tons of flanks and thighs, nates and breasts, laughing mouths and bouncing hair and shining eyes, but neither lust nor art can deal with a few thousand of them. Perceptions go into stasis. You cannot compare one with another. They become a single silken and knowledgeable creature, unknowable, a thousand-legged contemptuous

joy, armored by the total ignorance of the very young and
by the total wisdom of body and instinct of the female kind.
A single cell of the huge creature, a single entity, one girl,
can be trapped and baffled, hurt and emptied, broken and
abandoned. Or to flip the coin, she can be isolated and cher-
ished, wanted and needed, taken with contracts and cere-
monies. In either case the great creature does not miss the
single identity subtracted from the whole any more than
the hive misses the single bee. It goes on in its glistening,
giggling, leggy immortality, forever replenished from the
question of children plus time, existing every spring, un-
changingly and challengingly invulnerable—an exquisite
reservoir called Girl, aware of being admired and saying
"Drink me!," knowing that no matter how deep the
draughts, the level of sweetness in the reservoir remains the
same forever.

There are miles of beach, and there were miles of bunnies
along the tan Atlantic sand. When the public beach ended I
came to the great white wall of high-rise condominiums
which conceal the sea and partition the sky. They are com-
partmented boxes stacked high in sterile sameness. The bal-
conied ghetto. Soundproof, by the sea. So many conveniences
and security measures and safety factors that life at last is
reduced to an ultimate boredom, to the great decisions of
the day—which channel to watch and whether to swim in
the sea or the pool.

I found 8553. It was called Casa de Playa and was spray-
creted as wedding cake white as the rest of them. Twelve
stories, in the shape of a shallow C, placed to give a maximum view of the sea to each apartment even though the lot
was quite narrow. I had heard that raw land along there was

going at four thousand a foot. It makes an architectural challenge to take a two-hundred-foot lot which costs eight hundred thousand dollars and cram 360 apartments onto it, each with a view, and retain some elusive flavor of spaciousness and elegance.

Economics lesson. Pay eight hundred thou for the land. Put up two hundred thousand more for site preparation, improvement, landscaping, covered parking areas, swimming pool or pools. Put up a twelve-story building with 30 apartments on each of the floors from the second through the eleventh and 15 penthouse apartments on top. You have 315 apartments. The building and the apartment equipment cost nine million. So you price them and move them on the basis that the higher in the air they are and the bigger they are, the more they cost. All you have to do is come out with about a thirty-three hundred net on each apartment on the average after all construction expenses, overhead expenses, and sales commissions, and you make one million dollars, and you are a sudden millionaire before taxes.

But if the apartments are retailing at an average forty thousand each and you sell off everything in the building except ten percent of the apartments, then instead of being a million bucks ahead, you are two hundred thousand in the red.

It is deceptively simple and monstrously tricky. Meyer says that they should make a survey and find out how many condominium heart attacks have been admitted to Florida hospitals. A new syndrome. The first symptom is a secret urge to go up to an unsold penthouse and jump off your own building, counting vacancies all the way down.

As I did not care to be remembered because of Miss

Agnes, I drove to a small shopping center on the left side of the highway, stashed her in the parking lot, and walked back to the Casa de Playa.

On foot I had time to read all of the sign in front.

> Now showing. Model apartments. Casa de Playa. A new adventure in living. From $38,950 to $98,950. Private ocean beach. Pool. Hotel services. Fireproof and soundproof construction. Security guard on premises. No pets. No children under fifteen. Automatic fire and burglar alarm. Community lounge and game area. Another adventure in living by Broll Enterprises, Inc.

The big glass door swung shut behind me and closed out the perpetual sounds of the river of traffic, leaving me in a chilled hush on springy carpeting in a faint smell of fresh paint and antiseptic.

I walked by the elevators and saw a small desk in an alcove. The sign on the desk said: Jeannie Dolan, Sales Executive on Duty. A lean young lady sat behind the desk, hunched over, biting down on her underlip, scowling down at the heel of her left hand and picking at the flesh with a pin or needle.

"Sliver?" I said.

She jumped about four inches off the desk chair. "Hey! Don't sneak up, huh?"

"I wasn't trying to."

"I know you weren't. I'm sorry. Yes, it's a sliver."

"Want some help?"

She looked up at me. Speculative and noncommittal. She couldn't decide whether I'd come to deliver something, repair something, serve legal papers, or buy all the unsold apartments in a package deal.

"Well . . . every time I take hold of something, it hurts."

I took her over to the daylight, to an upholstered bench near a big window which looked out at a wall made of pierced concrete blocks. I held her thin wrist and looked at her hand. There was red inflammation around the sliver and a drop of blood where she had been picking at it. I could see the dark narrow shape of the splinter under the pink and transparent skin. She had been working with a needle and a pair of tweezers. I sterilized the needle in her lighter flame, pinched up the skin so that I could pick a little edge of the splinter free. She sucked air through clenched teeth. I took the tweezers and got hold of the tiny end and pulled it out.

"Long," I said, holding it up. "Trophy size. You should get it mounted."

"Thank you very very much. It was driving me flippy," she said, standing up.

"Got anything to put on it?"

"Iodine in the first aid kit."

I followed her back to the desk. She hissed again when the iodine touched the raw tissue. She asked my advice as to whether to put a little round Band-Aid patch on it, and I said I thought a splinter that big deserved a bandage and a sling, too.

She was lean, steamed-up, a quick-moving, fast-talking woman in her late twenties with a mobile face and a flexible, expressive voice. In repose she could have been quite ordinary. There was a vivacity, an air of enjoying life about her that made her attractive. Her hair was red-brown, her eyes a quick, gray-green, her teeth too large, and her upper lip too short for her to comfortably pull her mouth shut, so it remained parted, making her look vital and breathless instead of vacuous. She used more eye makeup than I care for.

"Before I ask question one, Miss Dolan—"

"Mrs. Dolan. But Jeannie, please. And you are . . . ?"

"John Q. Public until I find out something."

"John Q. Spy?"

"No. I want to know who you represent, Jeannie."

"Represent? I'm selling these condominium apartments as any fool can plainly—"

"For whom?"

"For Broll Enterprises."

"I happen to know Harry. Do the skies clear now?"

She tilted, frowned, then grinned. "Sure. If a realtor was handling this and you talked to me, then there'd have to be a commission paid, and you couldn't get a better price from Mr. Broll. There used to be a realtor handling it, but they didn't do so well, and I guess Mr. Broll decided this would be a better way. Can I sell you one of our penthouses today, sir? Mr. Public, sir?"

"McGee. Travis McGee. I don't know whether I'm a live one or not. I'm doing some scouting for a friend. I'd like to look at one with two bedrooms and two baths just to get an idea."

She took a sign out of her desk and propped it against the phone. "Back in ten minutes. Please be seated." She locked her desk and we went up to the eighth floor. She chattered all the way up and all the way down the eighth floor corridor, telling me what a truly great place it was to live and how well constructed it was and how happy all the new residents were.

She unlocked the door and swung it open with a flourish. She kept on chattering, following a couple of steps behind me as I went from room to room. After quite a while she ran out of chatter. "Well. . . . Don't you want to ask *anything*?"

"The floor plan is efficient. The equipment looks pretty adequate. But the furniture and the carpeting and the decorating make me feel sort of sick, Jeannie."

"A very expensive decorator did all our display apartments."

"Yeck."

"A lot of people are really turned on by it."

"Yeck."

"We've even sold some with all the decor intact, just as you see it. The buyers insisted."

"Still yeck."

"And I think it is absolutely hideous, and it makes me feel queasy, too. It looks too sweet. Cotton candy and candy cane and ribbon candy. Yeck."

"Got one just like this that hasn't been messed with?"

"Down on five. Come along."

We rode down three floors. The apartment was spotlessly clean and absolutely empty. She unlocked the sliding doors, and we went out onto the balcony and leaned against the railing.

"If the answers to the other questions make sense, Jeannie, my friend might be interested, provided you don't show her that one up on eight."

I asked the right questions. Was it long-term leasehold or

actual ownership with undivided interest in the land? How much a year for taxes? How much for the maintenance contract? What were the escalation provisions in the maintenance contract? How much did utilities run? Would the apartment be managed, be rented if you wished when you were not using it?

"How many apartments are there all told?"

"Counting the penthouses—298."

"How many unsold?"

"Oh, very few, really."

"How many?"

"Well . . . Harry might cut my throat all the way around to the back if I told anybody. But after all, you are my surgeon, and I have the scar to prove it. We've got thirty-six to go. I've been here a month and a half, and I get free rent in one of the models and a fifty-buck-a-week draw against a thousand dollars a sale. Between the two of us, Betsy and me, we've sold two."

"So Harry Broll is hurting?"

"Would your friend live here alone, Travis?"

"It would just be more of a convenience for her than anything. She lives in the British Virgins. St. Kitts. She comes over here often, and she's thinking about getting an apartment. I imagine she'd use it four times a year probably, not over a week or two weeks at a time. She might loan it to friends. She doesn't have to worry about money."

Jeannie Dolan made a small rueful face. "How nice for her. Will you be bringing her around?"

"If I don't find anything she might like better."

"Remember, this floor plan is $55,950. Complete with color coded kitchen with—"

"I know, dear."

"Wind me up and I give my little spiel." She locked up, and we rode down in the elevator. She looked at her watch. "Hmmm. My long, exhausting day has been over for ten minutes. I read half a book, wrote four letters, and got operated on for a splinter."

"There's some medication I want to prescribe, Mrs. Dolan. If there's an aid station nearby, I can take you there and buy the proper dosage and make sure you take it."

She looked at me with the same expression as in the very beginning: speculative, noncommittal. "Well . . . there's Monty's Lounge up at the shopping center, behind the package store."

Five

MONTY'S WAS NO shadowy cave. It was bright, sunny, and noisy. Terrazzo floor, orange tables, a din of laughter and talk, shouts of greeting, clink of ice. Hey, Jeannie. Hi, Jeannie, as we found our way to a table for two against the far wall. I could see that this was the place for a quick one after the business places in the shopping center closed. There was a savings and loan, insurance offices, a beauty parlor, specialty shops all nearby.

The waitress came over and said, "The usual, Jeannie? Okay. And what's for you, friend?" Jeannie's turned out to be vodka tonic, and friend ordered a beer.

In those noisy and familiar surroundings Jeannie relaxed and talked freely. She and her friend Betsy had come down to Florida from Columbus, Ohio, in mid-January to arrange a couple of divorces. Their marriages had both gone sour. She had worked for an advertising agency, doing copy and layout, but couldn't find anything in her line in the Lauderdale area. Betsy Booker had been a dental hygienist in Columbus but hated it because no matter what kind of shoes she bought, her feet hurt all the time. Betsy's husband was a city fireman, and Jeannie's husband was an accountant.

She seemed miffed at her friend Betsy. There was tension there, and it had something to do with Harry Broll. I tried to pry, but she sidestepped me, asked me what I did. I told her I was in marine salvage, and she said she knew it had to be some kind of outdoor work.

Finally I took a calculated risk and said, "If my friend likes the apartment, then I'll see what I can do with Harry Broll. Hope you don't mind hearing somebody badmouth him. Harry is such a pompous, obnoxious, self-important jackass, it will be a pleasure to see how far down he'll come on the price."

"You said you were friends, McGee!"

"I said I knew him. Do I look like a man who needs friends like that?"

"Do I look like a girl who'd work for a man like that?"

We shook hands across the table, agreeing we both had better taste. Then she told me that Betsy Booker's taste was more questionable. Betsy had been having an affair with Harry Broll for two months.

"Betsy and I were in a two bedroom on the fourth on the highway side, but she has gradually been moving her stuff up onto six into his one bedroom, apartment 61. I guess it hurt her sore feet, all that undressing and dressing and undressing and walking practically the length of the building."

"Bitter about it?"

"I guess I sound bitter. It's more like hating to see her be so damned dumb. She's a real pretty blonde with a cute figure, and she just isn't used to being without a guy, I guess. It isn't a big sex thing going on. Betsy just has to have somebody beside her in the night, somebody she can hear breathing. She makes up these weird stories about how it's all going to work out. She says he's going to make a great big wad of money on some kind of land promotion stock and because Mrs. Broll deserted her husband, he's going to be able to get a divorce and marry Betsy."

"Couldn't it happen like that?"

"With him? Never!" she said and explained how she hadn't liked Harry's looks and had checked him out. Her best source had been the housekeeper at the apartment building. Last November when the place had been finished, Harry Broll had taken over apartment 61. He had an unlisted phone installed. He did not get any mail there.

"It's obvious what he was setting up," Jeannie said. "The world is full of Harry Broll–type husbands. The housekeeper said some Canadian broad moved into the apartment a week later. Harry would take long lunch hours. But he must have slipped up somehow, because Mrs. Broll arrived one day about Christmas time and went busting in when Harry was leaving, and there was a lot of screaming going on. His wife left him, even though Harry had gotten rid of his girlfriend. Then Harry moved out of his house and into the apartment. Betsy saw his house once. He took her there and showed it to her. She said it's big and beautiful. She won't ever get to live there. He'll dump her when he gets tired of her."

She said two drinks would be plenty. I paid the check and took her out and introduced her to Miss Agnes. Jeannie was so delighted with my ancient Rolls that I had to drive her up to Pompano Beach and back. I let her out across from the Casa de Playa. I wondered if I should caution her about mentioning my name to Betsy, who might in turn mention it to Harry Broll, and turn him more paranoid than ever. But it seemed to be too long a chance to worry about and too little damage from it even if it did happen.

She gave me an oblique, quick, half-shy look that said something about wondering if she would ever see me again. I discovered that I would like to see her again. We said cheerful and conspiratorial good-bys. She walked around the front of Miss Agnes, waited for a gap in traffic, and hastened across the highway. Her legs were not quite too thin, I decided. The brown-red hair had a lively bounce. From the far curb she turned and waved, her smile long-range but very visible.

It was dark when I parked Miss Agnes. I walked to F Dock and on out to Slip 18 and made a ritualistic check of the mooring lines and spring lines, then checked to see how the *Muñequita* was riding, tucked in against the flank of the *Busted Flush,* fenders in proper placement to prevent thumps and gouges.

"Don't pretend you can't hear my foot tapping, you rude, tardy son of a bitch," Jilly said with acid sweetness. She was at the sundeck rail, outlined against the misty stars with a pallor of dock lights against her face.

I went aboard, climbed up, and reached for her but she ducked away. "What did I forget, woman?"

"The Townsends. I told you I accepted for both of us. Don't you remember at all?"

"What did we accept?"

"Drinks aboard the *Wastrel* and dinner ashore. They're over at Pier 66. Old friends, dear. She was the heavy little woman with the good diamonds."

"Oh."

"You're drawing a blank, aren't you?"

"I seem to be."

"Hurry and change and we can join them at dinner. And, dear, not quite as informal as you were at my little party, please?"

"Is she the woman who kept talking about her servant problem? No matter what anybody else was talking about?"

"Yes. That's Natalie. And Charles is hard of hearing, and he's too vain to admit it or buy one of those little electronic things. *Please* hurry, Travis." She eeled into my arms, pressed herself close to me. She smelled very good, and she felt springy and useful. "The sooner we go, dearest, the sooner we can leave their party and come back and have our own little party."

I gave her a good solid whack on the behind and said, "You go ahead and make excuses."

"Ouch! That was too rough, really. You'll be along soon?"

"Jilly honey, I don't know those people. I can't talk to them, and they can't talk to me. I could use up my life with people like that and never know where it went."

"They're my *friends*! I won't permit you to be rude to my friends. You accepted, you know."

"*You* accepted."

"But I expect you had to have some consideration for—"

"Don't expect anything from me, Jillian. Sorry I forgot. Sorry you had to hang around waiting for me. Now go to your party and have a good time."

"Do you mean it?"

"Why shouldn't I want you to have a good time?"

"I have *had* it with you, you bahstid!"

"Sorry, Jilly. I just don't go to parties unless I like the people."

She went clicking down the outside ladderway and clacked her way aft and off the *Flush* and down the dock and away into the night. I went below, turned on a few lights, built a drink, ran a thumb down the stack of tapes, picked Eydie, and chunked her into the tape player and fixed the volume.

Eydie has comforted me many times in periods of stress. She has the effortlessness of total professionalism. She is just so damned good that people have not been able to believe she is as good as she is. She's been handed a lot of dull material, some of it so bad that even her best hasn't been able to bring it to life. She's been mishandled, booked into the right places at the wrong time, the wrong places at the right time. But she can do every style and do it a little better than the people who can't do any other. Maybe a generation from now those old discs and tapes of Eydie will be the collectors' joy, because she does it all true, does it all with pride, does it all with heart.

So I settled back and listened to her open her throat and

let go, backed by the Trio Los Panchos, Mexican love songs in flawless Mexican Spanish. She eased the little itch of remembering just how good my Irish lady had smelled, tasted, and felt.

A lot of the good ones get away. They want to impose structure upon my unstructured habits. It doesn't work. If I wanted structure, I'd live in a house with a Florida room, have 2.7 kids, a dog, a cat, a smiling wife, two cars, a viable retirement and profit-sharing plan, a seven handicap, and shortness of breath.

God only knows how many obligations there would have been once we were living in the British Virgins. Sing to me, Eydie. I just lost a pretty lady.

Through the music I heard the bong of my warning bell. I put on the aft floods and trapped Meyer in the white glare, blinking. I turned them off and let him in. I could not use Eydie for background music, so I ejected the tape and put a nothing tape on and dropped the sound down to the threshold of audibility.

Meyer said, "I was here an hour ago, and there was a beautiful, angry lady here, all dressed up, with someplace to go but nobody to go with."

"Fix yourself a knock. She decided to go alone."

"I bet."

"I am a crude, selfish bastard, and she is through with me."

He came back with a drink. He sat and said, "They tell me that a ring in the nose bothers you for the first week or so and then you never notice it again."

"Until somebody yanks on the rope."

"Oh, she wouldn't do that without good cause."

"Who the hell's side are you on?"

"She'll be back."

"Don't put any money on it."

"Speaking of money . . ."

"Harry Broll?"

"Yes, indeed. I had a long, tiring day. I talked to twenty people. I lied a lot. This is what I put together. It is all a fabric of assumption and supposition. Harry Broll is a small-to medium-sized cog in the machine called SeaGate, Inc. It is Canadian money, mostly from a Quebec financier named Dennis Waterbury, and New York money from a syndicate there which has been involved in other land deals. They needed Broll because of his knowledge of the local scene, the local contacts, legal shortcuts, and so on. It is a privately held corporation. They are going public. The offering price has not been set yet, but it will be about twenty-six or twenty-seven dollars a share. Most of the shares will be offered by the corporation, but about a third of the public offering will be by the present shareholders. Harry will be marketing a hundred thousand shares."

Cause for a long, low whistle. Old Harry with two and a half mil before taxes was a boggling picture for the mind to behold.

"How soon does he get rich?"

"Their fiscal year ends the last day of this month. The national accounting firm doing the audit is Jensen, Baker and Company. They will apparently get a guaranteed underwriting through Fairmont, Noyes. I hear that it is a pretty clean deal and that SEC approval should be pretty much cut and dried after they get the complete audit report, the draft of the red herring."

I stared at him. "Red herring?"

"Do you know what a prospectus is?"

"That thing that tells you more than you care to know about a new issue of stocks or bonds?"

"Yes. The red herring is the prospectus without the per share price of the stock on it or the date of issue. And it is a complete disclosure of *everything* to do with the company, background of executives and directors, how they got their stock, what stock options they may hold, what financial hanky panky, if any, they've ever been involved in. Very interesting reading sometimes."

"Nice to see an old acquaintance get rich enough to afford a hell of a lot of alimony."

"When a company is in registration, they get very secretive, Travis. Loose lips can sink financial ships."

"What would he want Mary to sign? He said it was to protect his interest in SeaGate."

"I wouldn't have any idea."

"Can you find out?"

"I can try to find out. I suppose the place to go would be West Palm. That's where the administrative offices of SeaGate are. That's where they are doing the audit, starting early so that they can close the books as of April thirtieth. It would be futile to try to pry anything out of the Jensen, Baker people. But maybe somebody in the SeaGate organization might talk. What did you do today?"

I told him. It was complicated and a lot of it was wasted time and effort, so I kept to the things that had worked.

Then I got to my big question. I had been bouncing it off the back of my mind for an hour, and it was going to be a pleasure to share the trauma with someone else.

"Here is this distrait husband, Meyer. He says he doesn't chase women. The Canadian girl was an exception, a big mistake. He wants me to tell Mary he wants her back. They'll go on a nice trip together. He is so rattled and upset he takes out his little gun and tries to kill me. Suppose he had. His two and a half mil would do him no good at all. And Mary could do him no good by coming back. Okay. He stashed his Canadian tail in apartment 61 at his Casa de Playa, and it was right there that Mary caught him. Harry got rid of the girlfriend. Mary gloomed around for a time, and then she left him. He wants her back. He's sending messages through me, he thinks, to get her to come back to him. Let's say she decides to go back. She goes to their house and finds it closed up. She knows he has the apartment. So she'd go there next, and she'd find him all cozied up there with a blonde named Betsy Booker. Draw me some inferences, please."

"Hmmm. We'll assume that the Booker woman is living in Broll's apartment with him, and the signs of her presence are too numerous to eliminate with short warning. Thus, when Broll came to see you, he either was very sure that Mary *would* not come back to him or that Mary *could* not come back to him. Or, possibly, if Mary could come back to him and decided to come back to him, he would have an early warning system to give him ample time to get the Booker woman out of the apartment and maybe even move back to Blue Heron Lane. This would imply that he knows where she is and has some pipeline to her. In either case, there would be considerable insincerity in his visit to you. Yet a man playing games does not pause in the middle of the game to murder someone out of jealousy. So we come to a final postulate which is not particularly satisfying. We assume that he is and was sincere but is too comfortable with his current living arrangement to want to think it through and see how easily it could spoil his second chance with Mary."

"He's not that dumb. Dumb, but not *that* dumb."

"Logic has to take into account all alternatives."

"Would you consider eating Hungarian tonight?" I asked him.

"Considered and approved."

"Poker dollar for the tab?"

"Food and drink, all on one."

Six

THE WAY YOU FIND MARY is the same way you find anybody. Through friends and neighbors. And patience. Through shopping habits, money habits, doctor, dentist, bureaucratic forms and reports. And more patience.

You reconstruct the events of three and a half and four years ago and try to remember the names and places, the people who could be leads. You find out who Mary used to be, and from that maybe you find out where she is.

To start with, she was Tina Potter's friend. Came down to see Tina and Freddie. Came down from Rochester, New York. It was just a visit, and then she got her own place. Had some money, some kind of income. Didn't have to work. Came down because she had just been through a jolting and ugly divorce action. She'd gotten her maiden name back by court order. Mary Dillon. Dillon and Dolan. I seemed to be working my way through the Ds. D for divorce.

A quiet young woman. We all got to like her. She had been putting the pieces of herself back together very very nicely. Then something happened. What the hell was it?

At last I remembered. Tina Potter had come over to the *Flush* late one afternoon and asked me if I could sort of keep an eye on Mary. Freddie had a special assignment in Bogota, and Tina would go with him only if she was sure somebody would watch over Mary. The incident which had racked her up had been the accidental death of her divorced husband a few days before. A one-car accident on a rainy night somewhere near Rochester. Left the road and hit a tree.

I remembered Tina's earnest face as she said, "Two-bit psychology for whatever it's worth, McGee. I think Mary had the idea, hidden so deep she didn't even realize it, that one day her Wally would grow up and come back to her and then they'd have the kind of marriage she thought they were going to have the first time around. So with him dead, it can't ever be. She's trying to hang on, but it's very white-knuckle stuff. Would you mind too much? She trusts you. She can talk to you."

So I had spent a lot of time with Mary. Beach walking, driving around, listening to music. But if she laughed, she couldn't be sure it wouldn't turn into tears. She had no appetite. The weight loss was apparent. A drink would hit her too hard.

I suggested the aimless cruise. Get away. No destination. Mary knew by then it wasn't a shrewd way of hurrying her into the sack, because had that been the target, it would have happened one of the times when her guard was way down. She agreed without much enthusiasm, provided she could pay her share of the expenses and do her share of the chores aboard.

After two weeks she had really begun to come out of it. At first she had slept twelve and fourteen hours a night, as if her exhaustion was of the same kind that happens after an almost mortal wound. Then she had begun to eat. The listlessness had turned to a new energy. She could laugh without it turning to tears.

One day when we were anchored a dozen miles north of Marathon, among some unnamed islands, I took the little *Sea Gull* outboard apart, cleaned it, lubricated it, reassembled it, while she zipped around out there in the sailing dinghy, skidding and tacking in a brisk bright wind. When she came back aboard the *Flush* she was wind blown, sun glowing, salty, happy, and thirsty. Before she went off to take her very niggardly freshwater shower, she brought me a beer. She told me she hadn't felt so good in a long long time. We clinked bottles in a toast to a happy day. She looked, smiling, into my eyes, and then her eyes changed. Something went click. They widened in small shock and surprise, then looked soft and heavy. Her head was too heavy for her slender neck. Her mouth was softer. Her mouth said my name without making a sound. She got up and left me, her walk slow and swaying, and went below. It had been awareness, invitation, and acceptance all in a few moments, all without warning. I remember hastily fastening the last piece of the housing back onto the small motor and deciding that I could test it and stow it later. The lady was below, and there was a day to celebrate, a cruise to celebrate, a recovery to celebrate.

• • •

So try Tina and Freddie Potter. Long gone, of course. Scrabbled around in the locker where I throw cards and letters. Found one a year old. Address in Atlanta. Direct-dialed Atlanta information, then direct-dialed the Potter house. Squeals of delight, then desolation that I wasn't in Atlanta. Freddie had just gone off to work. She had to quiet the kids down, then she came back on the line.

"Mary? Gee, I guess the last I heard was Christmas time, Trav. She wrote kind of a short dreary note on the back of a New Year's card. She sounded pretty depressed, so I wrote her, but I didn't hear from her. What's the matter? Why are you looking for her?"

"She left Harry Broll early in January."

"That doesn't surprise me much. I never could understand why she married him. Or the first one, Wally, either. Some women seem to have to pick losers every time. Like some women pick alcoholics every time. But . . . I'd think she'd get in touch with you or with us. But you know Mary. Doesn't want to be a burden to anyone."

"How about family?"

"Well, there was just her mother up in Rochester, and she died two years ago. That was all she had, Trav. Gee, I can't think of who you could ask. But I'd think she'd have some friend she'd talk to. A neighbor or something."

She couldn't contribute anything more. She wanted me to let her know when I found out where Mary was, and she wanted me to come to Atlanta and stay with them and tell them all the news about everybody around the marina.

I couldn't use the Rolls pickup to visit the neighbors along Blue Heron Lane. There aren't any cover stories to fit that set of wheels. And housewives are very edgy these days. They have little peep holes set into the doors and outdoor intercom speakers and little panic buttons to push if they get too nervous. Respectability is essential. Nothing eccentric please.

So I borrowed Johnny Dow's Plymouth sedan, and I wore pressed slacks, a sincere jacket, an earnest shirt, and a trustworthy necktie. I carried a black zipper portfolio and a dozen of my business cards. I am Travis McGee, Vice President of CDTA, Inc. It is no lie. Meyer incorporated the company a few years ago, and he keeps it active by paying the tiny annual tax. CDTA means nothing at all. Meyer picked the letters because they sound as if they have to mean something. Commercial Data Transmission Authority. Consolidated Division of Taxes and Audits. Contractors' Departmental Transit Acceptance.

In my sincere, earnest, trustworthy way I was going to hit the neighborhood on this hot Friday morning with a nice check which I had to deliver to Mrs. Harry Broll in settlement of her claim and get her to sign a release. I used one of the checks Meyer had ordered. It was on an actual account. Of course, the account was inactive and had about twelve dollars in it, but the blue checks were impressively imprinted with spaces for his signature and mine. He borrowed a checkwriter from a friend in one of the shops, and we debated the amount for some time before settling on a figure of $1,093.88.

"Good morning, ma'am. I hate to bother you like this, but I wonder if you can help me. My name is McGee. Here is my card. I've got out a check payable to Mrs. Harry Broll in full payment of her claim of last year, and I have a release here for her to sign, but the house looks as if they're off on a long trip or moved or something. Could you tell me how I could find Mrs. Broll?"

It was not a long street. Three short, curving blocks. Large lots, some of them vacant, so that the total was not over twenty-five homes right on Blue Heron Lane. The Broll house was in the middle of the middle block on the left. The canal ran behind the houses on the left hand side, following the curves. Dig a canal and you have instant waterfront.

I made the logical moves. I parked the Plymouth in the Broll driveway, tried the doorbell, then tried the neighbors, the nearest ones first.

"I can't help you at all. We moved in here three weeks ago, all the way from Omaha, and that house has been empty since we moved in, and from any sign of neighborliness from anybody else around here, all the houses might as well be empty, if you ask me."

"Go away. I don't open the door to anyone. Go away."

"Mrs. Broll? Someone said they split up. No, we weren't friendly. I wouldn't have any idea where you could find her."

At the fourth front door—the fifth if you count the place where nobody answered—there was a slight tweak at the baited end of my line.

"I guess the one to ask would be Mrs. Dressner. Holly Dressner. She and Mrs. Broll were all the time visiting back and forth, morning coffee and so forth. That's the next house there, number 29, if she's home. She probably is. I didn't hear her backing out."

After the second try on the doorbell I was about to give up. I could hear the chimes inside. No answer. Then the intercom speaker fastened to the rough-cut cypress board beside the front door clicked and said, "Who is it? And, for God's sake, just stand there and talk in a normal tone of voice. If you get close to the speaker and yell, I won't understand word one."

I gave my spiel, adding that the lady next door told me she would be the one to ask. She asked me if I had a card, and she had me poke it through the mail slot. I wondered why she sounded so out of breath.

I heard chains and locks, and she pulled the door open and said, "So come in." She wore a floor-length terry robe in wide yellow and white stripes, tightly belted. Her short, blond, water-dark hair was soaked. "I was in the pool. Daily discipline. Come on out onto the terrace. I'm too wet to sit in the living room."

She was a stocky woman with good shoulders and a slender waist. She had a tan, freckled face, broad and good humored, pale lashes and brows, pretty eyes. The terrace was screened, and the big pool took up most of the space. Sliding glass doors opened the terrace up into the living room. The yard beyond the screening and beyond the flowerbeds sloped down to a small concrete dock where a canopied Whaler was moored.

She invited me to sit across from her at a wrought iron table with a glass top.

"Try that on me again, Mr. McGee. Slowly. Is this the check?"

She picked it up and put it down and listened as I went through it again. "A claim for what?" she asked.

"Mrs. Dressner, it's company policy not to discuss casualty claims and settlements. I'm sure you can understand why."

"Mr. McGee, may I ask you a personal question?"

"Of course."

"How come you are so full of bullshit?"

I stared at her merry face and merry smile. But above the smile the hazel eyes were expressionless as poker chips.

"I . . . I don't quite understand."

"Go back to Harry and tell him that this didn't work, either. What does he think I am? Some kind of idiot, maybe? Good-by, Mr. McGee."

"This isn't for Harry. This is for me."

"So who the hell are you?"

"How friendly are you with Mary anyway?"

"Very very very. Okay?"

"What happened to her when Wally got killed?"

She frowned at me. "She came apart. She flipped."

"And a man took her on a boat ride?"

"Right. And the way she talked about him, that's the one she should have played house with instead of Harry Broll."

"I almost thought about it seriously."

"You?"

"Travis McGee. The *Busted Flush*. Cruised the Keys and up the west coast to Tampa Bay. Taught her to sail. Taught her to read a chart. Taught her to navigate."

She put her determined chin on her fist and stared at me. "That *was* the name. You, huh? So what's with the funny games, coming here with your funny card and your funny check? If you knew we're close friends, why not start honest?"

"I have not seen her or talked to her in over three years, Holly. And don't jump on my knowing your first name and try to make anything out of it. The woman next door clued me."

"Hitting the whole neighborhood?"

"One at a time. Mary is . . . low-key intense. She hides a lot of herself. She doesn't make friends easily. But she needs people, so I thought she'd have to have a friend in the neighborhood. A friend, not an acquaintance. Right?"

"So right, McGee. Coffee and tears. Most women bug me. Mary doesn't. I . . . still don't feel right about you. About taking you for granted. It *could* be some kind of a trick. I want to ask you things, but I can't think of anything to ask that you couldn't have gotten from Harry."

"He's trying to find her."

"You know it! I thought the silly son of a bitch was going to try to shake it out of me."

"When was this?"

"A couple of weeks ago. He'd had a couple. He got all weepy. He insisted I had to know where Mary is."

"Do you know where she is?"

"McGee, I know why Harry wants to find her. He wants her to come back to him and sign something and live happily ever after."

"It might be an ugly shock if she did come back."

"How?"

"She'd find the house empty, and she'd go look for Harry at the Casa de Playa, where he just so happens to be shacked with a divorcing blonde named Betsy Booker. In apartment 61."

I couldn't read her expression. "So?"

"So isn't that where Mary found him with the Canadian?"

"Only two people could have told you that. Or three. Harry, Mary, or Lisa—the Canadian quiff."

"Wrong."

"The hell you say."

"I got it out of Betsy Booker's best friend, Jeannie Dolan, also from Columbus, who got part of it from Betsy and part of it from the housekeeper. Jeannie and Betsy take turns manning the sales desk at the Casa de Playa."

I saw her buy it and give a small nod. "So help me. That rotten Harry. Jesus! The way I read it, Lisa was not the first. Just the first she caught him with. He really is one sorry bastard."

"How did she find out?"

"She thinks it was one of the girls in his office or a girl he'd fired, trying to make things rough for him. She got a phone call. The person on the other end whispered. Mary said it was spooky. Something very much to the point. 'Mrs. Broll, your husband has loaned apartment 61 in his new building to Lisa Dissat, and he'll be taking another long lunch hour today so he can drive out there and screw her.' So she drove out and hid somewhere until he arrived and went upstairs. Then she went up to the sixth floor and waited around until the door opened and he started to come out. She took a quick run at the door and knocked it open and charged past him and found the bareass Canadian getting ready to take a nice nap. I take it there was a certain amount of screaming going on for a while."

"Then Harry got rid of the girlfriend?"

"She was packed and out of there the next day. Back to

Canada, Harry told Mary. He confessed his sad story. He had gone to Quebec for business conferences with his Canadian partners. He had to dictate new agreements. They sent the secretary to the hotel. They worked very late. He was too tired to think clearly. She was pretty and available. It went on for the three days he was up there. He came back. Two days after he was back, she phoned him at his office from Miami. She had quit her job and followed him back to Florida. So he told Mary that while he was trying to talk Lisa into going back, he put her up at the apartment. I guess he was having a hard time convincing her. He talked from the end of November till two days before Christmas. That's a lot of long lunches and a lot of evening conferences."

"But Mary didn't leave him until January fifth."

"Harry told you that?"

I laughed. "I thought the silly son of a bitch was going to try to shake it out of me, too. This was just the other day. And he got weepy."

"So you're finding her for him?"

"May I ask you the same personal question you asked me?"

"Okay. Okay. I'm sorry. Why then?"

"For myself. Pride, I guess. Harry thought if she was really in trouble, she would come running to me. And the more I think about it, the more logical it seems. That she would. Besides—" I stopped suddenly.

"What's the matter?"

"When was Harry here, did you say?"

"Oh, two weeks ago."

"Can you pin it down to a day?"

"Let me go take a look at my kitchen calendar and see."

She came back and said, "Less than two weeks ago. It was a Monday morning. April fifth."

"He told me someone had seen Mary with me on April second. He was wrong, of course. Why would he come after you instead of me if she was seen with me?"

"Maybe he hadn't been told about it before he came to see me," she said.

"And maybe he was trying to get you to admit she'd moved in with me or some damn thing. What difference does it make anyway? He didn't act as if he was thinking very clearly."

"Mary was thinking about getting in touch with you. She was sitting in my kitchen wondering out loud if she should. That was after she'd decided to take off. Then she decided it would be better to have some breathing space in between, some time to herself first. I thought she would have written you long before now. It's over three months."

"She writes you?"

"Don't get too cute, McGee."

"Okay. Do you know where she is?"

"Yes."

"And she is okay?"

"I have no reason to think she isn't. If I was Mary, I would be relishing every damn moment. The farther from Harry, the better."

"That's all I wanted to know, Mrs. Dressner. That she is okay. I had to hear it from somebody I could believe."

"Hey! You're spoiling the fun. You're supposed to worm the whole story out of me. Or try to."

"It's Harry who has to know where she is. Not me."

"Friend McGee, I am not about to get you two men confused, one with the other."

"So she is a long distance from here. And should be relishing every moment. Right?"

"I've gotten some comedy postcards."

"I believe you. There are people you believe and people you don't. I don't need to know any more than I know right now."

She looked rueful. "Everybody believes me. Everything I'm thinking shows. I've got one of those faces. I'd make a rotten spy. Hey, sit down again. I haven't offered you anything. Coffee, tea, beer, booze? Even some lunch?"

"No thanks."

"Believe me, I'm glad to have anybody show up here. This is one of the days when the house gets empty somehow. David—my husband—has been gone all week. He'll be home tomorrow, probably about noon. He's gone a week or more out of every month. Our two little gals are tennis freaks, so who sees them at all when the weather is like this? I miss the hell out of Mary, I really do. You could choke down some terrible coffee at least. Pretend it's delicious, and I'll tell you where Mary is. Even if you don't have to know."

She brought coffee from the kitchen to the glass-top table on the screened terrace. Moving around had loosened the hitch in the terry belt, and when she bent to pour my coffee, the robe suddenly spilled open. She spilled coffee, clutched frantically, put the pot down, and gathered herself together and tied the robe firmly, her face dark red under the freckles. It was obvious she had not contrived it.

"Some people are solitary drinkers. I'm a solitary skinny dipper."

"It's habit forming," I said.

She got paper towels and mopped up the spilled coffee and filled my cup the rest of the way. She sat and stared at me, lips pursed. Finally she said, "Thank you."

"For?"

"For not jumping to any conclusions, for which I could not exactly blame you. Good God, I tell you my husband is away, my kids are playing tennis, I'm lonesome. I beg you to stay for coffee and then damn near drop my robe on the floor."

"Some days are like that."

"I like the way you can smile without hardly changing your mouth at all. It's kind of all in the eyes. Mary said you're a doll. She said big and brown and sort of beat-up looking. But you're bigger and browner than the idea I had of you. About Mary. That was a sordid scene at the Casa de Playa. It shook her. Friendship is friendship, but you don't tell your friends what to do when it comes to big emotional decisions. Through Christmas and the rest of December she spent a lot of time over here. I let her bounce it all off me. She was thinking aloud, arguing it out. Taking one side and then the other, while all I did was say 'um.' But I could tell which side was winning. Finally she said that if she hadn't already had one divorce, she would definitely decide to leave Harry. It was a lousy reason to stick around, just to avoid being divorced twice, which has a kind of ring of failure to it, failure as a person or as a woman. So she was going to leave him and go away and, to be real fair, think it all through. But the way she felt, she'd probably sue for divorce after the waiting period. I waited for her to really make her mind up, and then I questioned her to make certain she was sure, and finally I told her about a little problem I had once with her husband. There'd been a party down the street and the four of us, the Brolls and the Dressners, had walked back together, a little tight. They came over here for a nightcap. There were supposed to be falling stars. It was in the paper. I wanted to see them. We put out the lights on the terrace, and I stretched out on a sun mattress beside the pool, right over there, to watch up through the screening overhead. David went to the kitchen to fix drinks, and Mary changed her mind about what she wanted and went in the kitchen to tell him. Harry was on a sun mattress near mine. All of a sudden he rolled over and put his big old cigar mouth on mine and pressed me down with his big belly and ran his big paw up under my skirt and started groping me. I froze with shock for about one second, and then I gave a big snap of my back like a huge fishing shrimp and bucked him into the pool in all his clothes. It turned into a big joke. He said he'd gotten up and tripped and fallen in.

"When I told Mary about it, she was furious with me for not telling her sooner. I told her I hadn't told David, because he would have tried to beat Harry to death. I said that now she'd made her mind up, I could tell her about what Harry pulled that time. Frankly, what I was doing was trying to lock her into her decision to drop that jerk forever. Having her own money made it easy for her to get away. She got it from her trust officer at the Southern National Bank and Trust in Miami. Cash. A lot, I think. She didn't want Harry tracing her through credit cards or personal checks. She told me she didn't want to hear his voice or see his face once she left. Not for a long time anyway. We sat right out here one afternoon, a warm day for early January, and we looked at the travel folders she'd picked up from some little travel agency where she wasn't known. She wanted to go to the islands. Between the two of us we decided that Grenada looked the best, and it was certainly far enough, way down there at the bottom of the West Indies, almost as far as Trinidad. So the travel agency sent wires and cables and got her set up at what looked like a very plush place, the Spice Island Inn. She's sent me those joke greetings. Four or five, I guess. Airmail takes eight days! That place is a real hideaway."

"Harry told me she left on January fifth. He said he came home from work and she was gone."

"I think it was an impulse. She wasn't going to leave until Thursday or Friday. I was out most of that afternoon. Maybe she tried to say good-by. I guess she probably drove down to Miami and stayed in a hotel or motel until her flight left."

"I wonder what she did with her car?"

"I think she was going to leave it at Miami International."

"Which is two fifty a day, no matter how many days, so she is up to a two-hundred-dollar parking charge."

"McGee, the lady had decided to go first class all the way. That is what ladies do when they get mad enough."

"What would Harry be wanting her to sign?"

"I haven't the faintest idea."

"Good coffee."

"Come *on*! It tastes like stewed tire patches."

She walked me to the door. She got ahead of me and

leaned back against the door and looked up quizzically. She stood a little taller than my elbow. "McGee, I just wondered. It seems like a hell of a lot of trouble you went to. The business cards and the funny check and the sales talk."

"No big thing, Holly. The cards and the checks were in the cupboard. I have to hunt for people sometimes. You learn to use something that works."

"Why do you hunt for people?"

"I do favors for friends."

"Is that a line of work with you?"

"I really wouldn't know how to answer that question."

She sighed. "Heck, I thought I could solve a problem for Mary. She never *was* able to figure out what it is that you do for a living."

"Salvage consultant."

"Sure. Sure."

When I glanced back, she was standing on her shallow front steps, arms crossed. Her hair was beginning to dry and to curl a little. She smiled and waved. She was a sturdy, healthy woman with a very friendly smile.

Seven

I WAS ON THE BEACH by three o'clock that Friday afternoon and that was where Meyer found me at a few minutes to four. He dropped his towel, sat upon it, and sighed more loudly than the surf in front of us or the traffic behind us.

There were nine lithe maidens, miraculously unaccompanied by a flock of boys, playing some game of their own devising on the hard sand in the foamy wash of the waves. It involved an improvised club of driftwood, a small, yellow, inflated beach ball, one team out in the water, and one on the beach. Either you had to whack the ball out over the heads of the swimmers before they . . . or you had to hit it past a beach player who then . . . Anyway, it involved a lot of running, yelping, and team spirit.

"A gaggle of giggles?" Meyer said, trying that one on me. My turn. "How about a prance of pussycats?"

"Not bad at all. Hmmm. A scramble of scrumptious?"

"Okay. You win. You always win."

He slowly scratched his pelted chest and smiled his brown bear smile. "We both win. By being right here at this time. All the strain of a long, difficult, and futile day is evaporating quickly. Meyer is at peace. Play on, young ladies, because from here on out life will be a lot less fun for most of you."

"Grow up and be earnest and troubled?" I asked. "Why does it have to be that way?"

"It doesn't. It shouldn't be. Funny, though. They take all those high spirits, all that sense of fun and play into one of the new communes, and within a year they are doleful wenches indeed. Somber young versions of American Gothic, like young wagon train mothers waiting for the Indians to ride over the ridge. And their men look like the pictures of the young ones slain at Shiloh. Idealism in our society is pretty damned funereal."

One of the players looked up the beach and gave a quick wave and then went churning into the water to capture the yellow ball.

"One of my constituents," Meyer said comfortably.

"You are a dirty old man."

"You have a dirty mind, McGee. I could not bring myself to ever touch the child. But in all fairness it does enter my mind. Lovely, isn't she?"

"Exquisite."

"Her last name is Kincaid, and I do not know her first name. She is known to everyone as Breadbox. She has an incredible appetite. She's an economics major at Yale. Quite a good mind. Her father grows tobacco in Connecticut. She drove down in a five-year-old Porsche with two other girls.

This summer she is going to work in a boutique aboard a cruise ship. She has a dog at home named Rover, which seems to have come full circle and is now an 'in' name for a dog. She is getting over a romance which ended abruptly and does not want to become interested in another man for years and years, she says. Tennis used to be her sport, but now she prefers—"

"So all right already, Meyer. Damn it."

"I think she was waving at someone behind us."

"What?"

"I never saw the child before in my life. I was just putting together into one package some of the things the other young ladies have told me."

"Have you been drinking?"

"No. But if you'd like to . . ."

With as little warning as a flock of water birds, the nine maidens dropped the club and went jogging north along the beach, one of them clutching the yellow ball.

Meyer said, "I did not do well today, Travis. Just a few small items. Dennis Waterbury is in his mid-thirties, bland, shrewd, tough, quick, merciless—and completely honest. He gives his word and keeps it."

"Listen. I was able—"

"Let me deliver my few crumbs first. Harry Broll's cost on his one hundred thousand shares was ten dollars a share, and his money and the money the others put in was used to acquire the land, prepare sites, build roads, start the utility construction, water, waste processing, and so forth. A very golden opportunity for a man like Broll to get his foot in the door with people like Waterbury and friends. But in order to make it big, he had to pluck himself pretty clean, I imagine, and borrow to the hilt. Put up one million and drag down two million and a half. The odds are splendid, the risk low enough."

"About Mary, I—"

"I can't seem to find out what she would have to sign. She wouldn't have to sign anything in connection with the stock. It's in his name. She isn't on his business paper."

"Mary is alive and well and living in Grenada."

"In Spain?"

"No. The island."

"Dear chap, the one in Spain is Gran-AH-duh. The island is Gre-NAY-duh. The British corrupted it with their usual mispronunciation of all place names."

"You've been there?"

"No."

"But you know a lot about it?"

"No. I happen to know how to pronounce it. One has to start somewhere."

"Let's swim."

After about ten minutes Meyer intercepted me fifty yards from the beach, to ask, "How come you could find that out and Harry can't?"

"I found the only person who might really know for sure, aside from the travel agent. A neighbor lady, who shows her good taste by disliking the hell out of Harry Broll. She thought for a while Harry sent me. I softened her up. She makes terrible coffee."

"Did Harry try to pry it out of her, too?"

"Yes. Nearly two weeks ago. With tears. Without the gun. But rough. She said she thought he was going to try to shake it out of her."

Meyer nodded and went gliding away, head up, in that powerful, slow, and tireless breaststroke that somehow makes me think of a seal when I see his head moving by.

When I came out of the water, he was sitting on his towel again, looking petulant, a rare mood for Meyer.

"Something bothering you?"

"Illogical actions and illogical emotions bother the hell out of me, Travis. His wife had been gone over three months. How about checking accounts, credit cards?"

I explained about the trust account and her taking cash so that she couldn't be easily traced by her husband. He said he knew one friendly face in the trust department of Southern National, but of course it would be Monday before he could learn anything there.

"Why bother?" I asked him. "I'm satisfied. We know where she is. I don't give a damn how jittery Harry Broll gets."

We walked back across the bridge together, squinting toward the western sun setting into its usual broad band of whisky soup. "I guess it doesn't matter in any case," Meyer said.

"What doesn't matter?"

"What happens to anybody. Look at the cars, McGee. Look at the people in the cars, on the boats, on the beach, in the water. Everybody is heading toward their own obituary notice at precisely the same speed. Fat babies, and old women like lizards, and the beautiful young with long golden hair. And me and thee, McGee. At tick-tock speed moving straight toward the grave, until all now living are as dead as if they had died in Ancient Rome. The only unknown, and that is a minor one, is how long will each individual travel at this unchanging, unchangeable pace?"

"Good God, Meyer! I was going to buy you dinner."

"Not today. This is not one of my good days. I think I'll open a can of something, go walking alone, fold up early. No need to poison somebody else's evening."

Away he trudged, not looking back. It happens sometimes. Not often. A curious gaiety, followed by bleak, black depression. It was a Meyer I seldom see and do not know at all.

Friday night. I took my time building a drink, showering, dressing, building a refill. Dark night by then, and a wind building up, so that the *Flush* moved uneasily, creaking and sighing against her lines, nudging at her fenders. I felt restless. I was wondering where to go, who to call, when Jillian came aboard.

She clung tightly and said she had been utterly miserable. She looked up at me with two perfect and effective tears caught in her lower lashes, her mouth quivering. The Townsend party had been desperately dull, really. She shouldn't have tried to force me to go. She shouldn't try to force me to do anything. She realized that now. She would not do it again, ever. Forgive me, Travis darling, please. I've been so lonely and so ashamed of myself etc., etc., etc.

Once forgiven, all the lights came on behind her eyes, and the tears were flicked away. Mood of holiday. She had been confident of reconciliation, she had brought hairbrush and toothbrush. And all the urgencies a girl could muster.

In the morning a rare April rain was coming down hard, thrashing at the ports beside the half acre of the captain's wrinkled and rumpled bed, bathing us in gray ten o'clock light.

"Is your friend in trouble?" she asked.

"Who?"

"That respectable married lady friend, of course."

"Oh. No, she's fine. It turns out she's hiding from her husband. She went down to Grenada."

She lifted her head. "Really? Henry and I went down there on the first really long cruise we took in the *Jilly III*. The Grenadines are one of the great sailing areas of the world. And the yacht basin at St. George's is really marvelous. You see people from everywhere, really. Yacht Services is very helpful."

"She's staying at the Spice Island Inn."

"Quite expensive. Is she alone down there?"

"Apparently."

"She can get into all kinds of delicious mischief if she wants. If she's even half attractive, she won't be lonely. The air is full of spice and perfume down there, dear. It's a fabulously erotic island. Always so warm and lazy, with the hot hot sun and the hills and jungles and the beaches. Quite near the equator, you know."

"I didn't know."

"Well, it is. Don't you think we should go there one day?"

"I guess so."

"You don't seem exactly overwhelmed with enthusiasm."

"Sorry."

"Are you going back to sleep, you wretch?"

"Not with you doing what you're doing."

"This? Oh, it's just a sort of reflex thing, I guess. Darling, if you're no longer worried about your friend, could we be ready to aim the *Jilly* toward home on Tuesday? I can get her provisioned on Monday."

"What? Oh, Tuesday. I guess so."

"You don't seem to keep track of what I'm saying."

"I guess I'm easily distracted."

"You're easily something else, too."

"What did you expect?"

"I expect, my dear, if we put our minds to it, we might make the Guinness Book of Records. Cozy? A nice rain always makes me very randy." After a moment she giggled.

"What's funny?"

"Oh, I was thinking I might decide we should go to Grenada during the rainy season, dear."

"Ho ho ho."

"Well . . . it amused *me*. When I feel this delicious, I laugh at practically anything. Sometimes at nothing at all."

The unusual cold front which had brought the rain ahead of it moved through late on Saturday afternoon. She went back to the *Jilly III*. She said she had a thousand things to do before we sailed on Tuesday. She said to come over on Sunday, sometime in the afternoon. She said I could bring along some of my clothes and toys then, if I wanted.

She left and I locked up again, hot showered, and fell into a deep sleep. I woke at ten on Saturday night, drank a gallon of water, ate half a pound of rat cheese, and dropped right back down into the pit.

I woke with a hell of a start at four on Sunday morning,

and thought there was somebody coming aboard. Realized it had been something happening in a dream. Made a grab for what was left of the dream, but it was all gone too quickly. Almost a nightmare. It had pumped me so full of adrenaline there was no hope of going back to sleep. Heart bumped and banged. Legs felt shaky. I scrubbed a bad taste off my teeth, put on jeans and boat shoes and an old gray sweatshirt, and went out onto the deck.

A very silent night. No breeze. A fog so thick the nearer dock lights were haloed and the farther ones were a faint and milky pallor, beyond tangible gray. I could hear slow waves curl and thud against the sand. The craft on either side of the *Flush* were shrouded in the fog, half visible.

Meyer's gloomy message had been delivered none too soon. Everybody else had been tick-tocked to the grave, leaving one more trip to complete—mine. Then, far away, I heard a long screeeeee of tormented rubber and a deep and ugly thud with a small accompanying orchestration of jangles and tinkles. The thud had been mortal, tick-tocking some racing jackass into his satin-lined box, possibly along with the girl beside him or the surprised folk in the other car.

A few minutes later I heard the sirens, heard them stop at what seemed a plausible distance.

So stop thinking about this and that, McGee, and think about what you don't want to think about, namely the lush future with the rich widow.

I climbed to the sun deck and went forward and slouched behind the wheel and propped my heels atop the instrument panel, ankles crossed.

That old honorary Cuban had simplified the question all

to hell when he'd said that a moral act is something you feel good after. Conversely, you feel bad after an immoral act. But what about the act that is neither moral nor immoral, Papa? How are you supposed to feel then?

Look, we are very suited to each other. There is a lot of control either way on both sides, so timing is no problem at all. She pleases me. She knows how to intensify it. I like the textures and juices, spices and rhythms of her, all her tastes and tastings. We truly climb one hell of a hill, Papa, and when we fall off the far side together, it is truly one hell of a long fall, Papa, and we land truly and well and as zonked out as lovers can get. We laugh a lot. We like to hold each other afterward. We make bawdy jokes. She has a lot of body greed and finds me a satisfying stud. In her gratitude she takes a lot of extra effort to keep things varied and interesting. So?

There's this little problem. I go into the head, Papa, and look at this battered and skewed beach-bum countenance of mine, reflected in the mirror, and my eyes look dull, and my mouth looks slack, and I am wearing the remnants of a doggy little smirk. I know she is in there, a-sprawl on the bed, drifting in and out of her little love doze, and I look truly and well at myself in the mirror, and I do not feel good about anything or bad about anything. I just feel as if I had made one of those little diagonal lines you use to keep track. You know—four little vertical lines side by side and then the diagonal that crosses them out and ends the group.

In the mirror my nose looks too big, and my skin looks grainy. I wear the doggy little grin. The smells of her cling to my body. There is the feeling of marking something off on a long score sheet. Something well and truly done that will have to be well and truly done for whatever years we both have left, because that is the bargain. Chop that cotton, tote that bale, plow that little acre of God.

What about it when you don't feel good and you don't feel bad? When you just feel that it's done for this time and done reasonably well, and later on the slack dangle of flesh will turn tumescent, and it will and can be done again, just as well as the last time? With proficiency, determination, patience, understanding, power and skill. Isn't lovemaking as good a way as any to pass the time for the rest of your life? It tones the body, and it's acceptable exercise, and it makes two people feel good.

If I don't grasp the opportunity, somebody will find some quick and dirty way to let the sea air through my skull.

I'm overdue. That's what Meyer says, and that's what my gut says in a slow cold coil of tingling viscera. Overdue, and scared, and not ready for the end of it yet. The old bullfighters who have known the famous rings and famous breeds despise the little country corridas, because they know that if they do not quit, that is where they will die—and the bull that hooks their steaming guts out onto the sand will be a poor animal without class or distinction or style.

An animal as ordinary as Harry Broll.

I shifted position, dug the keys out of the pocket, and found the keyholes in the instrument panel. It is one of the tics of the boatman, turning on the juice without starting up, just to check fuel levels, battery charge. By leaning close, I could read the gauges in the pallid light.

Maybe it isn't just the woman. This woman. Or a passing of time. It is the awareness, perhaps, of the grasshopper

years, of always pushing all the pleasure buttons. The justi-
fication was a spavined sense of mission, galumphing out to
face the dragon's fiery breath. It had been a focus upon the
torment of individuals to my own profit. Along with a dis-
interest in doing anything at all about all those greater ineq-
uities which affect most of us. Oh, I could note them and
bitch about them and say somebody ought to do something.
I could say it on my way to the beach or to the bed.

Who will know you were ever around, McGee? Or care?

Wait a minute! What am I supposed to be doing? Making
up the slogan I shall paint on my placard and tote in the big
parade? A parade is a group, and I'm not a group animal. I
think a mob, no matter what it happens to be doing, is the
lowest form of living thing, always steaming with potential
murder. Several things I could write on my placard and
then carry it all by myself down empty streets.

Up with life. Stamp out all small and large indignities.
Leave everyone alone to make it without pressure.
Down with hurting. Lower the standard of living. Do
without plastics. Smash the servomechanisms. Stop
grabbing. Snuff the breeze and hug the kids. Love all
love. Hate all hate.

Carry my placard and whistle between my teeth and
wink and smirk at the girls on the sidewalk watching the
nut with his sign.

Am I supposed to go out with my brush and yellow soap
and scrub clean the wide grimy world?

If you can't change everything, why try to change any
part of it, McGee?

The answer lit up in the foggy predawn morning, right over my head. A great big light bulb with glowing filaments, just like those old timey ones over in Boca Grande in the Edison place.

Because, you dumbass, when you stop scrubbing away at that tiny area you can reach, when you give up the illusion you are doing any good at all, then you start feeling like this. Jillian Brent-Archer is another name for giving up your fatuous, self-serving morality, and when you give it up, you feel grainy, studlike, secure, and that doggy little smirk becomes ineradicable.

You are never going to like yourself a hell of a lot, T. McGee, so what little liking you have must be conserved. To become Jilly's amiable useful houseguest and bedguest would turn you into something which you are not—yet have an uncomfortable tendency to become.

You retain the fragile self-respect by giving Them the increasingly good chance of ventilating your skull or scragging you through the heart. There have been some rotten little scenes with Jilly, but the next one will be the most memorable of all.

So Mary Broll is okay. And there is a good lump of cash money stashed behind the fake hull in the forward bilge of the *Flush*. But it would be a good time, a very good time, to go steaming out and find the plucked pigeon and clean up its little corner of the world by getting its feathers back— half of them, anyway. Get out there on the range and go down to the pits and stand up for a moment and see if they can pot you between the eyes. If they miss, maybe you'll get your nerve back, you tinhorn Gawain.

Eight

SUNDAY I DID NOT feel up to facing the predictable fury of Lady Jillian. She wanted me aboard for drinks Monday evening. Time enough, I told myself.

Meyer came over to the *Flush* on Monday morning at about ten thirty. I was punishing myself for recent sensual excess by polishing some neglected brightwork on the instrument panel, using some new miracle goop that was no more miraculous than the old miracle goop.

Without preamble he said, "I phoned the trust department of the Southern National Bank and Trust Company and told the girl to put me through to somebody who could give me a trust account number. When another girl answered, I said that my name was Forrester, and I was with Merrill Lynch. I said we had received a dividend which apparently should have been sent to Mrs. Harry Broll's trust account. I wanted to advise New York and mail the check along, and to prevent further confusion, I wanted the trust account number and the name of the trust officer handling that account. Mary Dillon Broll or Mrs. Harry Broll, 21 Blue Heron Lane, and so forth. She told me to hold, and in a minute or two she came back and said the number was TA 5391, and the trust officer was Mr. Woodrow Willow."

"Interesting, but—"

"I asked her to put me through to Mr. Willow. When he came on the line I introduced myself correctly and told him that I was a personal friend of Mrs. Broll, and she had told me before going away on a trip that he handled her account TA 5391. He said that was correct. He sounded guarded. Properly so. I told him that Mrs. Broll had asked me to give her some advice regarding rephasing her accounts to provide a maximum income, as she anticipated some possible change in her personal status."

"You are getting very crafty lately, Meyer."

"Please stop rubbing those damned dials and look at me. Thank you. He sounded huffy then and said they were perfectly competent to give all necessary investment advice. I told him I knew that and that was why I had called him. I certainly didn't want to usurp their authority and responsibility. I said I seldom make portfolio recommendations any more, only for old friends and at no fee, of course. I said that women often become confused about the way a trust account is set up. I said I understood she had discretion over it, that she could determine what she wanted bought and sold and so direct them. He said that was indeed the case. He sounded wistful, as if he wished it weren't true. I said that I had been trying to get in touch with her in order to clear my ideas with her before coming in to discuss them with him. I said her husband had been unable to help me. I said her house was closed, and her neighbors did not know where she had gone. I asked if he could help me. He said she had phoned him early in January and had come in and drawn out all the accumulated interest and dividends, a sizable amount, and told him she was going away for a month or six weeks. She did not know where. He said he wished he could help me."

"A month or six weeks?"

"Yes. Over three months ago."

"She could have decided to stay longer, you know."

"That's what Woodrow Willow said. He said she was quite upset when she came to see him. He said he could guess why she might be thinking in terms of independent income. So I said that, of course, maximizing income would enable her to live comfortably, but with a woman that young, inflation protection was important."

"Did it work?"

Meyer displayed an uncommonly wolflike smile. "He hesitated and I heard a desk calculator rattling and humming, and then he said that with her equities reinvested in income holdings, she'd have a pretax income of from twenty-five to twenty-seven thousand. So I told him that we should probably think in terms of eighteen to twenty or, in case of substantial alimony, consider tax exempts. He said he'd be delighted to talk to me about it, but of course he would have to have clearance from her to discuss her affairs. I said I realized that. He said he expected to hear from her very shortly, before the end of the month. Travis, I couldn't push him any further."

"I can see that. He was all set to snap shut at any moment. You got a hell of a lot out of him. Congratulations."

"I braced myself and took a risk. I said, 'Oh, yes, of course. To sign those things for Mr. Broll.' He hesitated and then said, 'It's inconvenient for her to come here in person. So she told me when she came in what Mr. Broll was asking of her. It's something that they did once before, and it was paid off. I had her sign the note. The loan was later approved by the loan committee and the board. A sizable loan, secured by the assets in her trust, with her signed authorization to me to deposit the loan proceeds in Mr. Broll's personal checking account. The effective date of the loan was to be April fifteenth, last Thursday. He requires the funds before the end of the month. She requested me to get it all set up but not to go ahead with it until she gets in touch with me and tells me to proceed or to destroy the signed documents and forget it. That's why I expect her to be in touch with me soon.' Travis, I remember you telling me to always press the luck when it is running your way. So I told him that I had heard that Broll was getting very agitated about getting the note and the authorization signed, so I imagined that Mr. Broll had been in touch with him. Mr. Willow has a very weary laugh. He said he hears from Mr. Broll almost constantly. He said he saw no reason to tell Mr. Broll everything was signed and ready to go, awaiting only authorization from her. I got the impression Harry tried to bulldoze him, and Mr. Willow got his back up. Then he began to realize he had told me more than he should. I could *feel* him pulling back. So I jumped in and said that actually the documents aren't signed until she says they are signed. Until then it is an approved line of credit, and if she doesn't care to use it, she doesn't have to. I told him he was quite correct, and I could feel him trying to persuade himself I was not working for Harry Broll. I hope he did."

I put the cap on the miracle goop and swabbed up the few white places where it had dribbled on the varnish, miraculously removing the gloss. I spun the helmsman's seat around and looked at Meyer.

I said to him, "You are pretty damned intense about something I don't understand. We don't know whether Mary wants him to have that money or not. We know she's in Grenada, knowing he's sweating it out, and she's probably enjoying it every time she thinks about it. We know that Harry is getting so frantic he's losing control. He isn't thinking clearly. Are you?"

"She's been gone over three months now. Harry is living in a way that means he doesn't expect her to come back. You thought she'd get in touch with you if she was in trouble. She didn't. Who saw her leave? What travel agency did she use?"

I reached into the back of my mind and swatted something down. It had been buzzing in circles back there. I picked it up off the floor and looked at it. "Meyer, once on that cruise years ago we bought provisions and got a lot of green stamps. I think it was in Boca Grande. They got wet and got stuck together. Mary soaked them apart. It soaked all the glue off. She dried them between paper towels. Then she got a green stamp book and some Elmer's, and she glued them into the book. Meyer, she didn't even *save* green stamps. Another thing. We spent a lot of time anchored out, as far from marinas and boat traffic and shore sounds as we could get. So she kept turning off the generator, the air-conditioning, even the little battery transistor radio. She made great things out of the leftovers from yesterday's leftovers. She's not stingy. If you asked for her last dime, she'd borrow two bits somewhere and give you thirty-five cents. But she has a waste-not, want-not twitch. I kidded her about it. She didn't mind. But it didn't change a thing. Holly Dressner told me Mary planned to leave her car at the Miami airport. Okay. Would Mary pay two and a half a day indefinitely? Ninety days is two hundred and twenty-five dollars. Not Mary. No matter how upset. She'd find out the rates and turn around, drive a few miles, make a deal with a gas station or parking lot, and take a cab back and catch her flight."

"If she had time."

"Unless she changed a lot, she'd get there two hours ahead when the ticket desk says one hour. She'd have time."

"So we should go look for her car?"

"Holly should be able to tell me what to look for."

"Travis, I don't want to seem efficient, but why don't we phone Mary in Grenada? I would rather go below and drink one of your Tuborgs and listen to you fight with the island operators than drive to Miami."

I struck myself a heavy blow in the forehead with the heel of my hand, said a few one-, seven- and ten-syllable words, and we went below.

I started at eleven thirty, and by the time I got the desk at the Spice Island Inn, I was in a cold rage. It was a radio link, and nobody seemed to give a damn about completing it. I had mentally hung Alex Bell and Don Ameche in effigy several times.

At last I got the faint voice of a girl, saying, "Spice Island Inn. May I help you?" It was the singsong lilt of the West Indies, where the accented syllables seem to fall at random in strange places.

"Do you have a Mrs. Broll registered? A Mrs. Harry Broll?"

"Who? I am sorry. What last name, sir?"

"Broll. Bee-are-oh-el-el. Broll."

"Ah. Broll. There is no Mrs. Harry Broll."

"Was she there? Did she leave?"

"There is a Mrs. Mary Broll. She is here since many weeks."

"From Florida?"

"Yes. She is here from Florida."

"Can you put me through to her, please."

"I am sorry."

"Do you mean you can't?"

"There is the instruction, sir. Mrs. Broll does not take overseas calls. Not from anyone, sir."

"This is an emergency."

"I am sorry. I can write down for her your name and the number of your telephone. I cannot say if she returns the call. She does not wish to be disturbed by telephone calls from overseas. If you can give me your name?"

"Never mind. Thank you for your help."

"I am sorry." She said something else but it faded away into an odd, humming silence. There were loud clicks. Somebody else said, "Code eighteen, route through Barbados, over."

I said, "Hey! Somebody."

The humming stopped and the line went dead as marble.

I hung up. I stood up and stretched. "Mrs. Mary Broll has been there for a long time, but she doesn't take overseas calls."

"In case one might be from Harry, I suppose."

"That takes care of it. Right, Meyer?"

"I suppose so."

"It was your idea. I phoned. She's there."

"I know. But . . ."

"But?"

"The known facts now seem contradictory."

"Meyer, for God's sake!"

"Now listen to me. She wants to hide from her husband and think things out. She does not want to take any overseas calls. What would it cost her to get the operator and the desk clerk to deny that she's even registered? Ten Biwi dollars each, ten U.S. dollars total? No more, certainly. If she was sure her husband couldn't trace her, then the only call she *could* get would be from her friend Holly Dressner, and she would want to take a call from her I'd think. If she set it up so that he *can* find out where she is, then the refusal to take calls would mean she wants him to fly down, and the bait would be the loan he needs."

"First you simplify things, Meyer, and then you complicate the hell out of them. I don't know what to think now."

"Neither do I. That's my problem."

"So we drive to Miami anyway?"

Holly was home, and she was very helpful about the car. "It's one of those Volks with the fancy body. Oh, dear. What in the world are they called?"

"Karmann Ghia."

"Right! Two years old. Dark red. Hard top. Believe it or not, I can give you the license plate number even. We were shopping, and we went to the place you get the plates together, and mine is about the same weight, so we were in the same series. Hers was one digit more than mine, so hers is 1 D 3108."

We drove down to Miami in Miss Agnes, and I jammed her through the confusions of the cloverleaves and put her in one of the new airport parking buildings, halfway up the long wide ramp leading to the third level, nosing her against the wall between two squatty Detroit products which made her look like a dowager queen at a rock fest. A mediocre hamburger, gobbled too hastily on the way down, lay like a stone on the floor of my stomach.

I pointed out to Meyer how our task was simplified. Apparently there was some kind of stone-crushing plant in operation not too far from the open parking garages. The longer any car had been parked there, sheltered from the rain, the more white powdered stone dust it had all over it. And Mary's would be one of the whitest of all.

There were more than enough ramps and levels and separate structures. Finally, on a top level on the side furthest from the entrance and exit ramp, I saw Karmann Ghia lines, powdery white as a sugar doughnut. Even the plate was powder white, but the bas relief of the digits made it readable as I neared it: 3108. Three months of sitting and accumulating stone dust and parking charges.

Meyer drew in the dust atop the trunk. It would have

been a childish trick except for what he drew. A single large question mark. I wiped the windshield with the edge of my hand and bent and peered in. Nothing to see except a very empty automobile.

A police sedan drifted up and stopped close behind the Ghia. "Got a problem?" the driver asked. His partner got out.

"No problem, officer."

"Your car?"

"No. It belongs to a friend."

The driver got out. "And you can't quite remember the name of your friend, I suppose?"

I gave him my earnest, affable smile. "Now why'd you think that, officer? This belongs to Mrs. Mary Broll, 21 Blue Heron Lane, Lauderdale, for sure."

"Girlfriend?"

"Just a friend, officer."

"Doesn't your friend have anything to say?"

Meyer said, "I was not aware that you were addressing me with any of the prior questions, officer. I happen to have here—"

"Easy. Bring it out real slow."

"I happen to have here a page from a scratch pad which, if you will examine it, gives the name of the owner and the license number and description of the vehicle."

The nearest officer took the note and looked at it and handed it back. "Repo?"

"What?" Meyer asked. "Oh. Repossession. No. We happened to be parked here, and we knew Mrs. Broll has been gone for three months, and we wondered if she'd left her car here."

The other officer had gotten into their car. I heard his low voice as he used the hand mike. He waited, then got out again. "Isn't on the list, Al," he said.

"Parked here, you say. Now both of you, let me see some ID. Slow and easy. Take it out of the wallet. Keep the wallet. Hand me the ID. Okay. Now you. Okay. Now show me your parking ticket. What kind of a car?"

"Officer, it is a very old Rolls Royce pickup truck. Bright blue. It's over there in that other—"

"I saw that, Al. Remember? That's the one I had you back up and see if it had the inspection sticker."

It stopped being confrontation and began to be conversation. "Nobody," said Al, "but nobody at all is going to arrive here in that freak truck to pull anything cute. Okay. For the hell of it, why were you wondering if this woman left her car here?"

"Not so much if she left it here, but to see if she was back yet. We were just wondering. If we didn't find it, maybe she left it someplace else, or she came back from her trip. But we found it, so that means she's still on her trip."

"She stays away too much longer, she can save money by forgetting the car." They got in and glided away without saying good-by or looking back. I guessed they cruised the garages from time to time, checking their hot car lists. It would make a good drop after a stolen car had been used for a felony. Leave it, walk across to the upper or lower level, leave the airport by cab or limousine. Or airplane. Or by private car previously stashed in the parking garage.

Meyer was very quiet, and he did not speak until we were approaching Miss Agnes. He stopped and I turned and looked back at him and strolled back to where he was standing.

"Are you going to break into tears?"

"Maybe. If you were as anxious to find your wife as Harry is, if it's financially important as well as emotionally important, wouldn't you report her missing and give her description and the description of her car with the tag number to the police?"

"I would think so."

"Then the number would be on their list, wouldn't it?"

"Yes. I mean, yes, damn it."

"And because you are thinking what I am thinking and because we happen to be right here, wouldn't it be a good time to find out about airline connections, McGee?"

"For two?"

"I have to finish my paper on the Eurocurrency which replaced the dollar. I promised the conference program chairman."

Nine

I SHOULD HAVE BOARDED my early afternoon BWIA flight to Barbados with stops at Kingston and San Juan, thoroughly, if not visibly, bloodied by Jillian. This was Tuesday, and I should have been sailing the sea not the air.

Cowardice is a very curious ailment. The attacks occur when you do not expect them. Instead of saying the rehearsed words, I heard myself say, "Jilly dear, the matter of the old friend has come up again. I wouldn't want to go cruising down to St. Kitts with that hanging over me. I wouldn't be able to stop thinking about it and wondering. It will take a few days . . ."

"Darling, I want you to be able to keep your mind on your work. Exclusively. Besides, the five-day forecast is foul. It might work out very nicely."

"No tantrum?"

"What sort of woman do you think I am, dear? That's

hardly flattering, you know. All evidence to the contrary, I am not a spoiled little bitch who goes about whining and screaming and drumming her heels. I'm grown up, you know. And more patient than you imagine. I have waited quite a while to have you all to myself."

"This shouldn't take very long."

"I'll be here when you return, dear Travis. Grenada?"

The habit of caution took over. It is an automatic reflex. Never tell anybody anything which they might in turn tell the wrong person. "No. That information is obsolete. San Juan."

"Of course. By this time, Grenada must be well emptied out. She could have more fun in Puerto Rico. Are you and she going to have a lot of fun, Travis? Just like old times?"

"I'm not planning to. But you never can tell."

"Really! You are the most—"

"You keep asking the wrong questions. It's a bad habit."

"As bad as giving the wrong answers."

For a moment the tantrum was on the edge of happening, but she forced it back, visibly, forgave me, kissed me a lingering farewell.

Now five miles over Cuba, I wondered if it would have been better for both of us if I had made it clear I was never going to become her tame houseguest. I wondered if it had been cowardice or if I was really, underneath, the kind of miserable son of a bitch who likes to keep something in reserve in case he happens to change his mind.

Our captain, being a pleasantly enthusiastic host, invited us to look down at Cuba. I was following the McGee rule of international travel and was in first class, alone in the window seat, the bulkhead seat on the starboard side. It was

British West Indian Airways, BWIA, and the leg room in the bulkhead seats on the 727 is good.

A clear and beautiful day. The tilled-field geometry of Cuba looked like the geometry of any other of the islands, from five miles up. We moved across the southern coastline, and the shallow sea was a hundred shades, from the pale pale tan of shallow sand through lime and lavender to cobalt.

"Sir?" the clear, young voice said. She was a small, dusky stewardess with a high forehead, a blue-eyed stare of calculated innocence, a dark spill of glossy black hair. Her skin was a matte texture, and it was one half-shade lighter than milk chocolate. She was the one with the absolutely great legs I had noticed when I had clambered onto their airplane. "You are going to . . ."

"Barbados."

"Ah, yes. Thank you, sir. Can I get you something to drink?"

"The last time I was on BWIA there was fresh orange juice. Do you still—"

"Oh, yes."

"With vodka then, please?"

"Oh yes, right away, thank you." She twinkled at me and spun away, the short skirt flirting and snapping. It is changing in the islands, same as everywhere. The conservative island politicians and the white businessmen try to tell you there is no racism, that black and white are treated alike and live amiably together in happy understanding and compassion.

But if you are observant, you notice that the more desirable the job, particularly the jobs women hold—stewardesses, cashiers in banks, clerks in specialty shops, hostesses in restaurants—the more likely they are to be bleached by past miscegenation. There are some true blacks in those positions, of course, but in a far lower ratio than exists in the general population. Look at the cleaning women, the cane-field workers, the laundry workers, to find the purest blacks in the islands. And the blackest blacks are, of course, probably seventy-five to eighty percent of the population of the West Indies, the Bahamas, the Windward and Leeward islands. The other twenty percent is a perceptible lightening of color, shade by shade, all the way to unleavened white. Regardless of all protestations, the whiter you are, the better you live. Blondes have the most fun. One of the most thoroughly ignored aspects of the Cuban Revolution is how happily the black Cubans embraced the new order. Though the percentage is smaller in Cuba than elsewhere through the Caribbean, the pattern of discrimination was the same. Black Cuba was entirely ready for anything at all which promised equality in education, jobs, and health care. It didn't have to be Khrush or Mao. They would have built statues to a big green Martian if it could have delivered on the promises.

The curious and immediate and personal result of the color prejudice in the islands was that my pale chocolate stewardess with the great legs identified with me. We were both part of the ruling cabal. There could be an earnest friendliness in her unlikely blue eyes, an uninhibited flirtatiousness.

Another little girl of exactly the same color, but a citizen of the US of A and working, say, for Eastern on a domestic run, would have been working hard on an Afro hairdo, would have given me the precise number of millimeters of

smile as prescribed by Eastern, would have been entirely
correct, but her eyes would have been as empty as the ice of
a long winter, concealing nothing more personal than a
propagandized hostility, a prepackaged contempt, an ability
to see me only as a symbol of oppression, not as a living
creature walking two-legged on the same untidy world,
trying to live through the weird years with a little bit of
grace and care.

Too bad, somehow. The real guilt is in being a human
being. That is the horrible reality which bugs us all. Wolves,
as a class, are cleaner, more industrious, far less savage, and
kinder to each other and their young.

When she came back with the screwdriver, she leaned
one round delicious knee on the empty seat beside me and
reached and put the glass and napkin on the small, built-in
service area between the seats. I could read her name tag.
Mia Cruikshank.

"Mia?" I said.

"Yes, sir?"

"I just meant . . . it's a pretty name."

She made a droll mouth. "Better than what it was, I
think. Miriam. Mia is smashing compared to that."

"Smashing indeed."

So we went humming down across the blue seas under the
blue skies of vacationland at approximately nine hundred
feet per second, which is the muzzle velocity of the .45 caliber Colt automatic pistol, an ugly and cumbersome
weapon. Our happy captain pointed out this and that. We
stopped at Kingston and San Juan and points south. We lost

more passengers than we took on. Each island had its quota of red tape, so that the stops were long.

Mia kept me happily supplied with drinks and food, and we found it easy to smile at each other. We stood together when the sun was low, on the little platform at the top of the rolling stairs at the little airport on St. Lucia.

"You are remaining at Barbados, sir, or continuing?"

"To Grenada tomorrow morning."

"Oh, yes. That is so lovely an island. Of course, Barbados is very nice, too. Just one night is a short time to stay."

"I didn't want to stay there at all."

"I know. There is no way. You fly with us or Pan Am to Barbados or Trinidad, from Miami everyone arrives too late for the last flight to Grenada. It has to be by daylight, of course, in the small aircraft. Where will you stay in Barbados?"

"I thought I would check it out after I get there."

"Oh, yes. The season is over. There is room everywhere. But really, there was room in most of the places during the season too this year. We did not carry so many people to Barbados this year."

"Why not?"

She glanced back over her shoulder and moved closer to me, lowered her voice. "I am not a rich, important person who owns a hotel, so perhaps they know what they are doing. But, sir, suppose this was in the season and you are traveling with a lady and you try to make a reservation for the two of you in Barbados, just to stay in a hotel room overnight to continue on in the morning. In your money, in US dollars, to stay at the Barbados Hilton, it will be seventy dollars for one night, and there will be ten percent service charge added to that, so that it will be seventy-seven dollars. Even were you to stay at the Holiday Inn, sir, it will be fifty-five plus ten percent, or sixty dollars and fifty cents."

"Without meals? You have to be kidding."

"Oh, no. You see, sir, they will only make reservations for you on the Modified American Plan, which includes breakfast and dinner, even when it is clear you will have dinner aboard this flight and leave so early the next morning there is perhaps time for coffee and rolls. This is happening in all the islands, sir. It is perhaps the worst in Barbados, the worst of all. It is a fantastic greed. It is like some terrible animal out of control, so hungry it feeds upon itself and is killing itself. I should not say so much."

"I won't turn you over to the tourist board, Mia."

"Oh, thank you." She hesitated and scowled. "There is something I am trying to think how to say. It is really what is wrong now with the islands. It is why each year there will be fewer people coming to these lovely places."

"It's a shame."

She turned to face me directly and looked up at me. "Seventy-seven dollars is over a hundred and fifty dollars in our currency. In Biwi dollars. A house servant in Barbados *might* make fifty dollars, Biwi, a month. A waiter or waitress *might* make seventy-five dollars, Biwi, a month. So how does a human person feel serving or cleaning up after another human person who pays two or three months' wages for one single night in a room? Sir, it is like such a terrible arrogance and thoughtlessness. It makes hate, sir. It makes contempt. So the cleaning is done badly, and the serving is done very slowly and badly, and there are no smiles. Then, sir, the person who is paying too much because the hotel owners are so greedy, he becomes very angry because, if he pays so much, the service should be of the very best, and everything should be very clean. When he is angry, then he seems to be more arrogant and rich and thoughtless, sir. Hate and anger back and forth, it is a terrible thing. There is no pleasure in work and no pleasure in vacationing here, and that is why each year, like this year, there will be fewer and fewer tourists, jobs, money. It is wicked. I keep thinking to myself, what can be done—what can be done? It is like the goose, sir."

"The goose?"

"The goose they killed to get at the golden eggs." She looked at her watch. An official was trotting up the stairs. "Now we will be going, sir."

After liftoff she gave me a final drink, and she and the other girls did their desk work and policed their area and changed to their ground uniforms. She had time to give me some advice. She told me that the nearest hotel to the airport was a five-dollar taxi ride, Biwi. The Crane Beach. She said the rooms were very small and primitive, but the beach was beautiful, and the food was excellent. She said the management was surly, and the waiters insolent, but it was only for overnight, and it would be almost empty. Besides, the Barbados Hilton and the other hotels were a lot closer to Bridgetown, and so were ten to fifteen Biwi dollars one way from the airport. In most of the islands it appears that committees of taxi drivers determine airport locations.

"Just laugh at whatever they want to charge you at the Crane Beach, sir. The season is over. Put down ten dollars, Yankee, and tell them the service charge percent is included, not extra. They will show you a rate schedule and tell you it is official and they cannot change it. Just laugh. They will take the money and give you a room. It is not so easy to get a taxi in the morning early from there. Just tear a Yankee dollar in two pieces and give half to the taxi driver and tell him when to come in the morning. He will be certain to return. Do not tip anyone at that hotel. They are shameless, and it is all included in the price of everything anyway."

I was genuinely grateful to Mia. I thanked her and said, "I hope I will get a chance to tell you how I made out."

"Perhaps, if you fly BWIA back to Miami, I will serve you again. How long shall you be in Grenada, sir?"

"A few days. Any idea where I should stay?"

"Oh, no. I do not know that island so well. This is not a vacation for you. Business, yes?"

"How do you know?"

"I think I can tell if a man is not one who would take a vacation alone, sir. Good luck, sir."

My taxi man arrived the next day three minutes before the stipulated hour. He smiled broadly when he saw me standing in the early morning light outside the hotel gates with my single piece of carry-on luggage. He decided that it was a splendid idea, the half of the paper dollar. It left each of us with an investment to protect. He had brought some tape, and he put his dollar back together before we started off. His name was Oswald, and he was a thin old man with several gold teeth. He drove his elderly white Plymouth with that kind of care which is more involved with not breaking anything than not hitting anybody.

I took LIAT, a BWIA subsidiary, to Grenada, a direct

flight of about forty minutes. It was an old Avro with the rows shoved closer together to increase capacity, so that the little oval windows did not match the seat positions. Two big propjet Rolls Royce brutes powered the small aircraft. The stewardess was about the same size and shape as Hubert Humphrey. The pilot had Walter Mitty dreams of being a fighter pilot. It was an interesting takeoff and an even more interesting landing.

At Grenada's grubby little airport I once again had to show my driver's license and turn over that card form which serves as embarkation and debarkation permit, depending on how you fill out the blanks.

And then came a fascinating ride in a taxi. The island is only twenty-one miles long and twelve miles wide. The airport is about as far as it could possibly be from the principal town, St. George's. The morning ride took one full hour, and I would not have wanted my man to have tried to shave five minutes off the elapsed time. I helped with the brakes so continuously that my right leg was nearly paralyzed when we finally came down out of the mountains to sea level. The driver—he gave me his card—was Albert Owen, and he had a Chevrolet assembled in Australia with a suspension system designed for the Outback of Australia. He had put fifty-three thousand incredible miles on it on that improbable road system, using up God only knows how many sets of brake linings. Drive on the left. Average width of road—one and a quarter lanes. No shoulders. Blind corners. Big lumps, deep potholes, children, dogs, pigs, donkeys, bicycles, trucks, buses, motorcycles. So honk the horn almost continuously, shift up and shift down, swerve, leap, squeal, slide, accelerate—and all the time Albert Owen was hollering back over his shoulder at me, pointing out bah-nah-nah tree, almond tree, sugar cane, sar. Over there mammy apple, coconut plahntation sar, cocoa, also you are seeing nutmeg, sar. Many spices.

Once when a small insane truck came leaping at us on the wrong side around a bend, Albert swerved smartly. It missed us by the thickness of a coat of paint. Albert laughed and laughed. He said, "That is one foolish driver, sar. He nearly mosh us."

But nobody actually did mosh us. It was hard to believe they were not trying. Were the fates to put Albert down on any weekday morning on the Palmetto Turnpike heading into Miami with the inbound torrent, the terror of it might put him into a dead faint. A Miami cabdriver suddenly transported into Albert's mountains might conceivably run weeping into the jungle.

People certainly did go about moshing people. The dead cars amid the lush vines and wild shrubs were proof enough of that.

Albert asked me where my reservation was as we plummeted down toward the town and blue late-morning sea beyond. I said I had none but would look about a little. He said there were no problems this time of year. There had been trouble with the government water supply. When the hotel cisterns had run out, many people had left. Now the water was on again, but there were not so many tourists as in other Aprils. I found out that the Grenada Beach Hotel was the place most centrally located on Grande Anse, the two miles of crescent beach just south of the town, looking westward. I asked him if he would wait there for me. We made certain financial negotiations.

I left my single piece of luggage with him. He parked in the vehicle circle outside the main doors. I walked in and through an open lobby area and found a thatched bar off to the left, open to the outdoors, looking out across a long expanse of green lawn and tall, graceful coconut palms toward the garden of beach umbrellas, toward the bright colors of beach chairs and towels on the distant sand.

A bored bartender in a red coat appeared from some unknown hiding place, yawning. He made me a delicious rum punch with grated nutmeg afloat on it. He asked for my room number, and I paid cash for my drink, then gifted him with some of the Biwi I had picked up at the moneychanger's booth in the temple of Miami International. He brightened visibly, and I asked him if he had a phone back there, and he said he did, and he said he would be glad to phone the Spice Island Inn for me. He did so and handed me the phone.

"What number is Mrs. Broll in, please? Mrs. Mary Broll?"

"Ah . . . yes, she is in cottage 50, sir. Shall I ring her for you?"

"No thank you," I said and hung up.

I finished my drink very very slowly. It is a very strange reluctance, a curious hesitation that can immobilize you at such a time. You are eager to prove to yourself that you've been quite wrong, that you've taken too many small things and built them up into a fantasy structure that cannot be true.

Yet, if by some chance the fantasy proves to be reality, most of the game is still left to play, and an ugly game it can be.

It could be a delicious surprise. I could see the shape of

Mary's familiar mouth, the wide and startled eyes, and then the rush of pleasure, the embrace.

"The Spice Island Inn is close by?"

"That direction. Very close. A small walk, sir. Two minutes."

But in the hot tropical blaze of April a man in slacks and sport shirt, socks and shoes would be as conspicuous on that beach, I found, as in a Mother Hubbard at a nudist camp. I went back through the hotel and found Albert dozing in the shade. I woke him, and we got into the broiling taxi and rode south to the entrance to the Spice Island Inn.

Meyer and I had tried to cover all eventualities in the long planning session we'd had before I left. In the islands there appeared to be so little interest in any verification of identity that the risk factor seemed very minor indeed. If we were wrong, I was going to feel a little foolish. But if we were right, there was a chance I could feel something beyond mere foolishness.

And so, in Albert Owen's backseat I switched the cash money, all of it, from one wallet to another and became Gavin Lee. Known as Gav. Known as Mr. Lee. This follows Meyer's theory that when you pick a new name, pick one that has the same basic vowel sounds. Then you will react if you hear somebody behind you say your assumed name.

I was going to carry my own suitcase in. Albert did not think that was appropriate. The desk was very cordial. Nothing creates such a flavor of genuine, heart-felt welcome as a nearly empty hotel. They showed me the rates. They told me I had a choice of plans. They showed me a map of the place with all manner of accommodations. What would please Mr. Lee, the ostensibly vacationing land developer from Miami, Scottsdale, Acapulco, Hawaii, Palm Springs, and Las Vegas? Well, I'm kind of curious about those with the private pool. These here on your map. Just this row of them, eh? How about this one right here on the end? Number . . . I can't read it upside down. Thank you, 50. Full. Are all these full then? Just 50, 57, and 58. Well, in the middle then, as far from the occupied ones as . . . 54? I can see there are two bedrooms, but I don't see any one bedroom ones with the walled garden and the pool, so. . . . Now what will it be on . . . a European Plan? After a few days I may change, depending on how the dining room is here. Of course. I'm sure it's marvelous. All right. Quote me on a per day. . . . That's $28, single? That's US? Hmmm. Plus ten percent service charge and five percent tax, which is . . . $32.34 per day. Look, I'm carrying a bit more cash than I intended. Would you mind taking this hundred-dollar bill for three days in advance? And I'll bring you an envelope to put in the safe.

I paid Albert off and told him I would keep his card and I would certainly get him to drive me back to the airport some day. A bellhop led me down a long long path to the newest line of attached bungalows, the ones with the pool in the garden. The row was a good two hundred and fifty yards from the hotel proper. He demonstrated the air-conditioning, the button to push for food service, the button to push for drink service.

Then he went away. I was left in silence, in the shadowed coolness of the tourist life.

Drive the clenched fist into palm. Pock!

"Be here, baby. Just *be* here!"

Ten

THE ROW OF TALL attached cottages with a double peak on the roof of each one was set at a slight angle to the beach, so that architecturally they could be set back, one from the next, to provide total privacy for the individual walled gardens where the small swimming pools were.

The row of cottages was back a hundred feet and more from the beach. Between the front gates of the cottages and the beach itself was a private expanse of sand, landscaped palms, sea grapes, almond trees with sun chaises spotted about at intervals far enough apart for privacy.

I put on swim trunks and took up a position on a chaise fifty feet from my front gate, turning it in such a way I could watch the gate of number 50. By then it was past noon. The tropic sun had such a hefty sting I knew that even my deep and permanent tan would not be immune, not without a little oil and a little limitation on the exposure time.

At twenty minutes to one the gate opened, and a young woman came out. She was of medium height, delicately and gracefully built. Her dark hair was quite long, and she had a white band above her forehead clipping it in place. She seemed to be somewhere in her twenties. I could not make a closer guess at that distance. She wore eccentric sunglasses with huge round lenses in dark amber. She wore a don't-swim-in-it bikini fashioned of white elasticized cord and swatches of watermelon-colored terrycloth. She was two shades darker than Mia Cruikshank, a perfect and even tan which could only have come from untold hours of total discipline and constant care.

A man came out with her. Youngish, lithe, laughing and saying something which made her laugh. Awesomely muscled, moving well so that muscles bulged and slid under the red-bronze tan. A Riviera swimming outfit, little more than a white satin jockstrap. She walked a few steps and then turned in a proprietary way and went back and tested to see if the gate was locked. She looked in her small white Ratsey bag, apparently to make sure that her key was there. Then they walked toward the hotel.

My heart had turned heavy, and there was a taste of sickness in my throat. But you have to be certain, terribly certain. Like a biopsy. Make absolutely sure of the malignancy. Because the surgery is radical.

I gave them five minutes and then followed the same route. I found them in another of the ubiquitous thatched bars, having a drink at a shady table and still laughing. A cheerful pair. I went to the bar and ordered a drink. When I had a chance, I asked the bartender if the woman at the table was a certain Lois Jefferson. He looked troubled. He said he knew them by the numbers. Just a moment, please. He went to the other end of the bar and came back with a signed drink tab. Mary D. Broll. Number 50. He showed it to me. I thanked him, said I was wrong. I winked at him and said, "But that is not Mr. Broll?"

He had a knowing smile. "It is just a friend. He has been a friend for a week, I think. He works, I think, on a private boat. That is what I hear. It is easy to make friends here."

I picked my drink up and moved along the bar to a stool that was about a dozen feet from their table. I turned around on the stool, my back to the bar, and looked at her with obvious and amiable and very thorough appreciation. She was worth appreciating, right from her brown, slender, tidy little ankles right on up—not too quickly—to a ripely cushioned little mouth, dark eyes set at an interesting tilt, a broad, immature, and vulgar little nose.

She put her glasses back on and leaned over and said something to her nautical friend. He put his drink down and turned around and stared back over his shoulder at me. I smiled and nodded at him. He had a Prince Valiant hair-cut, and his hair was the dark molten shade of some golden retrievers. His face had a tough, pinched, disadvantaged look which did not go with the Valiant hair or the beachboy body. I do not make any judgments about hair length, mine or anyone's. I own some Sears electric clippers with plastic gadgets of various shapes which fit on the clippers to keep you from accidentally peeling your hair off down to the skull. I find that long hair is a damned nuisance on boats, on the beach, and in the water. So when it gets long enough to start to make me aware of it, I clipper it off, doing the sides in the mirror and the back by feel. The sun bleaches my hair and burns it and dries it out. And the salt water makes it feel stiff and look like some kind of Dynel. Were I going to keep it long, I would have to take care of it. That would mean tonics and lotions and special shampoos. That would mean brushing it and combing it a lot more than I do and somehow fastening it out of the way in a stiff breeze. Life is so full of all those damned minor things you have to do anyway, it seems nonproductive to go looking for more. So I go hoe the hair down when it attracts my attention. The length is not an expression of any social, economic, emotional, political, or chronographic opinion. It is on account of being lazy and impatient. No reason why the male can't have long, lovely, dark-golden hair if he wants it. But it is a personal decision now, just as it was during the Crusades and the Civil War.

He kept staring right at me, and I kept smiling at him. So he got up fast and rolled his shoulders as he covered the twelve feet to stand in front of me, bare feet spread and braced.

"Chief, stop the birddog routine. You're annoying the lady."

"Me? Come *on* now! Don't let her kid you. Lois and I have known each other for a long time. She knows I like to look at her. Always have. And I know she likes being looked at. Right, dear?"

"You're out of your tree, chief. Knock it off. She isn't Lois."

I stood up. "She's Lois Jefferson. Believe me!" I edged by him as he tried to block me away from the table. "Lois, honey. It's Gav Lee, for God's sake. It was a good joke, but let's not run it into the ground."

She took the glasses off and looked up at me. "Really, I'm not Lois. I'm Mary Broll. Really."

I boggled at her. "Not Lois Jefferson from Scarsdale? Not Tom's wife?"

It sucked in the fellow nicely. He was all alerted for games. When you roam in public with an item like that woman, you keep the guard way up. "Honey," he said, "how about this clown? You get it? Tom Jefferson. Thomas Jefferson. Stop annoying us, chief, or I'll call the—"

I turned on him. "Really. Would it put too much of a strain on you to have a little common courtesy? Her husband has always had the nickname Tom, for quite obvious reasons. His real name is . . ." I turned back to her. "What *is* Tom's real first name, dear?"

She laughed. "But I am really *not* your friend!"

I stared at her. "That can't be possible. It's the most fantastic look-alike. . . . You wouldn't believe. . . . Miss Broll, would you—"

"Mrs. Broll."

"I'm sorry. Mrs. Broll, would it be rude of me to ask you to stand up for just a moment?"

"I guess not."

"Now just one goddamn—"

I turned on him again. "What harm can it do, Mr. Broll?"

She stood up beside her chair. I moved closer to her, and I stared into her eyes from close range. "By God, I *am* wrong. I would never have believed it. You are a little bit taller than Lois, and I think your eyes are a darker shade, Mrs. Broll."

"Now go away," the man said.

As she sat down she said, "Oh, shut up, Carl. You get so boring sometimes. The man made a mistake. All right? All right. Please forgive Carl, Mr. . . ."

"Lee. Gavin Lee. Gav to my friends."

"I don't see any friends of yours around here," the man said.

She gave me a very pretty and well-practiced smile. "Gav, this rude animal is Carl Brego. Carl, shake hands nicely with Gav, or you can damned well take off."

I saw the little tightening around his eyes and knew the childish bit he was going to try. So when he put his hand out, I put my hand into his much too quickly for him to close his hand to get my knuckles. I got my hand all the way back, deep into the web between thumb and finger. Then I could just maintain a mild, firm clasp and smile at him as he nearly ruptured his shoulder muscles trying to squeeze my hand to broken pulp.

"Sorry about the little misunderstanding, Carl," I said. "I'd like to buy you two nice people a drink."

He let go of my hand and sat down. "Nobody invited you to join the party, chief."

He had fallen into that one, too. He was scoring very badly. I said, "I don't expect to sit down with you, Carl. Why should I? I was going to go to that table way over there and have my own drink over there and send two to this table. You act as if I'm trying to move in on you. How far would I get, Carl? As you are not Mr. Broll, then this lovely lady is a friend of yours. You are having lunch together. Just the two of you. If I were having lunch with her, I would be very ugly about anybody trying to move in. I just think you overreact, Carl. I made a little mistake. You keep getting rude for no reason. But I'll still buy those drinks. I was thinking of it as an apology, not a ticket to the party."

So saying, I gave the lady a little bow and marched on over to my distant table and told the waiter to give them anything they might want. I sat with my back toward them.

It did not take her long. Four minutes, I think it was, before he appeared beside my chair, standing almost at attention.

"Excuse me. Mrs. Broll would be very happy if you would join us for lunch."

I smiled up at him. "Only if you are absolutely certain you don't mind, Brego."

It hurt his mouth to say it. It hurt his whole face. "Please join us, Mr. Lee."

All through lunch I knew Brego was waiting and planning. When I saw that he wasn't at all upset that I was living just a few doors—or a few gardens—away from his pretty friend, I could almost guess the kind of routine he had figured out.

And during lunch I had managed to steer the conversation in a direction that gave me a chance to awaken more than a flicker of interest in her eyes and at the same time gave her a chance to shove a little blade into Carl Brego and give it a twist.

I said, "I take little flyers in island property sometimes. Actually, that's why I'm here. Some associates said I ought to take a look at this one. Anyway, usually I like to pyramid, but quite a while ago I got into Freeport up in the Bahamas at the right time and got out at exactly the right time with much more than I'd expected, so I thought I'd give myself a little present. So I bought this great big, ridiculous brute of a schooner in Nassau and had the yard that sold it to me hire aboard a crew, and I actually set out for *this* island. But the guest I invited aboard for the trip became terribly seasick. We made it as far as Great Inagua and got off, both of us, at Matthew Town and arranged passage from there back to civilization. I had the crew take the boat back to Nassau. As I remember, my accountants told me the net loss was something like thirteen thousand dollars after I had the yard resell the schooner. But it would have been cruel and unusual punishment to have made the young lady sail one more mile."

Something behind her dark eyes went ding, and a cash drawer slid open in her skull. She counted the big bills and shut it again and smiled and said, "Carl knows all about yachts. He sails one around for a very fat rich lady, don't you, darling?"

"That must be very interesting," I said.

"He's waiting on Grenada until she arrives with friends," the woman said. "You know. Like a chauffeur, parked somewhere."

"Knock it off," Carl said in a small humble voice.

"Please?" she said.

"Please."

And that made it even more imperative. I decided I was reading her well enough to see that she knew the direction the tensions would take and would give the ceremony a chance to get under way at the first opportunity. And would want to watch.

When we got to her gate, there was no one in sight. The breeze had stopped. Sweat popped out immediately on all three of us. I felt it run down my back.

"Do come in, Gav," she said. "Do join us."

She was starting to unlock the gate. Carl said, "So it's enough already."

"Enough?" she said blankly. "Enough?"

"Honey, the guy is taking a cheap shot, and I'm going to run him off."

She licked her mouth. "Carl, sweetie, why do you have to be—"

"You can go in out of the heat, or you can stay and watch how it's done, Mary. Either way I run this smartass off."

"Any special direction?" I asked.

"Pick the one you like best, chief," he said with a jolly grin of anticipation. "Start now and save yourself grief."

"Take your best shot, Brego." He took it. I was worried that he might know too much about what he wanted to do. If he did, it was going to take a long time in the hot sun, and if he didn't, it could be reasonably quick.

He did a little bounce, a little prance. He pawed with the clumsy, measuring left and then came leaping in, following up on the right hook that he had brought up from about five feet behind him, practically at ground level. He did not know what he was doing. People who know do not go around taking the chance of hitting the solid bone of skull or jaw with the bare fist. A broken hand is incapacitating. It takes a long, tiresome time to heal. He wanted to pop me one and let the momentum carry him into me so he could get his hands and arms on me and put those muscles to work. He gave me lots of time for a decision. If I fell back away from it, he was going to tumble onto me. That way I might get a thumb in my eye before I could unwind and unravel him. The footing in the soft sand was a little uncertain for savate. So I moved forward, a little to my right, to take me inside that long, sweeping hook.

I felt it go around me, and I let his momentum then drive me back. I drove both hands, fingers spread, into his long hair, I clenched hard and went down pulling him on top of me but getting my knees up against my chest in time. One shoe slipped off his sweaty body, but the sole of the other stayed in place against his belly, and momentum gave me enough leverage to push him up and over. It was a good, high kick, and he spun well. By then I was on my back with my hands straight up over my head.

He hit the soft sand flat on his back with one hell of a whump. It exploded the air out of his lungs. I was up first, and I moved into position, waiting for him. He got up slowly, gagging for air. As he pushed up, I cranked his arm around behind him and put my other hand on the nape of his neck and ran him into the weathered boards of the garden fence, quite close to the woman. He splintered a board with the top of his head. She squeaked and chewed her fist. I dragged him back by the ankles, face down. I picked him up and stood him on his noodle legs and slapped him until he started to come around. Then I bent him over and ran him into the fence again. I dragged him back again, and I turned his feet until he rolled over onto his back. I slapped him where he lay, and when he stirred and his eyes came into focus, I levered his mouth open by bracing the heel of my hand against his chin. I packed his mouth full of soft hot sand, from the back of his throat to his pretty, white teeth.

He came sputtering and gagging onto his hands and knees and coughed himself sick. I grabbed the hair and pulled his head up and back.

"Nod if you can understand me, Brego." He nodded. "Do you want me to break any bones? Do I have to do that?" He shook his head. "She isn't your woman any more. Understand?" He nodded. "Now I am going to start kicking your ass. You better head for the beach. If I ever see you back here, I'll break some bones."

I went around behind him and got a pretty good soccer kick into it, using the side of my foot. On the upswing. It slid him onto his face. He came scrambling up with more energy than I expected, but I got him again just as he got his feet under him and his hands free of the sand. Three running steps and he landed on his face again but didn't spend any time resting. He got up and went into a wobbly scuffling run, fists against his chest, not daring or wanting to look back.

I watched him and then turned and looked at the woman. She gave me a very uncertain smile. There was an unhealthy skin tone under that deep lovely tan. "I . . . I thought you were going to kill him."

"Kill him? What in God's name for?"

"Well . . . it was so quick and so terrible."

"He won't be back, Mary. Are you going to miss him, particularly? You going to be lonesome?"

"That would depend, wouldn't it?"

"Is there any of his stuff in there?"

"Not much. A few things."

"Anything worth his coming back after?"

"I wouldn't think so. No."

"Now you can invite me in again."

Her color was back. "You take a hell of a lot for granted."

I put a knuckle under her chin and tilted her face up and looked at it inch by inch, a long and interested search. "If you want, girl, I can throw you back, like an undersized mackerel. The world is full of Carl Bregos. It's up to you."

She twisted her chin free. "I guess I wouldn't want to be thrown back, Gav. I guess it wouldn't fit my image. Was there really a Lois Jefferson?"

"If you think there was."

"I don't think so."

"Then there never was such a girl."

"Poor Carl. Do you always get what you want?"

"I usually get what I *think* I want."

She tilted her shoulders one way, her hips the other. Her look was challenge. "And sometimes you find out you didn't really want it after all. Me, too. Win a little, lose a little, huh?"

"If you wanted Brego, you'd still have him. I wouldn't have gotten to say more than two words to you."

"Like I was saying when we were so rudely interrupted, you want to come into my house? It's hot out here when the wind quits."

So we went in, and I wondered why I could find no trace of a Canadian accent. She had to be Lisa Dissat.

Eleven

THOUGH THE PLANTINGS were different, the patio furniture of a different style and arrangement, the pool and the cold water shower head were placed just as in my rented garden. I went to the shower and turned it on and sluiced off the sand that had caked thickly on my sweaty back and on my left side where I had rolled to get up quickly. The woman stood and watched me and then took a big, striped beach towel from a stone bench and brought it to me as I stepped out of the spray and turned the shower off.

As I dried myself, I realized how sexually aware of her I had become. Physical readiness. All her honey-brown curves and cushions were there, appropriate, ready for more.

It is such an old old thing, the pattern of male conflict that wins the female. It is deep in the blood and the secretions, a gut knowledge. We are mammals still caught up in all the midbrain mechanisms of survival. The bison female stood long ago and watched the males thud their brute heads together, tear up the sod with their hooves, watched the loser lope heavily away, and then she waited patiently to be mounted by the victor. The stronger the male, the stronger the calves, and the better protected the calves would be during the long months of helplessness. The victorious male, turning from battle to the prize of battle, would be physiologically ready to mate her and have no question about her readiness.

I knew the musky readiness of the woman. She told me in the way she stood, in the way she looked at me, in the shape of her placid mouth. Maybe ten percent of what we can say to each other is with words, and words can conceal as easily as they can reveal. The rest of it is body language, our cants, tilts, postures, textures.

And who can prove there is not an actual telepathic signal being transmitted? Tiny electrical discharges occur in the living mind in great and complex profusion. Strong emotion, tautly focused, may send out an impulse so strong it can be read. Hate, fear, anger, joy, lust . . . these all seem contagious beyond all objective reason. I knew she was so swollen, so moist, so ready, that if I trotted her into the shadowy coolness of the apartment and into her bed, there would be no time or need for foreplay, that she would cling and grind and gasp and within a minute begin to go into a climax.

The violence had caught us up in the first act of the fleshy ceremony, and I wanted to take that quick, primitive jump so badly I felt hollowed out by the ache of it. Bed was her country. That was where, after the first great surge, she would take command. I would become what she was accustomed to and lose any chance of keeping her off balance. I shook myself like a big tired Labrador after a long swim, balled the damp towel, and flipped it at her face. She moved in her slow sensuous dream, getting her hand partway up before it hit her squarely in the face. It fluttered to the floor.

"Hey!" she said, frowning. "What's that for?"

"Pick it up!"

"Sure," she said. She picked the towel up. "What are you sore about? Why are you getting ugly and spoiling the fun?"

"He was supposed to hammer me to bloody ruin out there. That was supposed to be the fun. Thanks a lot."

She came toward me. "Darling, you've got it all wrong. I was getting *bored* with him! I was *so* glad you came along."

"Sure, Mary. Only I know the Bregos of this world. They don't start anything they don't think they can win. Their cheap women chouse them into it because they like the blood. You set me up by reacting to me. If you'd cooled it, there'd have been no fight. He was going to smash me around and that was going to turn you on for him, so you'd hustle him into your sack for a quick hump. A little midday entertainment. No thanks."

She leaned forward from the waist, face contorting, voice turning to a squalling fishwife. "*Goddamn* you! You moved in on us with all that crap about me looking like somebody else. *You* thought I was worth the chance of getting your ass whipped. Don't slam the gate on the way out, you son of a—"

Her lips started to say the obvious word, but I had fitted my big right hand to her slender throat, just firmly enough to cut off her wind, not firmly enough to crush any of the tender bones and cartilage. The ball of my thumb reached to the big artery in the side of her throat under the jaw hinge, and my first and middle finger reached to the artery on the left side of her throat.

Her eyes went wide, and she dropped the towel and put her nails into the back of my hand and my wrist. I pinched the arteries gently, drastically reducing the flow of blood to the brain. It gave her a gray-out to the edge of fainting. Her eyes went out of focus, and her mouth sagged. When I let up, she tried to kick me, so I pinched again. Her arms fell slack to her sides. When I released the pressure, adjusting my hand enough so that she could breathe, she raised her hands and then hung them upon my wrist.

I smiled at her, pulling her a half-step closer and said, "If you get loud and say nasty things, dear, if you get on my nerves, I can hold you like this, and I can take this free hand and make a big fist like this, and I can give you one little pop right here that will give you a nose three inches wide and a quarter inch high."

"Please," she said in a rusty little voice.

"You can get a job as a clown. Or you can see if you can find a surgeon willing to try to rebuild it."

"Please," she said again.

I let go of her and said, "Pick up the towel, love."

She coughed and bent and picked it up and backed away. I turned away from her and went to the cottage apartment and pulled the door open and went in. I went to the kitchen alcove and checked the bottle supply. I heard her slide the glass door shut again.

I fixed some Booth's with Rose's lime juice and a dash of bitters, humming softly but audibly. I took my glass over to the couch and sat and smiled at her and said, "Did I ever tell you I read minds?"

"You must be some kind of a crazy person." It was not said as an insult. It was said softly, wonderingly.

I pinched the bridge of my nose and closed my eyes. "Many messages are coming through. Ah, yes. You are wondering if you can get the hotel management to throw a net over me and get me out of here. No, dear. I think they would believe me instead of you. If they make life difficult, I could go down to the harbor and find your friend Brego and bounce him up and down until he agrees to write out a personal history of your touching romance and sign it. Then I could go find your husband and peddle it to him. It would cut the heart out of any alimony payments."

"I just want you to—"

"Where and when did you meet Brego?"

"On the beach. Over a week ago. My neck hurts."

"Of *course* it hurts a little! How could I do that without giving you a sore neck? Let me see. What else is in your mind? You're wondering if I'm going to lay you and if I'll be nicer to you afterward. The answer to both questions, dear, is: time will tell."

She went over to the kitchen bar. Ice clinked into a glass. She came back with a drink and sat on a hassock five feet away from me. Her eyes looked better. Her confidence was coming back. She squared her shoulders, tugged the bikini top and bottom into better adjustment, tilted her head, and risked a meager smile. "I guess all that lunch talk about land investments was a lot of crap, huh?"

"What makes you think so? It's what I do."

"You don't act like it's what you do. Like the way you

were with Carl and with me, Gavin. I mean . . . well, it's like you enjoyed hurting."

"Well . . . let's suppose there's a man with a good idea where a new interstate is going or a new jetport, and suppose we teamed up, and you had some nice long weekends with him, and he clued you about where to buy the raw land. Mary, I just couldn't stand having you get tricky with me about something like that. I wouldn't want to worry about you selling that information to somebody else. I'd have to have you so trained for the work that if I just stare at you for ten seconds, you start to have the cold sweats and the gags. Hurting is purely business. I guess I enjoy anything that helps make money."

She thought that over, sipping, frowning. "But it's not as if I was going to work with you, Mr. Lee."

"Time will tell."

"You keep saying that. Well, I'm not going to work with you or for you. For that kind of work you're talking about, what you want is some kind of a hooker, it seems to me."

"Does it seem like that to you? Really? I wouldn't say that. You're built for the work. You have just enough cheap invitation in the way you look and the way you handle yourself to keep a man from wasting a lot of time on unnecessary preliminaries."

"Now wait one goddamn minute—"

"Are you still with Brego? No. Then shut up."

"I'm sorry. Don't get sore."

"Fifty bucks makes you a hooker. For five hundred you're a call girl. Five thousand makes you a courtesan."

"What's that?"

"Never mind. But when we move the decimal point one

more place, your end of the arrangement is fifty thousand. That makes you a career woman."

The pointed tongue moved slowly across the underlip. She swallowed and said, "I've got my own thing going, thanks."

"Alimony is a cheap hustle."

"It all depends."

"On how much he's got? On the evidence? On the law? It has to be a cheap hustle, because when there's enough money involved, there's more profit from going in some other direction."

I had wanted to test just how deep the hardness went. Her eyes changed. She slopped some of her drink onto her bare knees, wiped it off with her hand. "That's crazy talk."

"Not for careful people who've got the right contacts."

"For me, no thanks. I just wouldn't have the nerve, Gav."

I got up and moved around, carrying my drink. I did not know where to take it from there. I could guess that she had been ordered to keep to herself in Grenada but had finally gotten so bored she had become reckless and picked up Brego. Now the Brego game had mushroomed into something a lot less comfortable for her. If she could live quietly at the inn for the length of time she was supposed to, she could get away with it. She wasn't too much shorter than Mary or too much younger. Dark hair. All American women look alike to the help.

I hadn't wanted to let myself think about Mary. From the physical description the housekeeper had given Jeannie Dolan, this woman was the Canadian, Lisa Dissat. If she was here, Mary was dead. I had the beginnings of an idea. I went back to the conversations at lunch. Neither the first name of her supposed husband nor her Stateside residence had come up.

After mental rehearsal and rewrite I sat once again and looked placidly at her and said, "The way you spell that last name is bee-are-oh-el-el?"

"Yes."

"Kind of unusual. It rings a bell someplace. Mary Broll. Mary Broll. It's been bothering me ever since I met you in the bar."

"Why bother with it? Want me to fresh up your drink?"

"Got it!"

"Got what?"

"Where'd you register from? One buck will get you five it's the Fort Lauderdale area. Sure! We had a syndicate set up a couple of years back and we wanted a builder in the Lauderdale area who could put up a hotel and marina complex in a hurry. Heavy-set fellow name of Broll. Big. Not old. Frank? Wally? Jerry? . . . Harry! Damn right. Harry Broll."

"Maybe there's more Brolls than you know, Gav."

"Bring me your purse, honey."

"What?"

"Go get your purse. Your pocketbook. Your handbag. Bring it to dear old Gavin Lee so he can look at your ID, dear."

She gave me a broad, bright smile, and her teeth chattered for a moment before she got herself under control. "Okay. My secret is out. You are speaking of the man I used to love."

"How long have you been married to him?"

". . . Nearly four years."

"Any kids? No? Lucky. Kids seem to get the rough end of the stick. Bring me the purse, honey."

"Why should I? I told you, didn't I?"

"Honey, if we stop getting along, we're going to have to hurt your neck a little until we get squared away."

"Please. It makes me sick to my stom—"

"Get the purse!"

She brought it to me. I found the billfold. I examined the identification. I looked at the signature on the driver's license. I knew my Mary had signed it, and I knew, looking at it, that she was dead.

"Honey, go over to that desk and take a piece of paper and sign your name on it. Mary D. Broll. And bring it back here to me."

"Who *are* you? What do you want?"

"I am the fellow who sat across the table from Mary D. Broll at Le Dome of the Four Seasons in Lauderdale two years ago last month. There were about ten of us at that dinner. Harry was making the big gesture, trying to sucker us into letting him build for us. I spent the evening trying to make his wife. She wouldn't give me a clue. I always have a better memory for the ones who get away. Here's her signature right here. Go over there and forge it for me, honey."

"Who *are* you?" she demanded, close to tears.

I gave her a broad, egg-sucking smile. "Me? I am the fellow who all of a sudden owns himself a whole woman, right from dandruff to bunions and everything in between. Broads like you don't play games like this unless there's money in it. And now it's *our* money, dear. I am the fellow who is going to get it all out of you, and I am going to beat on you until you convince me there's nothing left to tell. Me? Hell, baby, I am your new partner."

"Please. Please. I can't tell you—"

"The little lady in this corner is getting one chance and one chance only, to go over to the desk and sign her real, true, legal name to a piece of paper and bring it back to the gentleman. And if it turns out that it is not her real true name, it is going to be one of those long afternoons. We're going to have to stuff a towel in the little lady's mouth so the screaming won't spoil anybody's vacation."

She walked to the desk, her back very straight. She wrote on a piece of paper and brought it back and handed it to me and began to weep. She covered her face and ran for the bedroom. Damned few women look well from a rear elevation, running away from you in a bikini. She was not one of them. She had written her name neatly. It was a schoolgirl neatness. Lisa Dissat.

I slowly crumpled the sheet of hotel paper. I felt tired. I got up and walked back to the bedroom where she lay upon the unchanged sheets she and Brego had stained, sweated, and rumpled. She was on her side, knees hiked up, clenched fists tucked under her chin. She made sucking sounds, whining sounds. Fetal agony.

In the better interrogations there is always a good guy and a bad guy. I had been the bad guy. Time to change roles. I went into the bathroom and took a hand towel and soaked it in cold water. I wrung it out, took it to the bed, sat on the side of the bed, and cupped my hand on her shoulder and pulled her toward me. She resisted and made protest sounds, then let herself roll onto her back.

I hitched closer and gently swabbed her face and forehead. Her eyes went wide with astonishment. The last thing she had expected was gentleness. She snuffled. Her face looked touchingly young. Tears had washed away the challenge and the hardness.

"Have you got anything with you to prove your name is Lisa Dissat?"

"N-no."

"And you're pretending to be Mary Broll?"

"Yes. But I—"

"Does Broll know you're impersonating his wife?"

"Yes."

"Were you having an affair with him?"

"Yes."

"Where's the real Mary Broll?"

". . . I don't know."

"Lisa?"

"I didn't know what he was going to do! I *didn't*!"

"Lisa!"

"I couldn't have changed anything."

"Just say she's dead, Lisa. Go ahead."

"I didn't know he—"

"Lisa! Say it!"

"She's dead. Okay. She's dead."

"Harry killed her?"

She looked startled. "Oh, no!"

"Who killed her?"

"Please, Gavin. If he ever knew I told anybody—"

"You're in a real box, dear. You can worry about what's going to happen in the future, or you can worry about what's going to happen in the next ten minutes."

"I don't even know if he really meant to."

"What's his name?"

". . . Paul. Paul Dissat. He is . . . my first cousin. We worked for the same man. In Quebec. Mr. Dennis Waterbury. Paul got me the job there. I'm a secretary. I was a secretary. Paul is an accountant. He is . . . very trusted. I think he might be crazy. Really crazy. Maybe he really planned to kill Harry's wife. I don't know. I don't even know if he knows."

"How much money is involved?"

"An awful lot. Really, an awful lot of money."

"Stop crying."

"I want to talk about it, and I don't want to talk about it. I've been scared for so long! I *want* you to make me tell you all of it, but I'm afraid to tell you."

Twelve

IT WAS A VERY LONG AFTERNOON for both of us. But longer for Lisa Dissat, because from time to time she tried to get cute. But the more she tried it, the more conditioned she became, and the more quickly she would correct herself.

At last I was able to bring the complex, wandering, fragments of the story into reasonably sharp focus.

Paul Dissat had hungered for a long time to share in some of the large profits Dennis Waterbury made on his varied operations and investments in resort lands, oil and gas drilling programs, new urban office structures, tanker leasing, and so on. Paul Dissat was well paid. There were staff bonuses when things went well. Paul Dissat was shrewd enough to realize that without investment capital he had no chance of participating in the profits and that if he used his skills to tinker with the records of the various corporations and their shifting, changing bank balances, sooner or later an audit would catch him.

He was single, she said, and did not look like anybody's idea of an accountant. Bachelor apartment, sports car. She said he was a superb skier, proficient at downhill racing and slalom. She said that three years ago, when she was twenty-three, she had run up bills she was unable to pay. She was afraid of losing her job. She had phoned Paul. She had not seen him in several years. He had taken her to dinner and back to his apartment and made love to her. He had paid her overdue accounts and arranged for her to be employed by Waterbury. After they had been intimate many times, he had told her of his plan to share in some of the fat profits from Waterbury's operations. He would arrange the necessary leverage through her. He said he would let her know when the right opportunity came along.

He arranged for her to seduce the particularly unattractive minor partner in one of the Waterbury developments and to pretend infatuation. Paul prompted her during the affair, telling her what her lines should be. Eventually, in order to safely end the affair without Lisa going to his wife, the man deposited a substantial amount of cash in her savings account. Paul told her that the cash was the proceeds from the stock in a Waterbury enterprise that the man had sold to get the money to buy her off. Paul had taken all of the cash except a thousand dollars.

They had done it once again prior to her affair with Harry Broll and made a little more than the first time. Paul explained to her that a man who has suddenly made a substantial profit tends to be generous with a mistress who is becoming too demanding and possessive.

I wanted to know why she kept so little of the take and let her first cousin have all the rest. She said it was because she was in love with him. At first.

"The third one was Harry," she said. "I went to the hotel and took dictation. Just like the first two men. Ten minutes after I looked at him in a certain way and told him how real brilliant he was, I was helping him take off my bra, because his hands were shaking so bad. Then after Harry went back to the States, Paul made me quit my job and follow him. I didn't want to. He said this could be the big one, worth a big risk. So . . . I did what he said. Harry got jumpy when I phoned him last November from Miami. He was glad, but he was nervous, too. I told him I had followed him because I was so in love with him I couldn't live without him, and I was putting my future in his hands."

Harry had set her up in the apartment in the Casa de Playa. At about that time Paul Dissat had been transferred to the administrative offices of SeaGate, Inc. in West Palm Beach, just as he had planned and expected. SeaGate was a large, complex situation with very complicated financing and special tax problems. Paul had been involved in it from the beginning.

"I called Paul once, but he got very angry. He told me to keep on following orders. The orders were to make myself just as agreeable as I possibly could, to make Harry as happy as possible, to really work on the sex part of it and do anything and everything to give him so much pleasure he'd never be able to get along without me. That wasn't easy, because Harry worked hard and he didn't keep in shape and didn't have much energy left for bed. But after I learned what turned him on the most, it got better for both of us. I had to pretend to be passionately in love with him. You know, it wasn't such a bad life. Go shopping, go out on the beach, get your hair done, watch your weight, do your nails, take naps. Not a bad life. Then a few days before Christmas, Paul wanted to know when Harry would be with me, definitely. I said I could make sure he'd come in the middle of the day on the twenty-third and spend an hour and a half with me. He told me not to be surprised if Mrs. Broll showed up. I couldn't understand what Paul was trying to do. He told me to shut up and do what I was told. She came barging in as Harry was leaving. Better looking than I'd thought from what Harry had told me about her. She called me some things, and I called her some things, and she went away crying."

Harry Broll had then become very upset. He had told Lisa Dissat that he needed her, that he wanted to get a divorce from Mary and marry her, but he couldn't do that yet. He had to make up with Mary, humble himself, promise never to see Lisa again. He said he had to do that because without her financial backing he was going to miss out on his great opportunity at SeaGate. He said he had to move her out of the apartment and be very careful about seeing her. He said it might last until May, but then he could leave Mary and marry her.

On the night of January fourth, shortly before midnight, Harry came to Lisa's motel, where he had moved her after taking her out of the apartment. He was drunk. He said that he and Mary had a terrible fight, and she was leaving him. As soon as Harry had passed out, Lisa phoned Paul to report, as required, any new development. Paul drove over to the motel, left his rented car there, borrowed

Harry's car and house keys, and told Lisa to undress the unconscious Harry and keep him quiet for as long as she could manage.

"He wouldn't tell me what he was going to do. He acted all . . . keyed up, excited, on top of the world. He came back at daylight. He seemed very tired and very relaxed. He helped me get Harry up. Harry was confused. He knew Paul, of course, because of SeaGate and knew he was my cousin. But that was the first he realized that Paul knew about Harry and me. Paul pretended to be very upset about the affair, I guess to keep Harry off-balance. The three of us went back in Harry's car to Harry's house on Blue Heron Lane. Paul kept telling Harry he was in trouble. Paul made me wait in the living room. He took Harry into the bedroom. Harry made a terrible sound. A kind of bellowing groan. I heard heavy footsteps running, and then I heard Harry throwing up. When Paul brought him back into the living room, all cleaned up, Harry was like a sleepwalker. Paul kept saying it was an accident, and Harry kept saying anything like that just couldn't be an accident, and Paul kept telling him that everything could be worked out for the best if Harry would just pull himself together. Paul had me make coffee, a lot of it."

Mary had, of course, been interrogated by Paul Dissat and murdered by Paul Dissat when he finally had everything he needed—the air reservations and tickets from the travel agency, the hotel reservation, the complete details of her arrangement with her trust officer, the fact that only one friend knew where she was going and why: Holly Dressner at 27 Blue Heron Lane, a few doors away. And he had the ninety-two hundred dollars in cash she had drawn from the income account of TA 5391. Mary was half packed for the trip. She had bought resort clothes. At Paul's order Lisa finished the packing, hunting through Mary's belongings for what she thought she would need.

"It was weird with her on the bed all covered up. I tried some of the stuff on in her dressing room. She was a little hippier than I am. I mean some of the things were a size ten when I'd be better off in an eight. Harry was like a very sick person. He couldn't seem to get himself out of it. Tears kept rolling down his face. Once he just sort of hung on me. He grabbed me and put so much weight on me he nearly rode me right down on to the floor. He was asking me something, mumbling about how could Paul do that, how could he. They had a terrible argument later on. I couldn't hear most of it. It was about what to do with her body. Harry said he couldn't stand having her buried on the place. There was something about the seawall and a transit mix truck. Paul told Harry she was going to be buried right on the property, then Harry would not go back on any promises, ever."

She was given her orders, and Paul made her repeat them until there was no chance of her forgetting them. Drive to Miami International. Find accommodations for the night of the fifth and sixth. Stay in the room. Use Mary's ticket on the seventh. Use Mary's driver's license as proof of birthplace when needed. Use her immunization certificate if needed. Use her hairstyle. Wear big dark sunglasses. Travel in her new clothes. Go to Grenada. Register as Mary Broll. Live quietly. Keep to yourself. Send some postcards to Holly Dressner. Pick the kind which do not require a message. Sign with a little drawing of a smiling face.

"I *did* try to keep to myself. But, God, I've been here a long long time, Gav. I really have."

"What do you do next? What are Paul's orders?"

"On Monday, next Monday, I'm supposed to send a cable. Paul dictated it to me." I made her get it. It was to Woodrow Willow at Southern National in Miami. PROCEED WITH LOAN AS ARRANGED EARLY JANUARY. HAVE ADVISED HARRY BY PHONE. HOME SOON. MARY BROLL.

Harry's part in it would be to phone Woodrow Willow that same day, Monday, April twenty-sixth, and tell him that Mary had reached him by overseas phone call from Grenada to tell him she had cabled Willow to go ahead, tell him not to worry, tell him she would be home soon. He would inform Willow that Mary had given him the name of the travel agency she had used and had told him that her neighbor, Mrs. Dressner, had known all along where she was.

Very nice. If Willow felt like double-checking after he got the cable, he could call the travel agency and call Mrs. Dressner.

"Can't they check back on an overseas call?" I asked.

"Sure. That's why I call him at his office next Sunday afternoon. I've got the number. He'll have a secretary there. It will be person-to-person. Mrs. Broll calling Mr. Broll. That's for afterward, in case they do a lot of checking."

"Checking what?"

"I'm reserved to leave here on Monday, the third of May. Paul just didn't have time to work everything out before I left. But the way he wants it to happen, Mary Broll will have some kind of accident. He's going to get a message to me telling me what to do. I just . . . leave everything of hers and arrive back home as myself somehow. Maybe a towel and a beach bag left on the beach, and nothing missing but a swim suit and a cap."

"Where does the money come from?"

"The way I understand it, Gav, Harry invested seven hundred thousand in SeaGate. The letter of agreement said that on or before April thirtieth, he has to pay in another three hundred thousand to make one million dollars. There is a block of stock escrowed for him and a note escrowed, saying SeaGate owes him seven hundred thousand plus interest. It is an . . . indivisible block. He takes it all and wipes out the money SeaGate owes him and pays three hundred more. If he doesn't, he just gets his seven hundred back with interest, and the hundred thousand shares go to increase the number of shares the corporation is selling to the public and to reduce the number the stockholders will offer. There is no way in the world Harry can get that money except from the bank on a loan on Mary's trust. He can't get an extension, and he can't cut down the number of shares he'll take. And he is borrowed to the hilt everywhere else."

"So he had to keep Mary alive for about four months after she died?"

She shivered. "Or lose a big profit, a million and a half."

"How much to your cousin?"

"He said a million. He didn't say that in front of Harry. I think he could get it all out of Harry." She frowned. "The thing about Paul, he stopped giving a damn *what* he does. It doesn't matter to him any more. It scares me. Once when

I was little, a deaf boy took me to the movies, and he laughed when nobody else was laughing. Paul is like that now, sort of."

"And I suppose Harry has been making a big fuss, storming around, shaking up Mary's friends, demanding they tell him where they're hiding her."

"Maybe. I don't know. I guess it would make him look better later on, if people could testify to that. I don't know how he is. I keep wondering how he'll sound on the phone."

Her voice dragged. Her face looked puffy with fatigue. Her eyes were irritated because of the many times the tears had come. There wasn't much left of the day. She said, "Can we go for a walk on the beach? Would that be okay, Gavin?"

She got up and got a gaudy print dashiki and pulled it over her head, pushed her hair back into semiorder, put her big glasses on. "Gee, I feel emptied out, as if it's out of my hands somehow. I should be scared, but I'm too beaten down to be scared. You're in charge, Gav. You've taken over. I don't know where we're going, but you're running the ship."

It was so nicely done I had my mouth all set for the bait and the hook. Poor little victim of a sordid conspiracy, clinging to the first man who'd give her the benefit of the doubt.

Sweet little immature face and a busy, nimble little butt and all the conscience and mercy of a leopard shark. Let me be your little pal, mister. Nobody else has ever understood me but you. She had slipped up on one little detail, but it was a bad slip. She let me see how she must have looked trying on Mary's new resort clothes while Mary lay dead. Probably Lisa turned this way and that, looking in the mirror, smoothing her rear with the backs of her hands, wishing the damned dead woman had bought the cute clothes one size smaller. She tried on clothes while the men argued in the next room. "Look at it this way, Broll. You had a look at her an hour and a half ago. They'll want to know why you waited so long before reporting it. What do you tell them?" While Lisa hummed and bit her lip and frowned at herself and wondered if the colors were right for her.

Thirteen

WE WALKED UP THE BEACH in the orange and gold light of tropic sunset. The tide was moving out and the packed sand was damp and firm under our tread, a coarse, yellow-brown sand. The sun was behind us setting into the sea just out beyond Long Point. Far ahead, beyond the rocks that marked the end of Grand Anse beach and beyond St. George's harbor, was the toy-town look of the town at evening, spilled up the green slopes, small formal shapes with windows looking toward the sea.

We walked past the Grand Anse Hotel, the Grenada Beach Hotel, the Holiday Inn. Cars had come down to the public areas to park under the sea grapes and the almond trees. People swam in the relative cool of twilight, and people walked the long broad promenade of packed sand. Sloops and ketches and multihull sailboats were anchored off the two-mile crescent of beach. A fast boat was pulling a limber black girl on water skis between the anchored sail-boats. Behind us was the blinding dazzle of the sun's path on the quiet sea, and our shadows ahead of us were long in a slanting pattern against the damp sand.

"You were going to talk, I thought?"

"I am. I am." She moved closer, linked her arm through mine, hugged it against her body, and looked up at me. "I have to, I guess. Do you know how things can happen to your life that . . . don't fit it somehow? Then everything else isn't real. When you forget, then everything around you is real again, but what happened doesn't seem as if it could have ever happened. Do you know what I'm talking about?"

"Not yet, girl. Not yet."

"I guess in my own way I was as numb as Harry was. It seems like ten years ago, practically."

"Didn't you think it was pretty damned stupid for Paul to kill Mary Broll? Didn't you tell him it was stupid?"

She had to wait until we had passed a group of people strolling at a slower pace than ours. She indicated a stubby cement pier at the far border of the Holiday Inn property. It projected only to the surf line and seemed to have no pur-pose other than as some sort of groyne to retain the sand. We went up the slope of beach, stepped up onto it, and walked out to sit near the end, our backs to the sunset.

She laced her fingers in mine, tugged at my hand, and rested it palm upward against the smooth, round brown of mid-thigh. She frowned toward the town.

"I've thought about it and thought about it, Gavin. I guess it got to be pretty obvious to Paul that an affair with me wasn't going to be enough leverage on Harry. Harry and his wife weren't getting along so great anyway. There wasn't anything real important to expose, you might say. So why did he tip off Mary Broll so she'd catch me and Harry together? Why did he make sure she *would* catch us? Why did he tell me to yell at Mrs. Broll and make a big scene out of it? Motive, right?"

The point was well taken. Mary would certainly confide her problem to someone. The scene at the apartment had attracted so much attention that even Jeannie Dolan heard about it later. Of late, Harry had been blustering around, threatening people, trying to locate his dead wife.

If the police were tipped, dug for Mary, and found her, even the most inept state's attorney could put together a case F. Lee Bailey couldn't successfully defend.

"So, Lisa, you think Paul had decided to kill her when he made the phone call to her. Does that make sense? He didn't know then she'd decided to go away. He didn't know then what she'd arrange about the loan. She could have left without any warning at all. He'd have to be some kind of warlock, reading the future."

"I know. I think about it until my head starts to hurt, and then I give up."

"Did you think he'd ever kill anybody?"

"You don't go around wondering whether people you know can kill other people, do you? I knew he was mean. I knew how nasty he could get. I knew there was something kinky about him, the way he got something special out of sleeping with me and then making me sleep with those older guys. It was something to do with him never getting married, I think. We look alike, like brother and sister. His eyes are the same as mine, the same dark dark brown and long black lashes and—see?—the left one set straight, and the right one slanty. His mouth is like mine, a lot of natural red to the lips, and the mouth small, and the lower lip heavy and curling out from the upper lip. We both look younger than we are, but that's always been true of the whole family. Aside from that there isn't the least thing feminine about him. Even my eyes and mouth don't look girlish on Paul, somehow. Except when he's asleep. That's strange, isn't it? I'd watch him sleeping, and then his eyes and lips would look the most like mine and make me feel strange. He is big! He's almost as tall as you are and as big through the chest. But he moves a lot quicker. I guess I mean his normal way of moving is quicker. Nobody is quicker than you were with Carl. Jesus! You looked kind of dumb and sleepy, as if you couldn't believe he was really going to beat on you. Then you were something else."

"I want to know more about Paul. How old is he?"

"He'll be coming up onto thirty-seven, I think in July. Yes. Other companies have tried to hire him away from Mr. Waterbury. So I guess he's a good accountant. He stays in great shape all year. He does competition slalom in the winter and tennis in the summer. His legs are tremendously powerful, like fantastic springs."

"An exercise nut?"

"With weights and springs and pulleys and things. And a sun lamp that travels by itself from one end of you to the other and turns itself off. He's really happy about those legs. One funny thing, he's as dark as I am, and he has to shave twice a day when he goes out in the evening, but on his body, except for those places where everybody has hair, he hasn't any. His legs have a really great shape, and there isn't any hair on them or his chest or his arms. The muscles are long and smooth, not bunchy. When he tenses them, his legs are like marble."

"You called him kinky."

She frowned and thought for a little while. I saw the point of her tongue slowly moisten the curve of underlip. "No. That isn't the right word. The whole sex scene isn't a big thing with him. I mean it's there, all right. It was something we would do. You know, when he couldn't unwind and get to sleep, he'd phone me to come over to his place down in the city. We were five blocks apart. He makes me feel . . . I don't know . . . like one of his damn exercise machines, something with a motor and weights and springs, so that afterward he could put it in his exercise log. Ten minutes on the rowing machine. Eight minutes on the Lisa machine."

"I can't really get the picture of you two."

"What's so difficult, honey?"

"You move to Quebec and change jobs because he tells you to. You come over whenever he phones you. He tells you to seduce Mr. X and then Mr. Y and tells you how to extort money from them, and he takes most of it. He tells you to seduce Harry, quit your job, and follow Harry to Florida, and he tells you to come here and pretend to be Mary. You are awfully goddamn docile, Lisa."

"I know. I know. Yes. It's funny about him. He's just so absolutely positive you're going to do what he tells you to do, it's a lot easier to do it than try to say you won't."

"Did you ever try to say you wouldn't do something he asked you to do?"

"God, yes! In the very beginning, before he even got the

job for me. I was at his place, and he asked me to get him something from across the room. I was sitting at the table, and I said something like 'You're not a cripple, are you?' He got up and went behind me and hit me on top of the head with his fist. I blacked out and fell off the chair and cut my chin. It did something funny to my neck, pinched a nerve or something, and I was in bed for three days with it, practically in agony. He was a darling. He waited on me hand and foot. He was so sweet and considerate. I guess . . . it's easier to do what he says, because you have the feeling that neither of you knows what he'll do if you say no. At work he's another person."

"How do you feel about the way you're crossing him?"

"It keeps making me feel as if I'm going to throw up."

She looked up at me with a piquant tilt of her dark head. "It's funny," she said. "I never saw you before today. Then you scared me so. You really did. Now you're so nice and understanding. I can really talk to you. About everything."

Her fingers were laced in mine, and she pressed down on my hand, holding the back of my hand against the round, tan thigh, slowly swinging her dangling leg as she did so. I felt the smooth working of the thigh muscles against the back of my hand. It was a sensuous and persuasive feeling. She was a pretty piece, making her constant offer of herself in any way that she could.

"Why trust me?" I asked her.

She shrugged. "I don't know. I guess I'm trying to. I guess I can't go it alone, no matter what it is. I appreciate you didn't mark me up any. I mean I hate to get belted in the face where it shows. It cuts a person's mouth inside, and there's a big puffy bruise and maybe a mouse comes under a person's eye. It's a bad thing to do to a girl. She goes around ashamed."

"Paul belted you?"

"Sometimes."

"But you trust him?"

"He's a blood relative. Maybe I shouldn't trust him at all. He's strange. He really is. It doesn't show. You have to know him."

"I keep thinking of how boxed in you are."

"How do you mean?"

"Suppose after you go back, Harry is picked up for killing his wife. They have her body. It's certainly no big problem finding the girlfriend and proving you were there. With that starting point, Lisa, how long before the state attorney's investigators learn about the impersonation? Would you want to explain on the stand why you took her money, her tickets, her reservations, her clothes, and her car?"

There was a sudden sallowness. "Come *on* now. Don't, honey! Jesus! I don't like jokes like that. We're in this together, aren't we?"

"Are we?"

"What do you *want* of me? What more do you want that I'm not ready and eager and willing to give, dear?"

"Do you think Cousin Paul is going to give you a short count on the money again?"

"If he gets the chance."

I pulled my hand away from her. "Now what would keep him from having the chance? Me?"

"Darling, please don't try to confuse me."

"How am I confusing you?"

"Well . . . you said you own me now, and you said there

had to be money in it. So I guess you'll go after the money. I guess you'd have to have my help."

"Doing what?"

"That would be up to you, dear."

"To figure out how you can help me get rich?"

"That's the name of your game, I thought."

"Maybe Paul's game is over."

"How do you mean?"

"Harry Broll is not a complete idiot. Why couldn't he have gone quietly to the police and managed to sell them the truth? So they lay back and wait for you to return and for Paul to make his move, and scoop you both up."

"Damn! I forgot to tell you about the letter I wrote Paul. He was right there when I wrote it. He found Mary Broll's personal stationery for me to use. He told me what to write. I had to do it over because he said it was too neat the first time. I dated it January fifth. It said that Paul had been right and I never should have gotten involved with Harry. It said Harry had done something terrible while drunk and had gotten me to his house afterward to help him but I couldn't. I said I was frightened and I was going away and to wait until I got in touch with him. He held it in front of Harry and made him read it. Then he had me seal it in an envelope and put a stamp on it and address it to Paul's place in West Palm Beach. Paul put it in his pocket to mail as soon as he could."

The sun was gone. The world was darkening. The sky was a dying furnace, and the sea was slate. We walked back the way we had come but more slowly.

"Gavin?"

"Shut up, Lisa. Please."

The beach was almost empty. The outdoor torches had been lighted at the Spice Island Inn. Birds were settling noisily to bed, arguing about the best places. Canned music was coming over all-weather speakers, a steel band playing carnival calypso.

When we reached her gate, she said, "Now can I say something? Like, please come in?"

"I want to sit out in the breeze, thanks. Over there."

"Join you?"

"Sure."

"Bring you a drink, maybe?"

"Thanks. Same as before."

I sat deep in a chaise, legs up, trying to work it out in every possible combination and permutation. With Mary Broll dead, Woodrow Willow was supposed to slam the lid on that trust account. Harry was probably the beneficiary under her will, possibly a coexecutor along with the bank. But had she died in early January, even in a traffic accident, the chances of processing the estate quickly enough for Harry to get his three hundred thousand before April thirtieth were very damned remote. She had to die later on.

So what if Meyer and I had not had all those vague feelings of uneasiness? What if we had accepted my phone call as being proof enough that she was alive and well and living in Grenada?

Then it would have worked like a railroad watch. The timely loan. The news of pending reconciliation. Enough supporting information for Willow to consider the cable legitimate authorization. Then the ironic tragedy. Estranged wife on the point of returning home to her contrite husband, missing in mysterious drowning incident. Search is on for body. However . . .

"Here you go," she said. I thanked her for the drink. She had brought one for herself. She sat on the side of the chaise, facing me. I moved my legs over to make room. The stars were beginning to come out. I could see that she had brushed her hair, freshened her mouth. The bright, block print dashaki had deep side slits, and she adjusted herself and it, either by accident or design, so that the side slit showed the outside of a bare thigh and hip as high as the waist, a smoothness of flesh in the dying day that was not interrupted by the narrow encirclement of bikini I had seen there before.

"You certainly do an awful lot of thinking," she said.

"And here I am, dear, alive and well."

"But you have been terribly terribly hurt a few times, Gav."

"The times when I wasn't thinking clearly."

"Do I keep you from thinking clearly? I'd sure like a chance to try. Would you mind if I ask you politely to please make love to me?"

"What are we celebrating?"

"You're *such* a bastard! Gavin darling, I feel very very insecure about a lot of things. I've been alone a long time. Now I want somebody to hold me tight and make love to me and tell me I'm delicious. For morale, I guess. Why do you even make me ask? It doesn't have to be any big thing, you know. It doesn't have to take up a hell of a lot of your time. Hitch over just a little bit, darling and let me . . ."

The way she started to manage it—to lie down beside me

and hike her dashiki up and tug my swim trunks down and simultaneously hook one brown leg over me—certainly wasn't going to take up a great deal of anybody's time, the way she was going at it.

I pushed her erect and pulled the trunks back up. "Very flattering. Very generous. But no thanks."

She laughed harshly and picked her drink up off the sand near her feet. "Well, comparing you to Carl, I can say this. You've got a different kind of attitude. If I hadn't uncovered proof, I'd be wondering about you."

"I'm busy pretending I'm Paul, wondering how he has it all worked out."

"Different strokes for different folks."

"I hang back and make sure Harry Broll follows orders. I check with him about the Sunday afternoon phone call from you. On Tuesday morning, the twenty-seventh, I will get in touch with Mr. Willow, in my capacity as an employee of SeaGate, to verify that Mr. Broll will indeed have the funds to pick up his escrowed block of SeaGate shares. I am assured. The money comes through. And I am very very busy right through the thirtieth and through the weekend, because that is the end of the fiscal year for SeaGate. Right?"

"I guess so, dear."

"Then I have to do something about Cousin Lisa. She's expecting a message from me. I'll have to deliver it in person."

"To tell me what to do next?"

"Old Harry is twitchy about his dead wife. And Lisa is twitchy about Harry's dead wife. Harry and Lisa could testify against me if they ever join forces. Lisa is wearing the dead woman's rings. I just have to arrange a nice quick safe way to meet her in the islands and blow her face off and blow her dental work to paste. Then there's no mystery about a body. I can settle down and separate good old Harry from every cent of his gain and every cent he has left over when that's gone. When Harry is empty, it will be time to lay him to rest, too. By accident. Just in case."

I reached an idle hand and patted her on the shoulder. She remained quiveringly still, then was suddenly up and away, to come to rest five feet from the chaise, staring at me.

"No! No, Gavin. He's my first cousin. No."

"He couldn't do that?"

"Absolutely not. Not ever. Not any way."

"Then why are you so upset?"

"Anybody would be upset, hearing something so horrible."

"You know you are supposed to fake Mary Broll's death. There's less chance of a hitch if somebody plays the part of the body. You've been Mary Broll since January. Why switch now?"

"Don't be such a bastard!"

"It's the way I have to read him from everything you've told me. A quirky guy but very logical. A good improviser. If one logical plan doesn't develop the way he wants it to, he thinks up an alternative just as good or better. And . . . Lisa dear, just what the hell good are you to him? The end of usefulness. He knows there's a chance you'll make new friends who'll hear about how you died and get very upset about it and might run into you in an air terminal somewhere a year from now. All you are is a big risk, and an unnecessary risk."

"Shut *up!*"

"Think about it."

"I *am* thinking about it."

"It wouldn't be *my* style, but I have to admire it in a way. It ties up the loose ends. No way out for Harry. Or you."

She found her drink had been kicked over. "Ready for another?"

"Not yet, thanks."

"Want to come in?"

"I'll stay here awhile."

"Be back soon, dear."

Fourteen

THOUGH LISA DISSAT was not gone for more than ten minutes, it was full night when she came back, a velvet beach under a brilliance of stars. There were lights behind us from the Spice Island Inn cottages. The lights made a slanting yellow glow against the sand.

She sat beside me again. She had changed to tailored white shorts, a dark blouse with a Chinese collar and long sleeves. She smelled of perfume . . . and Off. The white fabric was snug on the round hip that pressed warm against the side of my knee.

"Took off your instant rape suit, eh?"

She pulled her shoulders up slightly, and her drink made the sounds of ice as she sipped. "I guess you made me lose interest."

"Are you a believer now?"

"Up to a point. I can't see any percentage in taking dumb

risks. You are the loose end Paul doesn't know about. I guess I can be the bait in the trap. But we have to be awfully awfully careful. He's very sensitive to . . . what people are thinking. We can't give him any chance at all."

"How do you mean that?"

"If it's like you say, if that's what he's going to try to do, then he'll have it all worked out so there won't be any risk in it, hardly any at all. So if he really wants to kill me, we have to kill him instead, darling."

"Your very own first cousin?"

"Don't be a stinker, please. What other choice is there?"

"Then what?"

"Then we have to get me back into the States in some safe way. I guess there's no reason why I couldn't go back in as Mary Broll, come to think of it. What harm would it do?"

"None, if you don't try to keep on being Mrs. Broll."

"If he isn't thinking about killing me like you say, then we'll have to play it by ear."

"All goes well, and you and I are back in the States. Then?"

"We just go and see Harry. That's all. I'll tell him that unless he gives us lots and lots of money, he's going to have lots and lots of trouble. And you can beat him up if he tries to bluff us."

"How much money?"

"I don't think we should make him really desperate or anything. I think we should leave him with enough so he'll think he came out of it pretty well. I think we could ask for half a million dollars."

"Each?"

"No, dear. He has to pay taxes on the whole thing, you

know. I think with the holding period before the sale to the public, it will be long term. Yes, I know it will. He should get his money next December. Hmmm. His taxes will be a half million. That leaves him two million, and I know he owes four hundred thousand and he will have to pay back the three hundred thousand. So out of his million and three, we'll take five hundred thousand, darling, and he'll have eight hundred thousand left. It would be neater if we took six hundred and fifty and left him six hundred and fifty, don't you think?"

"A lot neater. And you want half?"

"What I want and what you'll let me have aren't the same, are they?"

"They could be with cooperation all the way."

"Moving money like that around without leaving traces that people can find later is very hard. Do you know anything about that kind of problem? I'd think you would."

"If Harry Broll will hold still for the bite, yes."

"There's no problem, Gav honey. None."

"Leaving only Paul."

She finished her drink, bunted me with her hip. "Scrooch over some, honey. Make room. No funny stuff this time, I promise."

She turned, lay back, and fitted her head to my shoulder, swinging her legs aboard.

After a while she said, "Want to order dinner in my place or yours, dear?"

"I don't know yet."

"I'm not hungry, either. Gee, look at all the damned stars. Like when I was a little kid, the night sky looked glittery like this."

"Where was that?"

"Way up in French Canada on the St. Lawrence, north of Riviere du Loup. A little town called Trois Pistoles. Ten thousand saints, ten thousand churches all over that country. Convent school, uniforms, vespers, acts of contrition, the whole scene. I ran away when I was fifteen. With my best friend, Diane Barbet. We got across the border and into the States. Things got kind of messy for us. You survive or you don't, I guess. I don't know what happened to Diane. I think about her sometimes. A guy in Detroit helped me really go to work on my hick Canuck accent. Movies, television, radio, and using a tape recorder. I think in English now, except if something startles the hell out of me or scares me. I get scared in French. Another man sent me to business school. To learn to be an executive secretary. That was in Cincinnati. He was a real old guy. He picked me up. I was hitchhiking. He took me home. He lived alone—his wife had been dead two years. He wanted me to stay there with him and pretend I was his grand-niece so the neighbors wouldn't turn him in. I wanted somebody to send me to school so I could be a secretary, so it worked out okay. He bought me pretty clothes. I was eighteen by then. He bought me a little car, even. He was retired. He cooked and kept the house clean and did the laundry and made the bed. He even ironed my things that needed it, and he rinsed out stuff. I was really pretty rotten to old Harv. He was forty years older than me. That is a lot of years. When he got on my nerves, I wouldn't let him touch me. I cut off the supply. He didn't really want me too often or give me much trouble. I finished school and got my certificate and got a job. The way I was living, I could put it all in the bank, and I did. I came home one evening, and he was on the floor in the utility room. His whole left side had gone dead. His eye drooped and spit ran out of the left side of his mouth, and he couldn't speak. He just made terrible noises when he tried. I packed all my things into the trunk of my car, and then I called the hospital. I parked in the next block and walked back to make sure they found him and put him in the ambulance. I went to a motel. I finished out the week after I gave notice. I got my money out of the bank. I left and went down to Mobile and sold the car there. You can sell cars easy in Alabama. Then I flew home to Canada and got a good job in Montreal. I kept missing old Harv. I still miss him, I guess. It was a pretty good way to live, you know? I wasn't very nice to him. If I had it to do over, I'd be a lot nicer. I'd never hold out on him the way I did. It never cost me a thing to make him feel good.

"Anyway, I had a wonderful life in Montreal. There was a great bunch of kids there. And then I fell really *really* in love. When my guy took off with a girlfriend of mine, I did what I always do when I hurt. Buy, buy, buy. Shoes, clothes, wigs. I like money. I guess I spend it to hurt myself. You know? I knew I was in real trouble unless somebody bailed me out. So I went up to Quebec and saw Cousin Paul. I think I could have gone the rest of my life without the kind of help *he* gave me. Hey, look!"

"Shooting star."

"I know. But such a big, bright, slow one, huh? It lasted forever."

"Did you make a wish?"

"Was I supposed to? Would it work?"

"The way to make a wish come true is to wish for something you're going to get anyway."

"Is it okay to wish a little late?"

"Go ahead. It wasn't my shooting star."

"Okay. I wished." My arm was around her. She turned in a twisting motion that slipped her breast into my hand. Under the thin fabric of the blouse she wore no bra, and in seconds I felt the nipple growing and hardening. "Does that give you a clue, friend? Something I'm going to get anyway?"

I sat up, raising her with me, slid my hands onto her waist, picked her up, and dropped her onto the sand beside the chaise.

"Ow! That made me bite my tongue, you son of a bitch!"

"Just be a good girl and stop trying to hook me on the product. It's there anytime I want it. Stop pushing it."

She stood up. "Don't be too damned sure it's going to be served up on a damn tray when you decide to ask for it, Gav. And I wasn't trying to hook you on anything. I just think it's friendly and nice to get laid. It isn't a big thing, is it? And it got me going, what I was talking about."

"Old Harv, for God's sake?"

"No, you dummy! The money. Big gobs of money, just thinking about it makes me feel all hollow and crawly inside, and I guess it's so much like the feeling you get when you know you're going to get laid, it works the same way."

"Go take a cold shower."

"You're terribly nice to me. You're oceans of fun. I'm going to walk up and down the beach and think about blizzards and icicles and catheters and having my teeth drilled. That takes me off the edge fast."

"I should think it would."

So she went walking out there, clearly visible, scuffing barefoot through the foamy water that came running up the wet slope after the thud of each slow, small wave. A girl walking slowly, slow tilting swing of hips, legs shapely and dark below the white glow of the shorts.

She had deftly pushed a lot of my buttons. She had worked on proximity, touch, forthright invitation. She had talked in areas that accentuated sexual awareness. She smelled good, felt good, kept her voice furry and intimate. I knew she wasn't being made wanton and reckless by my fabulous magnetism. We were moving toward an association, possibly profitable. For maximum leverage within that association of two, she wanted to put that weapon to work which had profited her in the past, probably in every relationship except the one with her cousin.

I was another version of good old Harv, whom we last saw on the floor with spit running out of his mouth. She'd pushed Harv's buttons and got her secretarial training and a car and a lot of clothes. Her libido certainly wasn't out of control. It was just a useful thing for her to do, a nice little inexpensive favor for her to grant, and if it clouded the recipient's judgment, eventual profit from the relationship might improve.

Were I a great ape, a giant anthropoid, munching stalks torn from the jungle, and able to lead her to forgotten treasure, Lisa would take her best shot at making everything friendlier and nicer. As she said about Harv, it wouldn't cost a thing to make that big monkey feel good.

But knowing how and why the buttons are pushed doesn't diminish the physiological after-effects of the button pushing. The tumescence is noticeable. The palm of the hand retains the shape of the breast—the precise size, warmth, and rate of erection. The eyes watch the slow walk, creating an increase in the heartbeat and rate of respiration and blood pressure and surface body temperature, as the conditioned mind anticipates the simple progression of events of calling to her, bringing her close, shucking her out of the shorts, pulling her astride, and settling her properly for that sweet, grinding task that would end so quickly the first time.

The buttons tripped certain relays. I had to go back into the mind, into central control, and reset those relays, compensate for the overload, switch the current back to those channels designed for it.

I went searching through the past for the right memory, the one which would most easily turn growing desire to indifference.

I thought a memory of Miss Mary Dillon long ago aboard the *Busted Flush* would do it. There were more than a few, but they would not come through vividly enough to achieve turnoff.

Lisa made it so damned easy, so completely available, there was no importance to it. And with no importance to an act, why did it matter whether or not it happened? Why did McGee need some cachet of importance in this world of wall-to-wall flesh in the weekend living room where the swingers courteously, diligently, skillfully, considerately hump one another to the big acid beat of the hi-fi installation, good from 20 to 20,000 cycles per second?

Is McGee still impaled upon some kind of weird Puritan dilemma, writhing and thrashing around, wrestling with an outdated, old-time, inhibiting and artificial sense of sin, guilt, and damnation? Is that why he couldn't accept the lifetime gift Lady Jillian offers? Is that why he has this sickly, sentimental idea that there has to be a productive and meaningful relationship first, or sex degrades? So bang the doxy, because easing the ball-pressure is reason enough.

Who needs magic and mystery? Well, maybe it is magic and mystery that an Antarctic penguin will hunt all over hell and gone to find the right pebble to carry in his beak and lay between the funny feet of his intended, hoping for her favor. Maybe sex is a simple bodily function, akin to chewing, sneezing and defecation. But bald eagles fly as high as they possibly can, up into the thinnest air, making the elegant flight patterns of intended mating all the way up, then cleave to each other and fall, fall, fall, mating as they fall fluttering, plummeting down toward the great rock mountains.

The way it is supposed to work nowadays, if you want to copulate with the lady, you politely suggest it to her, and you are not offended if she says no, and you are mannerly, considerate, and satisfying if she says yes.

But the Tibetan bar-headed goose and her gander have a very strange ceremony they perform *after* they have mated. They rise high in the water, wings spread wide, beaks aimed straight up at the sky, time and time again, making great bugle sounds of honking. The behaviorists think it is unprofessional to use subjective terms about animal patterns. So they don't call this ceremony joy. They don't know what to call it. These geese live for up to fifty years, and they mate for life. They celebrate the mating this same way year after year. If one dies, the other never mates again.

So penguins, eagles, geese, wolves, and many other creatures of land and sea and air are stuck with all this obsolete magic and mystery because they can't read and they can't listen to lectures. All they have is instinct. Man feels alienated from all feeling, so he sets up encounter groups to sensitize each member to human interrelationships. But the basic group of two, of male and female, is being desensitized as fast as we can manage it . . .

"What the hell is there about me that turns you off?" Lisa demanded. She had walked up the slope to stand by the chaise, blotting out a Lisa-shaped abundance of stars as she looked down at me with a faint angle of pale yellow light laying across her cheekbone and lips.

"I was wondering what you'd do if I picked up a pebble in my beak and put it between your feet."

"I've heard of a lot of ways guys get kinky, but that is—"

"Why do you want reassurance from me? Take my word for it. You are a fantastic piece of ass. Ask practically anybody."

"I don't know. I haven't checked it."

She stood there for a few seconds in silence. Then she said, "If you ever do want some, friend, you're going to have to take it away from me, because that's the only damned way in this world you're ever going to get any."

"Goodnight, Lisa."

She walked away from the shoreline, a silhouette moving toward the yellow lights.

Fifteen

THURSDAY I WAS UP EARLY. Awakening in a new place makes the day of arrival seem unreal. There had been no Carl Brego, no Lisa Dissat trying to be Mary Broll, no Lisa Dissat striding angrily away from me in the hot, buggy night. I went to my cottage after she left, swam in my mini-pool, two strokes per lap, changed, and went to the open dining room. The food was good, the service indifferent. There were some beautiful people there. A fashion photography team. Some yacht people. Some twosome guests had tried to get as far as possible from wherever they didn't care to be seen together. Some guests were ritualistic sun worshipers who had been there for many many weeks, using the intense tropic sun to add each day's tiny increment of pigmentation at the cost of blinding, suffocating, dazed hours and quarts of whatever oil they happened to believe in. Johnson's or coconut or olive. They were working toward

that heady goal of becoming a living legend in Bronxville
or Scranton or Des Moines.

"Tan? You think that's a tan? So you didn't see Barbie and
Ken when they got back from Grenada that time. Dark? I
swear to Christ, in a dark room all you could see were white
teeth. And Barbie's diamonds."

I took a cab into town, memorizing landmarks all the
way. I negotiated the rental of an Austin Moke. A Moke is a
shrunken jeep with a very attractive expression, if you look
at the front of it and think of the headlights as eyes. It looks
staunch, jaunty, and friendly. It is a simplified piece of ma-
chinery. Stick shift which, like the wheel on the right, you
work with the left hand. The horn, a single-note, piercing
beeeeep, is operated by pressing in on the turn indicator
with the right hand. A quick whack with the heel of the
hand is the approved method. Four speeds forward, small,
air-cooled engine, pedals so tiny that if you try to operate
one with your bare feet, it hurts like hell. Canvas top nobody ever folds down in the hot season, and all they have in
Grenada are two hot seasons, one wet and one dry.

With the tourist season almost over, there were a lot of
them in stock. I picked one with a lot of tread, and the
rental man and I walked around it and tested lights, horn,
directional signals, windshield wiper (singular). He wanted
his total rental in advance, which is standard for the area.
While we dickered, I practiced getting in and out of the
damned thing. I'd learned in Grand Cayman and Jamaica
that with the length of my legs there is only one possible
way. Stand beside vehicle on right side. Bend over at waist.
Reach across body and grasp steering wheel with right
hand, while simultaneously lifting left leg, inserting it into

vehicle so that foot comes to rest on the floor well beyond pedal area. Swoop your behind onto the seat and pick up right leg and lift over high broad sill (which contains gas tank). In driving position both knees are bent sharply, spread wide apart. Steering wheel fits between knees, and lower part of legs must angle in to assure foot contact with pedals. Adjust to inevitability of frequently giving oneself a painful rap on the left leg while shifting.

We arrived at a mutually agreeable fee of five Yankee—ten Biwi—dollars a day for a one week rental or any period of less than a week. I buy the gas. I will phone him when I leave and tell him to pick it up at the Spice Island Inn. I promise not to leave it at the airport. I tell him I would not drive it over that road to the airport for a hundred dollars a mile. Can I drive safely on the left side of the road? I suggest that perhaps no one in Grenada can drive safely on any side of the road. But yes, I have so driven on other islands of this British persuasion.

We accomplish the red tape, he gives me a free map of St. George's and environs. I note that, as expected, there is at least one half-pint of gas in the five-gallon gas tank. I edge carefully into the tourney and immediately am nearly bowled over and over by a small pale bus with a name across the front of it. The name is: I AM NOTHING.

After I have bought petrol and felt my way back into the center of town, avoiding too intimate a contact with a large gaudy city bus called LET IT BE ME, I park my Moke and wait until I am certain my legs will work. ("You will enjoy browsing in St. George's along the narrow, quaint streets.")

*   *   *

I changed another wad of Yankee dollars into Biwi at the Bank of Canada, picking that one from among all the shiny banks downtown, from Chase to Barclay's to the Bank of Nova Scotia, because there was a faint aroma of irony in the choice. The girl standing behind the money-changing counter was very dark, very thin, and totally antagonistic—so much so, there was no chance of ever making any kind of human contact with her unless you were her identical anthracite color.

I asked some questions and was directed to a big busy supermarket called EVERYBODY'S FOR EVERYTHING. As long as I had kitchen facilities and I could make my own ice cubes, it seemed useful to set up shop. Gin, rum, fruit juices from Trinidad, mixes, and a couple of large substantial drink glasses. I am a fussy old party about glassware. Nothing takes the pleasure out of drinking like the tiny dim glasses supplied by hotels and motels. I always buy heavy glasses, always leave them behind. Tiny glasses turn drinking from a pleasure rite to a quasialcoholic twitch.

The final purchase was on impulse at a shop I saw on the Carenage on the way home. A great big planter's hat of straw with a batik band. Put a man in a rental Moke with advertising painted on the side of it and put a funny hat on him, and he is a tourist. All tourists look alike. Regardless of age, sex, or the number of extra lenses for their cameras, they all look alike.

I found my way back out to Grand Anse to hotel row, and I found an overland way to get the Moke close to my cottage. I carried my box of stuff in. From the moment I had awakened until the moment I finished putting the stuff

away and sat down, I had not let myself think about Mary,
Lisa or the mechanics of impersonation.

It is a useful device. If you keep things in the front of
your mind, you worry at them like a hound chomping a
dead rabbit. Throw problems in the back cupboard and keep
them there as long as you can. The act of stirring around
seems to shuffle the elements of a problem into a new order,
and when you take it out again, there are new ways to handle it.

I tossed my sweat-soaked shirt aside. The air-conditioning felt good on my back and shoulders. Okay. Mary is
dead. I want Paul Dissat. I want him very badly. The money
is the bait, and Lisa is the bait in another sense. I want very
badly to convince Paul and Lisa and Harry Broll that, if
given a choice, they would elect retroactive birth control. I
want them so eager to be out of it they'd dig their own
graves with a bent spoon and their fingernails.

Secondly, as a professional, as a salvage consultant in
areas of considerable difficulty, I want to come out of this
with a little salvage for myself. If I walk away without a
dime, with only expenses I can't reasonably afford, then I
lose all respect for myself as a con artist. I would have kicked
the hell out of their little wagon just to avenge one hell of a
woman, Mary Dillon. Pure emotionalism is bush league.

So? So I do not advise Mr. Willow not to make the loan
on Mary's securities. They go to Harry eventually anyway.
That is, if Harry happens to be still around. The money has
to be loaned to Harry, and Harry has to pick up his block of
stock in time and get himself in position to make a great
deal of money when the public issue comes out. But that is

a long long time for me to wait for my money. I shall use the leverage to extract a reasonable chunk from Paul, maybe from Harry, maybe from both, before I set them to work with those bent spoons.

It may be enough to have Harry and Lisa dig their graves deep with the sides and ends properly squared off and stand in them without the slightest morsel of hope left. Then I walk away and leave them standing there. But Paul is something else.

Program: Lisa must perform exactly as instructed, make her phone call to Harry, and send the cable to Mr. Willow at the bank. I want her to be desperately anxious to tell me all the details of any contact by Paul Dissat. Then I will prepare to greet him. Here. There. Somewhere.

I pulled on my salty swim trunks and put on my big tourist hat and went looking for the lady. She was not in cottage 50. I trudged around, squinting into the hot glare, and found her on a sun cot at the top of the slope that led down to the beach proper. She was facedown. The bikini was yellow today. The top was undone, and she had rolled the fabric of the bottom so that it was about as big around as a yellow lead pencil where it cut across the tanned cheeks on her behind. She was glossy with oil. Her towel was on the sand. I sat on it. Her face was turned away.

"You wanna buy nice coconut, Miss lady? Peanuts? Nice spices?"

She slowly turned her heat-stricken, slack-mouthed face toward me. "I don't want any—" She shaded her eyes, squinted. "Oh. It's you."

"Me. Absolutely correct. Me, himself."

"Who needs you?"

She lay with her face turned toward me, eyes closed. "You need me," I told her.

"Not any more. Thanks a lot. But not any more."

"I don't mean that kind of need, honey. I'm talking about financial need. Commercial necessities."

"Thanks loads. I think I'd better take my chances with Paul."

"That should be a lot of laughs for both of you. I wrote an interesting letter last night."

She forgot her top wasn't latched. She sat up fast. "What kind of a letter? Who to?"

"What's the local policy about the tits on tourists?"

She picked up the top and put it on. "I know what *your* policy is, friend. You ignore them. What kind of a letter?"

"Double envelope. A sealed letter along inside the sealed letter. If he doesn't hear from me on or before May tenth, he opens the second letter."

"Then what?"

"He takes action."

"*What* action?"

"Oh, he just gets in touch with the right people at the SEC and says that it looks as if one Mr. Harry Broll bought himself into SeaGate, Inc. with a final three hundred thou fraudulently obtained and that this fact might not be uncovered by the accounting firm preparing the material for the red herring and they should check with a Mr. Willow regarding evidence as to whether or not Mrs. Broll was alive at the time he released funds at her earlier request. My friend is an attorney. He knows all the steps in the new registration folk dance. Delicate, these new issues. They can die of a head cold."

"Oh God! Why'd you think you couldn't trust me?"

"Who said anything about that?"

"Isn't that why you did it?"

"Lisa, Lisa, Lisa. What if we miss? Suppose your dear cousin nails us both, lays us to rest in a ceremonial boat, lights the pyre and sends us out to sea. The last few moments would be a lot more enjoyable knowing Cousin Paul would never make a profit on the deal."

She swallowed hard and looked unhappy. "Don't talk about things like that." I knew that behind her sun squint her brain was ticking away, weighing and measuring advantages. I reached under the sun cot and retrieved her big sunglasses from the magazine on which they lay and handed them to her.

"Thanks, dear," she said, putting them on. "Sure. I see what you mean. And if he catches us sort of off base, it could maybe be handy to tell him about your lawyer friend."

"Yes. I think so. If he gives me a chance."

"Can't you see why I thought you did it on account of me?"

I thought it over. "Well, I suppose I can in a way. If you *did* decide he represents a better chance, you could tip him off about me and he could . . . tidy up the situation."

She turned over and put her feet down on the sand near my legs. Her hairline was sweaty. Trickles of sweat ran down her throat, and a little rivulet ran between her breasts and down across her belly to soak into the narrow yellow bikini. Her knees were apart, and the cot was so short-legged that her knees were on the same level as her breasts. Her eyes were even with the top of my head.

She leaned toward me, forearms on her knees, and said in

a cooing voice, "You know, you act so weird about me, about us, that I'm afraid I'm going to keep on misinterpreting the things you say. We're going to keep on having misunderstandings. I waited a long time last night for you to come over to my place to say you were sorry."

I looked at her. Bright sunshine is as cruelly specific as lab lights and microscopes. There was a small double chin, caused by the angle of her head. There was a scar on her upper lip near the nostril. Her hands and feet were small, square and sturdy, nails carefully tended. Her posture made a narrow tan roll of fat across her trim belly. Her slender waist made a rich line that flowed in a double curve, concave, convex, into the ripe tan hip and thigh. She sat with her plump parts pouched into the yellow fabric, heavy and vital. Stray pubic hairs, longer than the others, curled over the top of the bikini and escaped at the sides of the crotch, hairs the color of dull copper.

Sweat, muscles, flesh, hair, closeness. So close the tightness of the yellow pouch revealed the cleavage of labia. This was the magic and mystery of a locker room, steam room, massage table, or of a coeducational volleyball game in a nudist colony. This was jockstrap sex, unadorned.

"Lisa, I guess we have to say things so carefully we won't have misunderstandings."

"Maybe I got the wrong impression yesterday. You wouldn't be queer, darling?"

"No more than any other true-blue American lad."

"Some kind of trouble? You can tell Lisa. Prostate, maybe? Or some kind of irritation?"

"I'm in glowing health."

"Honey, are you so strung out on some great broad that

you just don't want to make it with another girl? I could understand that. I've been through that."

"Nobody I've met lately has gotten to me."

Her mouth firmed, and her throat turned darker. "Am I some kind of pig woman it would turn your stomach to—"

"Whoa! It's just a little rule of mine. Save the dessert until last."

Her mouth softened into a sudden smile. "Dessert? Darling, I am also homemade soup, meat and potatoes, hot rolls and butter, and your choice of beverages. I am mostly meat and potatoes."

"There's another reason for waiting, Lisa."

"Like?"

She was ready again, I decided. Like training a mule. A good, solid blow between the eyes, and I should have her total attention.

"It's kind of a sad story, dear."

"I love sad stories. I love to cry and cry."

"Well, once upon a time there was this lovely, delicate little blond lady, and she and I were partners in a complicated little business deal. We took our plans and problems to bed, and talked them over during rest periods. I freaked over that little lady. She loved to make love. Then our business deal went sour. It fell apart. That was too damned bad because it was a nice piece of money for both of us. Well, one day a month later we romped all day together, happy as children, and that night I took her out in a boat, a nice runabout, out into the Atlantic. It was calm and beautiful, and I made her sit on the side rail, and I aimed a Colt .45 with the muzzle an inch from her pretty brow and blew the top of her head off. I wired the spare anchor to her waist and let her go in a half-mile of water, and the moon was so bright that night I could see her for a long way as she went down. Now you can cry."

Her mouth sagged open. She put a hand to her throat and in a husky whisper said, "Jesus H. Christ!"

"That idiot girl thought that by sleeping with me she was buying insurance, in case I ever found out she had gone behind my back and made her own deal for half again as much as she would have made as my partner. She was so convinced of it, she was starting to smile when I pulled the trigger. You're not crying."

"Jesus H. Christ!"

"You said that before, Lisa. After that I decided it's bad policy. I made the punishment fit the crime, but I hated myself. You know? I used to think of that little blonde a lot. It used to depress me. It seemed like a waste, all those goodies sinking to the bottom of the sea."

"What *are* you?"

"Me? I'm your partner, Lisa. And we trust each other, don't we? Nobody is going to try to be cute. But . . . just in case . . . let's save all the goodies until after we've made the money score?"

"T-that suits me, Gavin," she said. She clapped her thighs together so smartly they made a damp slapping sound. "L-later. I . . . I got to go for a minute. I'll be back."

"I'll probably be swimming."

She went off toward her place, walking slightly knock-kneed, head bowed and shoulders hunched.

An imaginary letter and an imaginary blond partner. I could imagine that dear imaginary girl sinking down down through the black water, hair outspread, getting smaller and smaller and more and more indistinct until she was gone out of my imaginary life forever. Poor kid. Gavin Lee was a mean son of a bitch. It made me almost want to cry. Now the Lisa-McGee contest could be declared no contest. The lady wasn't going to come out for the third round. She was cowed. She was going to do as she was told. She was going to have as much sex drive from here on as a harem guard. And at the first word from her cousin she was going to come on the run to tell me all about it.

That evening she was so prim it was as if she had never left the convent school. We walked on the beach and got back to the cottages just after dark. We went to her place. She unlocked the gate. We went in, and she screamed as the two dark shapes jumped me. It got very interesting. They both knew a lot more about it than Carl Brego had. If they had been ready and willing to kill, they had me. But they weren't. And that gave me a better chance than I thought I was going to get.

I took punishment and gave it back. Whistling grunts of effort. Slap and thud of blows. Scuff of feet. I took one on the shoulder, off balance, and fell and rolled hard and came up near a yellow light bulb. A half-familiar voice said, "Hold it! I said *hold* it, Artie! I *know* this joker."

The voice was suddenly very familiar. "Rupe, you dreary bastard, what are you trying to do?"

"A favor for a friend. Lady, if you can get some Kleenex and some rubbing alcohol or some gin, I'd be obliged. And turn on some lights around here."

I told Lisa it was all right. She turned on the garden lights and the inside lights. She had some alcohol and a big roll of paper towels. All three of us were breathing hard. We were all marked, one way and another.

I said, "Mary, this is an old friend of mine. Rupert Darby, a sailing man. Rupe, Mary Broll."

"Pleased to meet you, Mary. And this here, Mary, is Artie Calivan. Artie is mate on the *Dulcinea,* and I'm hired captain. And this big rawboned bastard it's so hard to get a clean shot at, Artie, is an old friend of mine from way back. Trav McGee."

"McGee?" Lisa said blankly.

"It's a kind of joke name, honey," I said. "It comes from an old limerick. Trav rhymes with Gav for Gavin. And McGee rhymes with Lee."

If it had just hung there, I couldn't have brought it off. But Rupe came in very smoothly. "I'd like to recite you the limerick, Miz Mary, but it's just too dirty to repeat in front of a lady. I use that old name on Gav when I'm trying to get his goat. I think I've got one tooth here that isn't going to grow back tight again, dammit."

I looked at his mate. "You brought along a big one."

"Seems he was needed. I needed two like him."

"You were doing fine with just one of him. But *why*?"

"Oh, that damn Brego. What did you think? He whined all day about how us hired captains ought to help each other out, and he said this big fellow, quick and mean as a sneak, had filched his piec—excuse me, Miz Broll, his lady friend. So finally I said to Artie here, let's take the dinghy and run over there to the inn and bounce this tourist around some. Had no idea it was you, Tr—Gav. None at all. Sorry. But not too sorry. First time I haven't been half asleep in two weeks."

I dabbed at a long scratch on my jaw and moved over to Lisa and put my arm around her waist. "Honey, have you got any message you want these fine men to deliver to Mr. Brego?"

"Rupe? Artie? Would you tell him that Mrs. Broll suggests he stop by again and try his luck with Mr. Lee?"

Rupe laughed. "Sure."

"Would you mind taking some of his things back to him?"

"Not at all."

"Let me go gather them up. It won't take a second."

Rupe sent the young man down to keep an eye on the dinghy. Rupe and I sat in a shadowy corner of the garden.

"What happened to the *Marianne*?" I asked him.

"Two bad seasons, and the bank finally grabbed her. I don't really mind a hell of a lot. I work for good people. Good wages."

"Thanks for the nice job of covering."

"That? Hell, that's what a good hired captain starts with or learns real fast. When somebody clues you, don't stand around saying 'Huh?' Run with the ball. No point in asking you what's going on. I certainly know something is going on, and that broad in there must be part of it. She looks good enough, but there's better on the island. Any time you have to scruff up a clown like Brego to grab yourself that kind of ass—"

"Like you said. There's more than meets the eye."

"By God, Trav, you know something? That was fun off and on."

"Glad you enjoyed it. How's Sally?"

"Fine, last I heard. She went back to her folks. She married a widower fellow with four kids. Our three plus his four makes a lot of family."

"Sorry to hear about that, Rupe. I really am."

"It hurt some. But I hate the land and everything on it. I hate a tree, and I hate a mountain. The only death worth dying is by drowning. With the licenses I've got I'll stay on the water all the rest of my time. When our oldest girl drowned, that did it for Sally. That finished her, up, down, and sideways. No more oceans. Next time I write the kids I'll put in a note to her saying I saw you. She always liked you, Trav."

Lisa came out with a brown paper bag and gave it to Rupe. "This won't be too much trouble?"

"Not one bit, Miz Mary."

"Thank you so much. Excuse me, but is that mate of yours a mute?"

"Artie just doesn't have very much to say."

We both walked Rupert down to the dinghy. He stowed the bag aboard, and they picked the little boat up and walked it out past the gentle surf, scrambled in, and started the little outboard and headed back toward the yacht basin.

"*Imagine* that Carl sending them to beat you up!"

"They gave it a good try."

"Did they hurt you, darling?"

"Hardly at all. A month in bed and I'll feel like new."

"I mean really."

"Honey, the adrenaline is still flowing. So the pain is suppressed. Tomorrow morning when I try to get out of bed I'll know how much damage they did."

"Rupe has really enormous hands, doesn't he?"

"And very hard, too."

"And that gigantic boy is *really* handsome. Did you notice?"

"I wasn't thinking in those terms. Want to eat in the dining room?"

"Let's order it sent to my place. It's so much nicer, really. We can fix our own drinks and be comfortable. I won't make any passes, Gavin. None at all."

She kept her word. Long after we had dined, when the nightcap was down to the dregs, she came over to me and bent and peered at my face, teeth set into the softness of her under lip.

"You are going to have one great big mouse right on that cheekbone, friend."

"I can feel it."

She straightened up. "I can't read you, McGee."

"McGee? Who he?"

"Like the limerick. Tell me the limerick, huh?"

"Tell the truth, I can't remember it."

"Was it real dirty?"

"Not very, as I remember. But insulting."

"Funny, you knowing him. I would have thought he would have told Carl you were an old friend. Carl would have told him your name, Gavin Lee, and described you and all."

"Lee is a common name."

"Gavin Lee sure the hell isn't. And how many people are your size anyway?"

"Lisa honey, what are you trying to develop here?"

"I don't know. Is there anything you ought to tell me that you haven't?"

"Can't think of a thing."

"What are we going to do after we get rich, dear?"

"Live rich."

"Like this place?"

"And Las Brisas at Acapulco. And Cala de Volpe on Sardinia. The Reina Cristina in Algeciras."

"In where?"

"Spain, near Gibraltar."

She sat on the couch a couple of feet from me, eyes hooded, mouth pursed. "Will we travel well together when we're rich?"

"Get along?"

"Do you think we will?"

"We'll have to try it."

"Are you terribly dog-in-the-manger about things?"

"Like what?"

"If we had something going for us and I happened to see somebody like Artie Calivan. As long as I didn't overdo."

"Get the guests?"

She shrugged. "When they come in pairs, dear. And both exciting."

"I don't like to set policy. Take each situation on its merits. Okay?" I put my glass down and stood up. Winced. Flexed my leg. It was going to stiffen up very nicely during the night. She walked me out to the garden gate. I kissed her on the forehead and told her to dream about being rich. She said she had dreamed about that ever since she could remember.

Sixteen

I CAME BOUNDING AWAKE in the middle of the night from a dream so horrible I couldn't remember any part of it. I was drenched with icy sweat and trembling badly.

The dream made me recall lying to Lisa about sending a letter. A letter would be a comfort. I couldn't wait until morning. Leonard Sibelius, Esq., attorney at law.

The sealed letter inside was about the same, but the cover letter for the sealed letter varied. I asked him to read the sealed letter if he did not hear from me by the last day of May and then give it to some colleague wise in the ways of the SEC and the NASD.

After the lights were out again and the letter tucked away, I thought of how ironic it would be if Harry Broll ended up being defended by Lennie Sibelius on a charge of murder, first. Lennie would get him off. He would extract every dime Harry had ever made and put a lock on every dime Harry might make in the future, but he would get him off.

I felt myself drifting off and wondered what the hell there had been in that nightmare that had so thoroughly chilled my blood.

I was up early again on Friday and made another exciting run into town. I stopped at the main post office and sent the letter to Lennie by air, special delivery, registered mail. I drove through the one-way tunnel that leads from the Carenage area under Hospital Hill to the Esplanade and the main part of downtown. The *Queen Elizabeth II* was in, and it was her last visit of the season. She had spewed about two thousand passengers into the town and onto the beaches. The ones in town were milling around, arguing with each other about the currency and looking for the nonexistent duty-free shops and being constantly importuned to hire a nice taxi and see the sights. The big single-stack ship was anchored out with fast launches running back and forth like big white water beetles.

I ambled around and admired one out of every forty-three tourist ladies as being worth looking at and did some minor shopping of my own, then tested my skill and reflexes by driving back to the Spice Island Inn.

It was on that twenty-second day of April that I risked two lives instead of merely my own and drove Lisa out toward the Lance aux Epines area and had lunch at the Red Crab—burly sandwiches on long rolls, icy Tuborg beer, green salad—eaten outdoors at a white metal table by a green lawn in the shade of a graceful and gracious tree. After lunch we went exploring. We stopped and looked at the sailboats moored in Prickly Bay. I drove past large, lovely houses, and we got out of the Moke at Prickly Point and walked down the rocky slope and looked over the edge at the blue sea lifting and smashing at the rocks, working away on caves and stone sculpture, biting stubbornly and forever at the land. A curiously ugly species of black crab, big as teacups, foraged the dry sheer stone just above the reach of wave and tide, scrabbling in swift hundreds when we moved too near.

I studied my map and found, on the way back, a turn that led to a stretch of divided highway, probably the only bit of it on the little island. Weeds grew up through cracks. It was the grand entrance to the site of what had been the Grenada Expo of several years ago. I had heard that few visitors came. Many of the Expo buildings were never completed. The ones which had been finished lay under the midafternoon hum of sun's heat, warping plywood shedding thin scabs of bright holiday paint. Some faded, unraveling remnants of festive banners moved in a small sea breeze. We saw a VIP lounge where the doorsill brush grew as high as the unused and corroded doorknobs. Steel rods sprouted from cement foundation slabs where buildings had never stood. We found a huge and elegant motel, totally empty, completely closed, yet with the lawns and gardens still maintained by the owners or the government.

I drove down crooked little dirt roads, creaking and swaying at two miles an hour over log-sized bumps and down into old rain gullies you could hide bodies in. She clung and laughed, and we made it down an angled slope to a pretty and private little stretch of beach where the almond trees and the coconuts and the sea grapes grew closer than usual to the high tide mark because of the offshore protection of some small islands.

I parked in the shade. We walked on the beach and found one of the heavy local skiffs pulled well up between the trees, with red and blue and green paint peeling off the old weathered wood. She hiked a haunch onto the gunwale, near the hand-whittled tholepin, braced herself there with one knee locked, the other leg a-swing. The breeze moved the leaves overhead, changing the patterns of sun and shade on her face and hair, on her yellow-and-white-checkered sun top, her skimpy little yellow skirt. The big lenses of her sunglasses reflected the seascape behind me. She sucked at her cigarette, looked solemn, then tilted her head, and smiled at me.

"I'm trying to figure out why it should be so much fun, just sort of churning around in the heat of the day," she said.

"Glad you're enjoying it."

"I guess it's because it's like a date. Like being a kid again in Trois Pistoles and going out on a date. It's a feeling I haven't had in a long long time. It's sort of sweet, somehow. Do you know what I mean, Gav?"

"Not exactly."

"Ever since I left when I was fifteen, I've been with guys I've either just been in bed with or am just about to get into bed with or both. And if it was a guy I'd already had or one I was going to have, if we were alone in a funny, private place like this, we'd be knocking off a stand-up piece right here. I was thinking I don't want you to try anything, because it would take away that feeling of being on a date. There's something funny and scary about it, like being a virgin again. Or maybe it's you that's scary to me, about that girl sinking in the ocean. I dreamed about her. Jesus! You really did that? Really?"

"It seemed like a good idea at the time."

She slid off the gunwale and snapped her cigarette into the surf line. She bent and picked up a coconut in the husk and threw it with a shotput motion. She was wiry, and she got surprising distance with it.

"So this is just a little bit of time when nothing happens and we just wait, Gavin."

"For your cousin. After you make the phone call and send the cable."

I leaned on the boat. Some palm fronds had been tossed into it. I lifted them and saw the battered metal fuel tank for the missing outboard motor, and I saw a spade with a short handle, sawed off where it had broken and decided it was a clumsy, improvised paddle. Clumsy but better than none at all. With all that weight and freeboard she would be a bitch to try to paddle against wind or tide.

"Head back?" I asked.

"Can we keep on being tourists, dear? Let's look at that map again."

We went back to the Moke, studied the map and decided to try the road out to Point Saline and look at the lighthouse. It was a road so wretched that by the time we were halfway I had decided only a jeeplike vehicle such as a Moke could make it. Then around the next hairpin corner I was shouldered into the shrubbery by three taxis coming back from the lighthouse, whamming and leaping over the ruts and broken paving, chock-full of tourists off the *QE2*.

My gratis map had little paragraphs on the back of it

about local wonders, so just short of the lighthouse hill we stopped and dutifully got out to walk for a moment on the white sand beach of the Caribbean, then crossed the road and went down a path for about fifty yards to walk on the black sand beach of the Atlantic. Then I roared the Moke up the twenty-degree slope to the lighthouse.

The attendant was there, obviously eager to be a guide, obviously eager for bread. We climbed the several flights to the glass enclosed top. The treads were very narrow, the steps very steep. Lisa was directly ahead of me, and I was staring at the backs of her knees as we climbed.

It was a view so breathtakingly, impossibly fabulous that it became meaningless. It was like being inserted into a living postcard. It does no good to stand and gawk at something like that. The mind goes blank as soon as you see it. Tourists take pictures and take them home and find out they have postcards. If they put Helen in front of the view, they have a postcard with Helen in it. The only way a person could accommodate himself to a place like that would be to live there until he ceased to see it and then slowly and at his own pace rediscover it for himself. When I found out what the attendant had to do to keep that fifty-mile light operating, I was happy to place some Biwi in his hand.

Lisa was quiet on the way back. When we were nearly back to the deserted Expo site, I glanced over at her and saw the tear running down her quiet cheek, coming out from under the sunglasses. I pulled over in a shady spot and said, "Hey!"

"Oh God, I don't know, I don't know. Leave me alone."

"Sure."

Glasses off. Dab eyes, snuffle, sigh, blow nose. Fix mouth.

Put glasses back on. Light cigarette. Sigh again, huffing smoke plume at windshield.

"Everything is supposed to be so great," she said. "Everything is some kind of a trick. Every time. Some kind of flaky trick, no matter what it is. Fifty-mile lighthouse! Good God! What the hell is a Fresnel lens?"

"A Frenchman invented it long ago. It focuses light into a beam."

"Nothing is ever what you expect. That's what got to me, Gav. A fifty-mile lighthouse and all there is up there is a mantle like off a Coleman lantern and not a hell of a lot bigger, and that poor scrawny black son of a bitch that has to get up every two hours all night long and run up there and pull on some goddamn weights like a big grandfather clock so his fucking light keeps turning around for another two hours. Fresnel! They fake everything in the world."

"What kind of a big deal did They promise you, Lisa?"

She pulled the glasses off and looked at me with reptilian venom and coldness. "They told me, friend, to sing in the choir, love Jesus, do unto others, pray to God, live a Christian life, and then live in heaven in eternal bliss forevermore. They forgot to explain that the choirmaster would give me free private voice lessons when I was fourteen and by the third lesson he'd have his finger up me. They didn't tell me that if I didn't report him, I'd lose out on all that eternal bliss. They didn't tell me that I wouldn't want to report him, because then he wouldn't have a chance to do it again. They didn't explain about it being the temptation of the flesh and how finally you get to the place where you either make a true confession or you run away. They were running their big lighthouse and making it look wonderful, shining its light all over the world to save souls. But it was just a gas mantle and weights and chains and a weird lens. The real thing they teach you without even knowing it is: do unto others before they do it unto you."

"My my my," I said in a gentle wonder, and the tears came again. She got them under control at last.

"Will you laugh at me if I tell you what I *really* want to do with the money, Gav?"

"I don't think I will."

"I want to join an order. I want to give the money to the order. I want to take a vow of silence. I want to kneel on stone floors and pray until my knees bleed and I faint. I don't ever want to be screwed again the rest of my life or be even touched by any man. I want to be a bride of Christ. Now laugh yourself sick."

"I don't hear anybody laughing."

"You think I'd go over the wall in a week, don't you?"

"Do you?"

"If I can find the guts to start, I'll never leave. Never. You're doing all this to me by making me feel the way I did a long long time ago. A lot of men ago. A lot of beds ago."

"I don't think people stick with projects they start because they think they should start them. That's image making. People stick to their truest, deepest gratifications, whether it's running banks, building temples out of beercans, stuffing dead birds, or telling dirty jokes. Somewhere early you get marked."

"I got it early. Stations of the Cross. Easter. Christ is risen. At about twelve I felt so marvelously pure. Jesus loved me, that I know."

"So you fight it all your life or go back to it. Either way, it is a deep involvement."

She found her glasses on the floor, picked them up and said wearily, "You know so goddamn much, don't you? You know something? You've got a big mouth. A great big mouth. Let's get back on the beach where I belong."

Seventeen

THAT RANDOM AFTERNOON had turned Lisa Dissat off in a way she either couldn't explain or didn't care to explain. It amounted to the same thing. We became like neighbors in a new suburb, nodded and smiling when we met walking to or from the main hotel building or up and down the two-mile beach or back and forth from sun cot to cottage.

I saw some of the cruise ship men, crew and passengers, take their try at her now and then when she walked the long wide beach alone. I saw male guests at our hotel and the other beach hotels make their approach, each one no doubt selecting the overworked line he thought might be most productive. They would fall in step with her, last about a half dozen steps before turning away. I followed her a couple of times and kept count. Prettier young women in bikinis just as revealing walked the beach unaccosted. It was difficult to identify those characteristics which made her such a frequent target. It was something about the tilt and position of her head, in relation to the shape in which she held her mouth while walking. It was challenge, somehow. A contempt and an arrogance. Try me, you bastard. Try your luck and see how good you are. Do you think you're man enough to cope, you bastard? There was both invitation and rejection in the roll of her hip. To describe everything that happened to tilt, curve, and musculature in one complete stride from start to finish and into the next stride would have taken a seventeen-syllable word. Provocative, daring, and ineradicably cheap. That was what Rupe had seen so quickly, wondering why I risked even a bruised knuckle to take ass like that away from Carl Brego. It was what I had seen when she sat with Brego for a drink and lunch.

It was a compulsive cheapness. I could not believe that it was deliberate in the sense of being something she had thought out. It had to be something she could not help doing, yet did not do out of some physical warp or out of any flaw in intelligence or awareness.

She had been uncommonly determined to give herself to me. It had been too early an effort. She wanted to be used, not loved. She wanted to be quickly tumbled and plundered. It was what she expected and what she wanted, and it was that need which exuded the musky, murky challenge.

I have a need to try to put people together out of the pieces they show me. The McGee Construct-A-Lady Kit. For those on a budget we suggest our cheaper, simpler Build-A-Broad Kit.

Once you Build-A-Broad, it pleases you more than it did before you took it apart and examined the components.

She had ripened young. They had drilled virtue into her so mercilessly that when she was seduced she believed herself corrupt and evil. Purity could not be regained. So she ran away and had spent a dozen years corrupting because she believed herself corrupt, debauching because she had been debauched, defiling because she was the virgin defiled.

When you cannot like yourself or any part of yourself in mind or body, then you cannot love anyone else at all. If you spend the rest of your life on bleeding knees, maybe Jesus will have the compassion to love you a little bit. She had been destroyed twelve years ago. It was taking her a little while to stop breathing.

I kept in close touch with her. She heard nothing. I killed time restlessly. So Saturday I got a clear connection and talked to Meyer. I told him to check out Paul Dissat in the SeaGate offices in West Palm. I had to spell the name in my own special kind of alphabet before he was sure of it. Detroit Indiana sugar sugar Alabama teacup.

"Dissat? Paul Dissat?"

"Yes. And be damned careful of him. Please. He bites."

"Is Mary there? Is she all right?"

"She's fine."

After all, what else could I say? Time to talk later.

Later on Saturday I drove until I finally found the way to Yacht Services. I parked the Moke and went out on the long dock and found the *Dulcinea*. She was a custom motor sailer, broad of beam with sturdy, graceless lines. Rupe Darby and Artie kept her sparkling, and she looked competent.

Artie had gone over to the Carenage in the dinghy to do some shopping. Rupe asked me aboard and showed me the belowdecks spaces, the brute diesels, all the electronics. He was fretting about the delivery of some highly necessary engine item. It was supposed to come in by air. They couldn't leave without it, and he didn't want to be late meeting his owners at Dominica. He hoped to be out by Wednesday.

I asked about Carl Brego, and he told me that Brego's rich lady had arrived with friends, and they had left early that morning for two weeks sailing the Grenadines.

A sunbrown and brawny woman in blue denim shorts and a dirty white T-shirt came along the dock and waved and smiled. She had a collie ruff of coppery gold hair, a handsome weathered face. Rupe invited her to come aboard and have some coffee with us. She did, and we sat in the shade of the tarp rigged forward. She was Captain Mickey Laneer, owner and operator of the *Hell's Belle,* a big businesslike charter schooner I could see from where we sat. Mickey had a man's handshake and a state of Maine accent.

"Trav, Mickey here has the best damned charter business in the islands, bar none."

"Sure do," she said, and they both chuckled and chuckled.

"Could be out on charter all the time," Rupe said.

"But that would take all the fun out of it, too much of the same thing," Mickey said.

"She charges high, and she picks and chooses and doesn't have to advertise. Word of mouth," Rupe said, and they kept chuckling.

"Five hundred bucks a day, US, and I don't take the *Belle* out for less than five days, and I won't carry less than three or more than five passengers. Price stays the same."

"That's pretty high," I said.

"I keep telling her she ought to raise the rate again."

"Would you two mind telling me why you keep laughing?"

Mickey shoved her hair back, grinning. "Rupe and I just enjoy life, Mr. McGee."

"She does a good trade with business meetings. Three or four or five busy, successful executives, usually fellows in their thirties or early forties, they come down to relax, get some fishing in, get a tan, do a little dickering and planning. You know."

"Why is everybody laughing but me?" I asked.

"She takes male passengers only, Trav."

I finally caught up. "I get it. Your crew is all female, Captain?"

"And," said Rupe, "all nimble and quick and beautiful and strong as little bulls. They range from golden blond—a gal who has a masters in languages from the University of Dublin—to the color of coffee with hardly a dab of cream. Eight of them."

"Seven, Rupe. Darn it. I had to dump Barbie. She was hustling a guest for extra the last time out. I've warned them and warned them. After I provision the *Belle*—the best booze and best food in the Windwards—I cut it down the middle, half for me and the boat, half for the gals. So on a five-day run, they make better than three hundred, Biwi. Everyone from golden Louise all the way to Hester, whose father is a bank official in Jamaica."

"You need eight crew to work that thing, Mick?"

"I know. I know. We're going out Monday for ten days. Four fellows from a television network. Nice guys. It'll be their third cruise. Old friends. That means my gals will be topless before we clear Grand Mal Bay."

"And bottomless before you get opposite Dragon Bay and Happy Hill."

"Could be, dear. Louise flew up to Barbados today. She says she has a cute chum who loves sailing. It's a way for a certain kind of girl to combine her favorite hobbies and make a nice living. I don't take hard-case types. I like polite, happy girls from nice backgrounds. Then we have a happy ship."

She got up and said, "A pleasure to meet any of Rupe's old friends, Travis. Hope you'll sail with us sometime. Rupe has."

"Mickey invited four of us captains to a free five-day cruise last year."

"I had a cancellation," Mickey said, "and we were all wondering what to give the other captains for a Christmas present. Well, nice to meet you."

After she was on the dock, she turned and waved and said, "Tell him our motto, Rupe."

He chuckled. She walked lithely away. He said, "Mickey likes you. In her line of work she gets to tell the men from the boys in a hurry."

"What's the motto?"

"Oh. It's on her letterhead. 'Make a lot of lovely new chums every voyage.'"

"Enjoy the cruise?"

"Oh, hell yes. By God, it is different. There's rules, and Mickey enforces them. None of her gals get slopped. Any and all balling is done in the privacy of your own bunk in your own stateroom, curtains drawn. No pairing off with any special gal, even for a whole day. If a gal is wearing pants, long or short, it means hands off. Otherwise, grab whatever is passing by whenever you feel like it. The gals don't make the approach. The things you remember are like standing aft with a big rum punch in a fresh wind with Mickey at the wheel really *sailing* that thing, putting on all the sail it'll take, and those eight great bareass gals scampering around, hauling on those lines, trimming sail. And like being anchored in a cove in the moonlight, the evening meal done, and those gals singing harmony so sweet it would break your heart right in two. Great food and great drinks and good fishing. Everybody laughs a lot aboard the *Belle*. Between all they got to do, those gals put in a day full of work for a day's pay. I can't understand that damned stupid Barbie. Why'd she want to try some private hustling? Her old man must own half the state of South Carolina. Barbie's been a sailboat bum all her life. And she gets this chance to make a good living doing the two things in this world she does best and enjoys most, sailing and screwing, and she blows the whole deal. It's hard to understand. Anyway, we were out five days, and it was like being gone a month, I swear. It's . . . it's something different. If you ever see the *Belle* coming in here or leaving, you wouldn't figure it out. Those gals look like some kind of Olympic people training for a race. Nimble and slender and tough and . . . fresh faced. Scrubbed. You know?"

• • •

On Sunday Lisa agreed without much argument to arrange her call so that I could hear both ends of the conversation. She placed it from the cottage. We had to wait a long time before the desk called back and said they had her party on the line. I sat close beside her, and she turned the phone slightly so we could both hear, my right ear and her left.

It was Harry's nervous, lying voice. "Mary, honey? Is that you, Mary darling?"

"Yes, dear. Can you hear me?"

"Talk loud. You sound a million miles away, honey. Where are you? I've about gone out of my head with worry."

I hoped he sounded more convincing to his secretary than he did to me. Lisa followed her prepared script, telling Harry to let Holly Dressner know she was all right and that she had phoned. She said she was afraid he'd find the travel agency she'd used. The Seven Seas. Down in Hallandale. Mrs. DeAngela had been very nice and helpful.

"Are you going to come home? To stay?"

"I think so, Harry. I think that's best, really."

"So do I. When, honey? When will you be home?"

"I've got reservations out of here May third. But don't try to meet me. I don't know when I'll get in. And I'll have my car. By the way, you don't have to worry about the money. Not any more. I'm going to cable Mr. Willow to-morrow to activate the loan and put the money in your account, dear."

"I've been getting pretty nervous."

"I can imagine. I guess I wanted you to sweat a little."

And on and on and finally it was over, and she hung up. She gave me a strange look and then wiped beads of sweat from her upper lip and throat.

"It spooked me."

"I know."

"If I'd been Mary, I certainly wouldn't arrange a loan for that son of a bitch. I don't see much point in that phone call, really. There's enough without that."

"His secretary will make a good witness. Mary Broll is alive and well and in Grenada. She'll be home May third. She can say she was there when Mrs. Broll called her husband. Probably Harry will have his secretary get Mrs. Dressner on the phone and make sure his secretary hears him give her Mary's message."

"I don't have to send her any more cards. If I was supposed to, Paul would have told me. He thinks everything out."

"It's a good way to be, if you like to kill people."

"It's weird. You know? I've thought and thought about what you said, Gav. The smart thing for him to do would be to kill me. Get word for me to meet him on the way back. Some other island. Arrange something. But I just can't believe he would. We're from the same town. We're family. I keep having this dream about him. He's standing watching me sleep, and I sneak my eyes open and find out he isn't really looking at me. He's looking the other way, and he has a mask just like his face that he wears on the back of his head. He's pretending to watch me, but he's looking at something else I can't see. When the dream wakes me up, I'm cold all over."

"We won't have long to wait, Lisa. After you send the cable to Willow tomorrow, you're no use to him."

"Stay close to me, huh?"

I reassured her. I wouldn't let the bad man get her. She'd be safe.

Sure.

Eighteen

I WAS UP VERY EARLY on Monday morning when the sun was still behind the green mountains. I swam. The tide was low and getting lower, still running out. I went back to take my shower before dressing for breakfast.

By then, of course, he had talked with Lisa long enough to discover I was one of his priorities. He had immobilized her and come after me. Usually I am pretty good at surprises. Some sense I cannot describe gives me a few microseconds of lead time, and when I get that kind of warning, the reaction time seems to be at its best. Perhaps it is hearing or the sense of smell at subliminal levels.

I don't know where he hid. There were good places in the garden. He could have crouched behind the bar in the service area or behind some of the bigger pieces of furniture in the living room. He worked it out well. He saw me go swimming, and he nipped over the wall unobserved. I'd locked the gate but not the sliding door. He could assume I would come inside to take my shower, and I would have no reason to close the bathroom door. Standard procedure is to reach in and turn the handles until you get the roaring water to the right temperature, and then you step in. It is a moment of helplessness, and there is a useful curtain of sound.

I remember that when I got the water temperature the way I wanted it, I straightened to strip the swim trunks off. The whole back of my head blew up, and I went spinning and fluttering down through torrents of white, blinding light.

I know what he probably used. I made things easy for him. I had picked up the piece of driftwood in the surf a few days before. It was iron hard, less than a yard long, a stick an inch and a half in diameter with a sea-polished clump of root structure at the end of it the size of a large clenched fist.

Because he did not give a particular damn whether he killed me or not, he waited for the water roar, then came prowling into the bathroom with the club cocked, poising like a laborer to sledge a stake into hard ground.

The brain is a tender, gray jelly wrapped in membrane, threaded and fed with miles of blood tubes down to the diameter of thread. The gray jelly is a few billion cells which build up and discharge very small amounts of electric impulses. The whole wet, complex ball is encased in this bone, covered with a rubbery layer of scalp and a hair thatch which performs some small shock-absorbing service. Like the rest of the body, the brain is designed to include its own spare parts system. Brain cells are always dying at a rate dependent on how you live but are never replaced. There are supposed to be enough to last you. If a stroke should kill all the cells in the right hemisphere involved with communication—hearing and speaking, reading and writing—there is a fair chance of dormant cells in the left hemisphere being awakened and trained and plugged into the other parts of the system. Researchers can run a very thin electrode into an animal brain and hit a pleasure center and offer a chimp two levers—push one, and he gets a little electrical charge that makes him feel intense pleasure; push the other, and he gets a banana. The chimp will happily starve to death, pushing the pleasure lever. They can make a rabbit dangerously savage, a cat afraid of mice. They can put electrodes against your skull and trace pictures of your brain waves. If you have nice big steep alpha waves, you learn quickly and well. People who smoke a lot have stunted alpha waves. People who live in an area with a high index of air pollution— New York, Los Angeles, Birmingham—have rotten little alpha waves that are so tiny they are hard to find. No one knows yet why this is so. It may be a big fat waste of everybody's money, time, and energy sending kids to school in Los Angeles, Chicago, and lately, Phoenix.

Anyway, if you take a club to all this miraculous gray tapioca with a good full swing and bash the back of the skull a little to the right of center where a right-hander is likely to hit it, it is not going to function at all for a while, and then it is going to function in some partial manner for a varying period of time, which could be for as long as it lives. If you have any blood leaking in there and building pressure between the bone and the jelly, then it is not going to live very long at all.

Even if there is a perfect, unlikely, one-hundred-percent

recovery, it is going to take a long time to gather up the scattered pieces of memory of the time just prior to the blow and the time just subsequent to the recovery of partial consciousness. The memories will never be complete and perfect. Drop one of those big Seeburg jukes off the back of a pickup truck, and you are not going to get any music at all, and even if it can be fixed, the stereo might not ever work too well.

Forget the crap about the television series hard guy who gets slugged and shoved out of a fast moving car, wakes up in the ambulance, and immediately deduces that the kidnapper was a left-handed albino because Little Milly left her pill bottle on the second piling from the end of the pier. If hard case happens to wake up in the ambulance, he is going to be busy trying to remember his own name and wondering why he has double vision and what that loud noise is and why he keeps throwing up.

Assembling the bits of memory into some kind of proper order is a good trick, too.

Here's one fragment. On my left side, curled up in a cramped, tilting, bouncing place where things dug into me. Very hot. Some fabric pasted to me with sweat. Head in a small place full of blue light. Something abrasive under my left cheek. Arms immovable, hands dead. Motor grinding. A woman making a keening sound somewhere near, a thin long gassy cry, over and over, not in fear, in pain, in sorrow—but as if she were practicing, trying to imitate something, like a broken valve in a steam plant. Blackout.

Another: being jounced and joggled, hanging head down, bent over something hard digging into my belly. Thighs clasped. By an arm? One brute son of a bitch to carry me that way in a walk, but this one was jogging! Begin shallow coughing that announces imminent vomit. Immediately dropped heavily into sand. Gag, choke, and drift back into the gray void.

There were others, more vague. Some were real, and some were dreams. The brain was trying to sort out the world and it took bits of input and built dreams. On patrol, clenching myself motionless against stony ground while the flare floated down, swinging a little, moving over to burn out against the shoulder of the hill that closed off the end of the valley they were using. A brilliantly vivid fragment of old nightmare of Junior Allen surfacing behind the cruiser, tough jowls wedged into the gap of the Danforth anchor.

Then along came a more detailed one that continued so long the brain was able to go to work on it, sorting out evidences of reality, comparing them to evidences of fantasy. I awoke slowly. I was sitting on sand, leaning back against something that felt like the trunk of a tree. My arms were fastened around behind me, painfully cramped. I tried to move them and could not. I tried to move my hands, wiggle my fingers, and I could feel nothing.

I stared down at familiar swim trunks and down the brown length of my very own legs with the curled hair sun-bleached to pure white against the brown hide. A quarter-inch-in-diameter nylon cord had been tied to both ankles. It had been pulled so tight it bit into the skin. My feet were puffed. There was a two-foot length of cord from ankle to ankle. My legs spraddled. A sea grape tree grew up out of the sand in the middle of the triangle formed by my spread legs and the ankle-to-ankle cord.

It took time to work it out. It was unlikely I had been

there so long the tree had happened to grow there. Do trees grow slowly? Yes. Very slowly. Okay, could I have been fitted over the tree somehow? Long, careful thought. No. Too big. The ankles had been tied after they had been placed on either side of the tree. By me? No, the cord was too tight. My feet were swollen and blood dark. By somebody else then. Untie the cord? Not with arms I couldn't move and hands I couldn't feel. Remove tree? No way. I was supposed to stay there. No choice about it. I turned my head to the left, slowly, slowly. I was in shade. Out there the sand blazed under a high sun. Blue waves, small ones, moved in toward the sand and lifted, crested white, slapped and ran up the sandslant and back into the next wave. I turned my head the other way as slowly and looked to my right.

A man was sitting there. He was sitting on a small, inflatable blue raft I had seen afloat in Lisa's pool. He had a weathered brown basket made of strips of woven palm frond, and he was pressing it back into shape and working new green strips of frond into it. He sat cross-legged, intent on his task. He had a trim cap of dark curls. He had dark eyes and long lashes. He had a plump red mouth. He wore white boxer shorts. He wore a gold cross on a chain around his neck. He wore a wristwatch with a stainless steel band and a complicated dial. That was all.

As he tugged and pulled at the stubborn fronds, a lot of useful-looking muscles bulged and writhed and slid around under the smooth skin of arms and shoulders. He rose effortlessly to a standing position and turned the basket this way and that. It was crude. Conical. Half-bushel size. His legs were slender, but the long muscles looked springy and powerful.

A name tugged at the edge of my mind until finally I could fit my sour mouth around it. An articulated croak. "Paul."

He looked at me. There is a way you look at people, and there is a way you look at objects. There is a difference in the way you look at objects. You do not look at your morning coffee cup, at a runover toad in your driveway, or at a flat tire the same way you look at people. This was the way a man might look at a flat tire that he was going to have to attend to in a little while. Not like the owner of the car but like a service station attendant. Damage appraisal, estimate of time required.

I managed another word. "Untie." I was becoming a chatterbox. He looked back down at his basket repair job. I couldn't understand why he wouldn't talk to me. Then gray mists came rolling in from some swamp in the back of my head, and the world faded away . . .

I was being shaken awake. I was going to be late for school. I was picked up and placed on my feet. I squinted into a dazzling world and saw Paul looking at me. I was leaning back against a palm bole, weak and dizzy. I looked down and saw the familiar length of cord from ankle to ankle. Where could my sea grape tree have gone? I could not imagine.

Paul pulled me away from the tree and turned me to face the sea. He walked me carefully, holding onto my upper arm with both hands, helping me with my balance. I had to take short steps. There was very little feeling in my feet. He guided me at an angle down the beach, the trees at my left, the sea at my right. We were out in the hot glare, away from the shade of the trees. He stopped me and said, "Sit." He helped me ease down onto the sea-damp brown sand, facing the basket I had seen him repairing. It was upside down on the sand, like a crude clown's hat. A wave slid up the sand and took a light lick at the edge of the basket and at my right foot.

With the slow grace that accompanies ceremony, Paul reached and plucked the basket away. It was a magic trick. Lisa's severed head was balanced upright on the sand, facing the sea. Magicians can fool you with things like that. He stood easily in front of her and extended his right foot and put his bare sandy toes against her left temple and slowly and gently turned the head so that it faced me. As he did so he spoke a rapid, guttural, unmusical French.

Lisa rolled mad and empty eyes toward me, eyes that looked through me at something on the other edge of the world beyond me and creaked her jaw wide and made a thin, gassy, aspirated scream, gagged for air, and screamed again.

He squatted, turned her head back, slid his palm under the chin to uptilt her face, spoke down at her, the French rapid but gentler, almost tender, chiding her.

A wave slid up and under him, and the edge of foam slapped the lower half of her face. She gagged and coughed. He stroked her dark, soaked hair back from her forehead with a tender and affectionate gesture, patted her cheek, said something else to her which ended with one word I understood. *Adieu.*

He moved toward me, and as he did so, I saw a bigger wave coming. She seemed to see it, too. She squeezed her eyes shut and clamped her mouth shut. It slapped against

my hip. It washed completely over her head and reached six
feet behind her and paused, then came sluicing back, leaving
two small divergent ridges in the sand from the nape of her
neck toward the sea, shaped like the wake of a boat. The sea
had combed her hair forward, left it pasted down over her
face.

He lifted me easily onto my feet, turned me to face up
the slope of sand, urging me on. By dint of great mental effort I put three words together. "She can't see." Meaning, if
she can't see, she can't see the wave coming the next time.

"Never mind," he said. His English was good, but there
was a trace of the French-Canadian accent which Lisa had
eliminated entirely. As we walked up the beach, I saw the
old boat and remembered the day with Lisa. So she had
guided Paul to this secluded spot. I saw the spade with the
short handle stuck into the dry sand near the trees. Easy to
dig a hole big enough for Lisa. With her knees against her
chest, her ankles tied to her wrists, it wouldn't take much of
a hole at all. I saw the Moke beyond the trees, on that rough
little sand road, parked almost where I had parked it on that
day of the lighthouse.

He helped me through the thick, dry sand and eased me
down in the shade with my back against a rough tree trunk.
"Dig her out?" I said. I was getting pretty good with three-
word sentences.

He sat on his heels, began picking up handfuls of dry
sand and letting it trickle out of the bottom of his fist. "It's
too late. Not that it would make any difference. I shouldn't
have used the basket. She hated the basket. She begged me
not to use the basket. But I had to be sure she told every last
thing. But something broke in her head. After she lost all

her English. Something gave way. I thought seeing you might put her back together. I guess it was the basket. I'll be more careful with you."

I looked out at Lisa. I saw the biggest wave yet of the incoming tide. It did not curl and smash down at the packed sand until it reached her; then it bounced high off that dark roundness sparkling in the sun, the way a wave will bounce off a small boulder along the shore.

It was hard to believe it was Lisa. From the back only the dark hair showed. Her head looked like some large nut covered with a dark growth that had fallen from a tropical tree and rolled down, coming to rest in the incoming tide.

"If she holds her breath at the right time, she could last a long time, perhaps," he said. "But she is dead. Just as you are dead."

"And . . . Mary?"

There was a slight Gallic shrug. "That was bad luck. I went to her to try to convince her to leave Harry for good. Why should a woman like that have been loyal to a man like that? I wanted her to run, because without her, Harry would have to find three hundred thousand somewhere else. I have that much. I was going to squeeze Harry for half his stock. Waterbury should have let me buy in. Then nothing would have ever happened."

"Bad luck?"

"She tried to run. The house was dark. I caught her, and we fell badly. Very badly. It was an ugly situation. She knew who I was. I couldn't call an ambulance, could I? She knew how bad it was. I had to find out a lot from her while she could still talk. She was stubborn. I had to . . . amplify the pain to make her speak." He frowned. "I thought it would sicken me to do that. But it was a strange pleasure in a little while. As if we were lovers. So that is bad luck too, I suppose, to learn that about oneself. Gratification is expensive and very dangerous, eh?"

He stood up, clapped his hands to remove the loose sand. "And it was the same pleasure with Lisa, and we will discover if it is the same with a man, too. I should not care to dig a hole big enough for you, Mr. McGee."

"McGee?"

"I am very good about details. Harry described you well enough. Mary is dead. Lisa is dead. McGee is dead. But we must find out who you sent the letter to and what it said. We shall improvise, eh? There is a tire pump and a jack in the tool compartment of that ugly little vehicle. Something will come to mind. There will be enough time to proceed slowly and carefully."

He walked up toward the car, a hundred feet away. The equation was very simple. No unknowns. I could spend the afternoon on this hideaway beach as Paul Dissat whiled away the lazy hours with a question-and-answer game with the penalty for wrong answers and right answers precisely the same. Improvised agony.

Or I could try to stand up. That was the first step. If I couldn't, there wasn't any point in wondering about step two. If I could stand up, then I had to see if I could walk down the beach and into the sea. I had to hurry, but with short steps well within the range of my constraining nylon cord, and I had to keep my balance. The third part of it was getting into the water at just the right place. I had seen the place when I had been out there near Lisa's head in the hot sun.

There is no such thing as an undertow. Not anywhere in the world. All you ever find is a rip. To have a rip, you have to have a partial barrier parallel to the beach. It can be a sandbar or a reef. The barrier has to be underwater. There has to be a hole or channel through it. A great volume of water comes in on wind and waves and tide over the barrier, rushing toward the beach with waves marching right along behind each other, hurrying in. Then that big volume of water has to get out to make room for the water coming in. So it goes flowing out through the hole or channel. A big volume and a narrow deep hole makes one hell of an outgoing current. It is sort of fan-shaped, wide at the beach end, narrowing toward the gap in the barrier, and going faster and stronger as it gets narrower.

You can read a rip on a sandy beach from the way it boils up the sand in a limited area and makes a foam line out toward the gap. If you get caught in one, you swim parallel to the beach until you are out of it, then turn toward the beach. Fight it and you can panic and drown, because they usually go faster than any man can swim.

I got up, scraping some hide off my back on the palm trunk. I went down the beach slope, stamping my feet wide for balance. The beach and the sea kept tilting, misting, merging, flowing. In nightmare slowness I passed the round, black, hairy thing, saw it vividly for just a moment. A wave had come in and covered it entirely. The top of it was a few inches under momentarily motionless water, at rest when a wave had come all the way in and gathered itself to run back out. Her black hair was fanned out, and in that instant of sharpened, memorable vision I saw the spume of sand drifting out of her open mouth, like a strange cartoon balloon, a message without sound. A sandy, tan farewell.

Paul was shouting above the wave noises. I was off balance, leaning forward. A wave slapped my chest and straightened me up. I took a deep breath and lunged forward. I counted on the exceptional buoyancy of the water, the high salinity of the dry season. I had to know if I was in the rip. I managed to roll and float and look back at the beach and saw him and the trees and the raft and the Moke moving into the distance at six or eight miles an hour. It was a good rip, and I hoped it was a long gap in a barrier reef, that the reef was well offshore, and that it would move me out into a current that would take me away from there. Any direction at all. Out to sea and drown while laughing at how Lennie Sibelius was going to nail Paul Dissat, nail him and sweat him and find out how it happened. All of it.

The swell had built nicely, and it was going to play hell on him, trying to find me bobbing around in all that blue and white sparkle. If the hands are dead, it is less burdensome to drown, but you try not to drown if you can help it. I could arch my back and float high, my ears full of the drum sounds of the sea, a wave slapping me in the face now and then. Lift my head, pick a direction, and go kicking along. When all the luck has gone bad, do what you can.

Nineteen

IT WAS A GOOD RIP that carried me way out and put me into a sea current that seemed to be taking me due north at a hell of a pace, increasing speed the further out I got. The water was warm, and the sky was squinty bright, and I was gently lifted and dropped in the swell. It had been a good way to live, and given a choice of dying, it was as good as any that came to mind. I wanted to stay aware of the act of dying as long as I could. I wanted to touch it and taste it and feel it. When it is the last sensation left, there is a hunger to use all of it up, just to see what it is like at the very end, if it is peace or panic.

I kicked my bound legs slowly and easily. When I lifted up, I could no longer pick out the beach area where Lisa had died. I looked to the southwest and saw the checkerboard pattern of the town of St. George's to the northeast growing more easterly as I floated farther. Finally, I began to see more and more of Grand Anse beach as I drifted further out from shore, and it came into view beyond Long Point. When all of the beach was visible, I estimated that I was two miles from land. I saw the bright sails moving back and forth in the bay when a wave lifted me high. I could not guess how long I had been floating because I kept fading into a semidazed condition very much like sleep. The sun was so high I guess it was past noon.

There was a change in the direction of the current. I believed it had begun to carry me northwesterly, but I was too far from any reference points to be sure. I was opposite the town by then, and as near as I could estimate, I was just as far from the town as I was from Point Saline. When I could no longer see much of the town, see only the green mounded hills, I knew I was at least three miles offshore, possibly four.

I came out of a daze and saw a tall ship bearing down on me about a mile away. There was just enough angle so I could make her out as a three-masted schooner, and she had all the canvas on her, all the fore and aft sails flying, tilting her on a long reach.

I knew it could be reality or fantasy, and the smart money would bet on fantasy. I guessed she had come out of St. George's, and from my estimate of the wind, if she was headed north to the Grenadines, she would stay on that course until she was far enough out to come about and put her on the opposite tack for a single long run that would clear all of Grenada and head her for Carriacou.

I felt remote, as if working out a problem that had nothing to do with me. My arms had no feeling. I moved up and down on big, slow, blue swells. The crests were not breaking. I kept kicking myself back to an angle where I could watch her, see the boil of white water at her bows. My chance of being seen was one in ten thousand, even if she passed by me fifty yards away.

But then I had an idea. I suppressed it because it was going to involve a lot of effort and any effort did not really seem worthwhile. There would be fishermen aboard, people who always scanned the sea even when there is no hope of stopping for a chance at whatever quarry they see. The big fish smash the water, whack it to foam, send the spray flying. Go to work. Make a fuss. Give them something to spot. Hard to do. Double up and snap. Get the bound legs up and whack them down. Get into a spin, writhing and turning the body, kicking. Duck under and come out and kick as high as you can. Dizziness then. Sickness. Vision going. A sound of sails slatting, lines creaking, a thin cry. Sound of an outboard nearby. Hands grasping, lifting me. Fall onto hardness, onto oil stink, fish smell, and vomit up quarts and quarts of sea water . . .

Then came that burlesque of fantasy, an ironic parody of the seafarer's paradise. I was on a low, broad hatch cover, and I could feel the motion of a ship under me. I squinted up into brightness to see, clustered close around me—all their lovely faces somber, all their girl voices murmuring of concern—the sirens of all the legends, seawind stirring their tresses, their lovely skin in shades from antique ivory to oiled walnut. They were close around me, a multitude of them, prodding and massaging calves, ankles, and puffy feet—forearms, wrists, and swollen hands.

One lifted my dead left hand, and I stared at it with remote interest. It was a dark purple rubber glove, over-inflated, with deep dimples where the knuckles had been.

Suddenly I screamed. It astonished me. I am not the screaming type. There was a pain in my right hand equivalent to having all the fingernails yanked off simultaneously. Pain shoved me far enough into sudden darkness so that the raw scream seemed far away and I could think of it as an angry white bird, clawing and flapping its way out of my open throat.

I came out of blackness in time to get myself braced for the next pain. It was again in the right hand, and as it faded, I got a big one in the left hand, which caught me off-balance and so I roared. The enchantresses moved back a little, looking down at me in worried speculation. They were all in little sleeveless blouses in bright colors, no two alike, all in little white shorts.

Captain Mickey Laneer came into view and perched a haunch on the hatch cover beside my hip. She wore a khaki shirt and a baseball cap. "What the hell have you been trying to do to yourself, McGee?"

"Hello, Mick. Lost an argument."

"Somebody throw you overboard?"

"Ran away, got into a rip, floated out from shore."

She stared at me. "From shore? Jesus! You could be a little bit hard to kill. Gals, this is an old and good friend of our old and dear friend, Rupert Darby, captain of the *Dulcinea*. Say hello to Travis McGee." They said hello in smiling musical chorus.

"McGee, clockwise around you, starting with Julia in the yellow shirt, meet Teddie, Louise, Hester, Janey, Joyce,

Margot, and Valerie. Teddie, get to the helm on the double and tell Mr. Woodleigh he's falling off to port, for chrissake, and bring him back on. Janey, Mr. McGee needs a big mug of black coffee with four ounces of Fernandez rum in it. Margot, you help me get Mr. McGee onto his feet, and we'll put him in my cabin while we run back in."

I started to say something to her, then had to clamp down on the pains. Very savage pain but not as bad as the first ones.

"Speak to you privately, Mickey?"

"Move back, gals."

"Somebody is going to make very damned sure I drowned. It could revise their plans if I didn't. They'll keep a watch on the hospital. They could get to me there, I think. It's a bad risk."

"McGee, I like you. But I can't get involved in anything. The government pretends I don't exist. They like the money I bring in. The black power types talk about me forcing blacks into prostitution. Bullshit! Hester is the only almost pure black, and there are three less than half. Every girl has freedom of choice, believe me. Any publicity of any kind, any infraction, they hit me with a heavy fine. Enough to hurt without driving me out of business. Don't kill the goose. But don't let her get fat. You need hospital attention for the head and the hands. So I'm going to come about and have a nice run back and turn you over to Rupe to put you in the hospital. I've got four good, regular customers aboard who've paid their money for a ten-day cruise. Sorry."

I started to fade out and couldn't have pulled myself back in time if a sudden pain hadn't hit my right foot, as if an electric icicle were being shoved through it.

"Mick. I'm . . . sorry, too. Rupe heading up to Dominica Wednesday. Take me up to Grenadines, set up a meet, transfer me. Reach him on radio?"

"Yes but, dammit—"

"Take me back, and I blow your tired businessman cruises right out of the water, captain. Sorry as hell. You probably fulfill a pressing need. No pun. Official complaint to your lady governor, if I have to. And the premier. And the *Miami Herald*."

"McGee, I like you less and less. You are a bastard!"

"Only when I have to be."

"But, damn you, you could *die* on me!"

"Sort of a risk for both of us."

"Valerie? VAL! Get it on over here, girl. This big ugly son of a bitch going to die on me? She was a nurse, McGee."

Valerie was of that distinctive and very special mix you see in Honduras. Mayan, Chinese, and Spanish. She looked at my hands and she had me roll onto my belly while she checked the back of my head. Her touch was firm enough to hurt but gentle enough to let you know the hurt was necessary.

They helped me onto my back again, and she bent close and thumbed my eyelids up and looked gravely into one eye and then the other, back and forth, several times.

"Well?" Mickey said impatiently.

"Eet wass a terrible blow on the head. I don't know. The pupils are just the same size. Probably no fracture because the skull is solid and thick right there. Concussion. Could be bleeding in the brain, captain."

"How do we tell? What do we do?"

"One girl has to be with him every minute, and what she

has to do all the time she is with him is count his pulse for
one full minute and write it down. Count his respiration for
one full minute. Write it down. Over and over. One hour
is the most a girl can do that and be accurate. Half-hour is
better."

"So we set up half-hour shifts."

"Then she must write down a column of figures. Suppose it is like . . . 71, 70, 72, 69, 71, 70, 69. Fine. Then it is
70, 69, 67, 68, 66, 67, 65 . . . right then the girl on duty
finds me and finds you, and we get a seaplane alongside to
take him to a hospital. They'll have to open his skull and see
if the clot is shallow enough so they can take it out and keep
him alive."

"My hands?" I asked.

"They'll hurt like hell," Valerie said. "Like living hell.
But you'll be fine. No nerve damage. No dead tissue. Good
circulation, so that even something that tight couldn't cut it
all off."

The pain hit again as I was fading, but it just held me on
the edge, and when it stopped, I went the rest of the way
on down. Blurred memories of being carried, of choking
on hot, pungent coffee, of hearing the hiss of water along
the side of the hull. Then memories of it being night time,
feeling that slow swing and turn of an anchored vessel,
hearing faint music from topside, of moving in and out of
sleep and seeing girls, sometimes the same one, sometimes a
different one, solemnly and intently taking my pulse, lips
moving, writing on a pad, then staring back and forth from
my chest to a watch, counting respirations, writing it down.
A Coleman lantern was hung from the overhead with an

improvised shade which left the bunk in relative shadow and filled the rest of the small cabin in harsh brightness.

I awoke to a gray morning light in the cabin. The lantern was out. A slender, dark-haired girl sat taking my pulse. She had a narrow, pretty face, sallow skin. Her forehead and the end of her nose were sunburned.

"Where are we?"

"I'm counting."

"Sorry. Tell me when you're through."

"You made me get mixed up."

I let her count, write it down. "We're at anchor in a cove by some pretty little islands north of Grenada. They're called the Sisters. Now I have to count your breathing."

"Who are you?"

"Joyce. I'm new. Hush, please."

"From Barbados, eh?"

It startled her. "How'd you know that?"

"I can even remember the words. You are Louise's 'cute little chum.' She flew up and talked to you about the job."

She blushed. "Yes. Let me count, please."

"Dear girl, do your counting, and then I have to get up and use the head."

She wouldn't let me without going and bringing Valerie back to check me over and give permission. I felt shaky and frail. When I came back from the nearby head, clutching at everything handy, Valerie was sitting on the bunk looking at the notebook tabulations, and Joyce was standing near her. They got out of my way, and I sighed as I got in and lay back.

"Now we can take you off the continuous count, I

think," Valerie said. "Do you feel dizzy? Do your ears hum?"

"No."

"I think we'll take a count every fifteen minutes. Joyce, your hour will be up in . . . ten minutes. Stay another hour, okay? I'll have Margot take over from you at seven thirty, and you can go help with breakfast then."

"You're a good nurse," I told Valerie. "Isn't there a shortage of nurses around the islands?"

She was so still for a moment her pretty face looked like a temple carving. Her Indian blood was more apparent. "Oh, yes. A shortage of nurses. And damn lots of patients. And not so many reasons for keeping them living, I think. The children die. The old ones come back, over and over, trying to die."

She spun and left quickly. I tried to smile at Joyce. Maybe I managed it convincingly enough. I think she smiled back as her face tilted and blurred and faded into gray-black. I had to say something to assure Joyce and myself I was not going sour on them.

"What did you do in Barbados, dear?" My voice seemed to come from the bottom of a brass barrel.

"Does it matter?" she said from the far end of a hundred-yard corridor.

"I'm interested. I'm curious. That's all."

She began to emerge out of the humming mists and the metallic distances. I saw her face again, shifting as if underwater, then firming up. "Are you all right?" she asked, frowning. I felt her fingertips moving on my wrists, seeking the pulse.

"I'm fine."

"You looked different. Your eyes were funny. I work in a boutique in Bridgetown. My husband worked at the desk in a couple of the good hotels. We could live on what we made if we were careful. Maybe he got tired of being careful. He left over a year ago, and I have no idea where he is. What else do you want to know? I'm English and Portuguese mostly with a bit of colored. I make about two hundred and seventy-five to three hundred Biwi a month in the season and a lot less when the tourists are gone. I can't quite live on it. I've sold the things Charles and I owned, like the music system we got on hire-purchase and was all paid for, and I let them come and take the things which weren't paid for. The last thing I let go, the last thing worth selling, was my little sailboat my father built for me before he died when I was twelve." Her words were coming faster and faster, and she had stopped searching for the pulse. Her thin fingers were wrapped around my lacerated wrist. "It was the only thing I could use to get away, to be someone else, and I took it out in a gale before I let it go, telling it to drown me, but it would not . . ."

"Hey, now," I said.

Her eyes had filled. "I mean there is no end to it, Mr. McGee. I've been a decent woman. I have no family at all. A fat political gentleman wants to give me a cottage in a development he owns. There has been one girl every two years, I understand. He is quite old. They each end up with a cottage and some sort of small pension. I imagine a long street of them with the years marked on little signs in the little yards, with all of us sitting on our little porches . . ."

"Joyce, honey. There, honey."

Kind words started the flood. She put her forehead down

into the bend of my elbow, and the stifled sobs wracked her thin body. I stroked her hair and made soothing sounds. I identified my own feeling of guilt. I had not really wanted to know about her life and her problems. I had been talking in an effort to keep the brassy mists from sucking me under. But the words had opened her up, and it had come spilling out.

She pushed herself away, stood with her back to me, blew her nose. "Why should you give a damn?" she said in a choked voice. "Why should anybody?"

"Is this cruise what your friend Louise described?"

She turned, snuffled, sat wearily in the chair. "Oh, yes. Louise didn't lie. She called a spade a spade. It's a ten-day trial, you might say. I will do deck duty, scut work, help with the food, drinks, laundry, scrubbing, and all that. But I don't have to be . . . available unless I decide to be and tell Captain Laneer first. The men really seem quite nice. I can keep my clothes on, thank God. Louise said it took her three days to get used to pottering about the decks and below decks entirely starko. I think it would take me forever, and even then I couldn't adjust. The girls are so much nicer than I imagined. But an entirely naked woman is not really erotic, do you think? Of course, in a cold wind or offshore insects or one's time of the month or coming into port, clothes are definitely required." She had a brooding look, frowning down at her knuckles. "It's rather difficult for one to imagine being quite ready for it. I mean if one has taken a bucket of scraps aft after cleaning fish, it is so abrupt to be suddenly tweaked, then taken by the hand, and led below." She roused herself and looked slightly startled. She had been voicing her internal monologue. "I go on, no?" She forced a wan smile. "At any rate, once the ten days are ended, I shall either go back to the boutique to stay or go back to quit my job and pack. I shall fret about it later, not now. Valerie told me that it would be good for you to get as much sleep as you can now. Can you sleep, dear?"

I could. I slept and slept and slept. The dull ache in hands and feet and head did not inhibit it. In too many of the sleep periods Lisa was way down below the velvet black, waiting for me on the bright beach, the severed head propped on the delicate bones of the jaw, smiling at me.

It was another morning, and Mickey Laneer brought me a stone mug of coffee, nudged me awake, and put the coffee in my hand after I had hitched up, knuckled grainy eyes.

"You are some kind of a sleeper," she said.

"A long swim with your hands and feet tied will do it every time. We moved again, didn't we? Where are we, and what day is it?"

"Anchored in the lee of Frigate Island at eight o'clock on the morning of Thursday, April twenty-ninth."

"Thursday! But couldn't you get in touch with—"

"He'll be off to the west of here about opposite us at fourteen hundred. We'll make a radio check on him an hour beforehand. No sweat. We'll run out and intercept and put you aboard *Dulcinea*."

"I've been a lot of trouble to you and your crew, Mick."

Her smile was sour. "Better this kind than the kind you were going to lay on me if I ran you back in."

"Hard feelings, captain?"

She grinned, punched me on the side of the thigh. "My

four passengers haven't made any complaints. Maybe because I run the only game in town. The gals have loved playing nurse. By doing it your way—with you having the grace not to die on me—I've kept my friendship with Rupe. And I put a high value on it. No, McGee. Except for having to give up my own cabin, no hard feelings. How do you feel anyway? Strong?"

I checked and tested. "Better than I should."

"You look good. If you feel strong enough, I can send you down a little sample of our recreation program here aboard the *Hell's Belle*. Courtesy of the management. Name your favorite nurse, man."

"Joyce?"

The taut smile was gone. "Now you really are a smartass, you know that? I know damned well you know that girl's arrangement aboard, because she told me about talking to you."

"I thought maybe she'd made her decision."

"And you were curious? I wouldn't want you aboard long. You'd make too much mischief. Nobody puts any kind of pressure on that kid. She works it out for herself. She makes her own decisions."

"What will she decide?"

Mickey Laneer stood up, looking weary and cynical. "She'll decide that every other choice she has is worse. I'll send your breakfast."

Teddie brought my breakfast. She was the big, creamy, Minnesota Swede who had learned her sailing on Lake Superior. She was the one who giggled. Her hair was sea-weathered to a harsh spill of pure white hemp. From the bulge of bland forehead down to the clench of prehensile toes, she was tanned to the shade of macaroons. She giggled as she presented the tray with the menu she had devised. Two giant rum sours. A stack of toast. A platter of flying fish, perfectly sautéed and browned, crisp and sweet. A big enameled coffee pot and two of the stone mugs. She latched the door, giggling, and we had breakfast. She took the tray over to the table and came back, giggling. In the moist hollow of her throat, from earlobe to collarbone and across the socket in front, around to the other earlobe, she smelled exactly like fresh cinnamon and Pears' Soap.

The rendezvous was made about fifteen minutes past two, an estimated seven miles due west of Frigate Island. I convinced Mickey that there was no need to use the tender to transfer me. It was a freshening breeze, the sea running sparkling high. I said that though I didn't want to test my skull by diving, I could certainly swim a little. Rupe put the *Dulcinea* dead in the water, rocking in the trough, and hung the boarding ladder over. Mickey at the helm took the *Belle* across the *Dulcinea*'s stern, laying her over so that as I sat on the lee rail and swung my legs around to the outboard side, my feet were but inches from the water.

I dropped and swam the fifty or sixty feet to the *Dulcinea*, bringing from the *Belle* no more than I had brought aboard—the swim trunks, leaving behind somewhere in the sea the scraps of nylon cord they had cut out of my flesh.

There was no hand extended to help me when I clambered aboard the *Dulcinea*. Rupe and Artie stood staring at the *Belle*, jaws slack, leathery paws dangling. Mickey saw no need to change the uniform regulations for an old friend like Rupe. Mickey showed off by taking the *Belle* fifty yards past us, coming about smartly, working hell out of her girls, and then coming back aslant, waving as she angled across our bows on a northeast course not over forty feet away. The girls shouted, grinned, laughed, and waved.

"Fool woman," Rupe said. "All sailor, that fool woman. Artie. Artie? ARTIE!"

"Huh? Me?"

"Bring in that boarding ladder and stow it right this time."

"Boarding ladder?"

"ARTIE!"

"Oh. Sure. Yessir, Rupe. Right away."

Rupe put the diesels back in gear, opened them up to full cruise, checked the chart and gave Artie the compass course, and left him at the wheel. We went below.

"Now what the *hell* is this all about, Trav?"

"It'll take some time."

"Time is what we've got the most of."

Twenty

RUPE LOANED ME the money to get home, and Artie loaned me the clothes, a set of fresh khakis that fit better than I would have guessed from looking at him. I had to buy straw sandals at Kingstown on St. Vincent. Customs and immigration clearance was at San Juan, and I had an interesting time there. People are supposed to have papers and luggage, a wallet and a toothbrush.

They wanted to take my citizenship away from me. I told them it was a little misfortune at sea. I told them we could make some collect phone calls. When I said a magic name they could call collect, they came to attention. They almost smiled. That was on Sunday, the second day of May. I pulled the home number, unlisted, out of the damaged recesses of memory and got his wife, then got him. He talked to the boss immigration fellow, and when they were through, the boss immigration type felt a compulsion to pump my hand and call me sir and ask me if there was any little thing he could do, anything at all.

Before my flight left, I tried Meyer again, and this time he was aboard his boat, and when he heard and recognized my voice, he said in a shaky voice, "Thank God. Thank God." I told him what I needed and what to do and not to be so sentimental, anyway.

It was a bright, clear day to fly across the Bahamas and the incredible tones and shades of the Bahama flats. I wanted to think but not very much. I wasn't very sure about being able to think things through. I wanted to depend on Meyer. The weather across my internal landscape wasn't very good. Patches of gray, like drifting clouds, obscured things I wanted to see. And sometimes in a waking state I would have the same feeling, the same jolt as when you awaken from sleep. For a little while I would not know where I was or where the plane would land.

I got off that flight and walked through the lower level and out to vehicle pickup, and there was Meyer, bless him, standing beside a dark blue rental Ford as ordered. A very anonymous car. I told him he had better do the driving, as I was not entirely sure of the circuitry in my head. He drove. I talked. We selected a ma-and-pa motel on the way into Lauderdale on Route 1, and he got me a room in the back with an air conditioner that sounded like an air hammer breaking up paving. I finished the story in the room.

I unpacked the stuff Meyer had brought from the *Flush,* using that spare key I gave him, which he keeps hidden aboard the *Keynes.* He had packed some Plymouth, which seemed a kindly gesture. He went and got ice from the machine, and we drank from sleazy disposable glasses that looked as though they were about five-room-guests over-due for disposal.

I sat on the bed, sipping the clean, cool taste of juniper. Meyer paced and paced. He would stop in front of me to ask questions. "I'm not clear on one point. You *did* write the whole thing to Lennie Sibelius, telling him to get moving, open the inner envelope if you hadn't checked in by the end of May?"

"I did. But I told Lisa the tenth of May. I wrote to Lennie later. And I did not tell her who I wrote to, of course."

"She believed you?"

"She very definitely bought it. And she told Cousin Paul everything he wanted to know. Assumption: he believed her the way she believed me. But by the time he found out about the letter, he'd gone too far with both of us to start making deals. His next step was to make me talk to him. And he could have. I'm stubborn, Meyer. Need I mention it? The pain threshold is high, as measured on the dolorim-eter. But I could have gotten so anxious to talk I would have fallen all over myself. He scares me. What was your reading on him?"

"Humble beginnings. Very bright, very reliable. Full scholarship to McGill. Went back to his village to work for the man who helped him. Worked for that man about three years, and then one of Waterbury's companies acquired the benefactor's business in a merger situation. Waterbury was impressed by Paul Dissat and took him into the Quebec headquarters. Dissat is thirty-six, single, conservative, de-vout Catholic. He doesn't drink or smoke. He's apparently managed his own savings very shrewdly. Handsome. Very fit. Superb skier and superior tennis player."

He paced and I sipped, and the air conditioner kept up its whangbangroaring, leaking condensation down the blue concrete-block wall.

He stopped in front of me, using his lectern mannerisms. "He functions very well in a highly pragmatic profession. He is perfectly aware of cause and effect. He can weigh the degree of risk he is willing to take. He will assume that the man who gets your letter will be competent. Can his whole plan stand determined investigation? No. Even without a link as weak as Harry Broll enough could be learned to bring it before a grand jury. What would this sort of scandal do to the SeaGate stock offering? It would come out that a fraud had been committed to get funds from a bank to pay for a preoffering block of stock. Waterbury could not afford to proceed. Both Jensen, Baker, and Fairmont, Noyes would recommend the applications be withdrawn. This would all happen, if your letter exists, with or without Paul Dissat on stage. See where I'm going?"

"I think so."

"With no public issue to raise money through the sale of stock, SeaGate comes to a shuddering halt. Harry's indivisible block becomes worthless. I can think of a Dissat-like solution."

"Grab the three hundred thousand from Harry?"

"Yes. But don't burn the bridges. Not all the way. Kill Harry because he is the last useful witness left alive. Then take a leave of absence on an emergency basis, somewhere out of touch. Lay back and listen. If there is no letter at all, if it was a bluff, then come back after the deadline and pick up the project again."

I toasted him. "To you, Meyer. If he has left already, I get the letter back from Sibelius, and we wait for him to reappear. If he's still here and working closer to the deadline of the tenth and if he hasn't gotten around to Harry, we pluck Harry away from him and take Harry to a private place and have a long chat about Mary and Lisa."

"If he has left, or is preparing to leave, and wants a door ajar so that he can get back just in case, then he'll have given Waterbury some sort of cover story, I imagine."

"Can we arrange a secret meeting with Waterbury?"

"Travis?"

"Why are you looking at me like that?"

"If we can't find Harry Broll anywhere and if Paul Dissat is still around and if Harry never did buy that block in SeaGate, even if Mary's body is dug up and identified, there's no way you can get Paul indicted. You probably can't even get him fired."

"He's got pretty legs."

"I don't want you to do some damned idiot thing."

"Long black eyelashes, Meyer. Red lips."

"Travis!"

"Maybe I want to dance with him. Maybe I want to whisper in his ear. But I don't want to have him come to me. You see, he's a careful man. He knows I'll come back if I didn't drown. That's why I told you to be careful about being seen going aboard the *Flush*. Am I overreacting?"

"No. You are not overreacting."

"Don't let him get to you, Meyer, when he starts looking for that letter."

"I've never seen you like this."

"He scrambled my brains. We should get away. I know a great cruise we could take."

"A cruise! A cruise?"

"It's different. I'll tell you about it later."

"Do that. There's been no report of Mary Broll's death from Grenada. It's taking a long time."

"A guest is charged for the cottage whether she uses it or not and charged for the food whether she uses it or not. And in the absence of a body it is the kind of island where, if a lady gets invited aboard a yacht for cocktails or up into the hills to an estate for cocktails, a lady could decide to spend a week being entertained. It is, shall we say, an impulsive place. A carefree isle."

"I phoned Mr. Willow last Wednesday. He got the cable from Mrs. Broll on Monday, and he talked with Harry Broll on Monday. On Tuesday morning he activated the loan papers and deposited the funds in Broll's personal account. I thought you'd like to know. That's when I started trying to get you on the phone. Wednesday, Thursday, Friday, Saturday. It was . . . pleasant to hear your voice."

"Paul sent the cable in her name. No problem. I should have realized how easily he could do that." I looked at Meyer's watch after first staring at my empty wrist for the thousandth time. "Five o'clock on Sunday afternoon. About the only thing we can do is try to find Harry."

"How?"

"There is a name in the back of this scrambled skull. All the file cards are spilled on the floor. Let me crawl around back there for a minute."

I retrieved the red-brown hair, pale green eyes, the vital and expressive face, the lean, quick-moving body. I let her walk around and smile, and then I knew her. "Jeannie Dolan think it was paid over to SeaGate. And I don't think it's still in the bank."

"How do you manage that?"

Meyer smiled an unexpectedly unkindly smile. "By almost giving Woodrow Willow a coronary. He deserves a jolt. One should not be able to con a trust officer out of any assets held in trust."

"I'm coming along."

"Do you think you—"

"In the disguise you're going to go out and buy me at Happy Sam's Giant Superstore Open Always Practically."

"And on the way back here I buy pizza and beer to go?"

The lobby of the Southern National Bank and Trust Company takes up half of the ground floor of their new building on Biscayne. It is like three football fields. People at the far end are midgets, scurrying around in the cathedral lighting. The carpeting is soft and thick, dividing the lobby into function areas through the use of colors. Coral, lime, turquoise. The bank colors are pale blue and gold. The girls wear little blue and gold bank jackets with the initials *SNB* on the pocket, curled into a fanciful logo, the same logo that's stitched into the carpet, mosaiced into the walls, embossed on the stationery, and watermarked into the checks. The male employees and officers up to ambassadorial rank wear pale blue and gold blazers. Everybody has been trained to smile at all times. The whole place looks like a huge, walk-in dental advertisement. There is probably also a bank song.

Meyer dropped me a block away, and while he found a parking space, I strolled back to the bank and went in. I wore a Hawaiian shirt, a straw ranch hat with a red band, a drugstore camera around my neck, sunglasses with big pale orange lenses.

A guard moved in from the side and asked if he could help me. I said I was meeting the little woman here because she had to cash a traveler's check, probably to buy some more of those damn silly hotpants, and where would she go to cash traveler's checks. He aimed me across a hundred yards of carpeting, under a forty-foot ceiling. Nobody else looked at me. Tourists are invisible, except to the man trying to sell them something. Otherwise, they are as alike as all the trees in the park. Only a botanist knows there is any difference between trees. Or an applegrower.

I kept moving, because if I stood still, one of the guards would come over and ask me if he could help me. I did not know how long it would take. Meyer said he would come in from the north side corridor after going up to the trust department and coming back down with Mr. Willow. Also, I kept moving because I wanted to make certain that by no ten-thousand-to-one-chance was Cousin Paul doing a little banking business this hot, windy Monday morning. Sometimes his face would be completely gone from memory, and that would frighten me. Then it would pop back like a slide coming into automatic focus.

At long last I saw Meyer coming toward me, striding right along, and I guessed that was Mr. Woodrow Willow a half step to the rear. I watched Meyer. He was going to rub his nose if he wanted me to join the act. He looked through me and did not see me at all. Woodrow Willow was not what I expected. This was a young man, tall, fresh-faced, snub-nosed, round-headed with the same mouth old Walt used to draw on his chipmunks. I sauntered after them, and caught up when they talked to a man who had his own big blond desk in a solitary, private thirty-by-thirty area of coral carpet right out in the midst of everything. The man used a phone. Soon a rangy woman came over walking like one of those heel-and-toe competitors, elbows pointed outward. She listened. She picked up the phone. A far younger girl came, carrying a ledger card. She jogged. Every part of her jogged.

After she left, Meyer shook hands with the man at the desk, and Meyer, Willow, and the rangy woman walked all the way across to a line of teller's stations on the far side of the bank. The rangy woman spoke to a slender girl with brown hair. Then she spoke to a man patrolling behind the cages. The slender girl closed her window and came around and out onto the bank floor. Meyer turned toward me and rubbed his nose. The rangy woman was leaving.

I walked up, and Meyer said, "Mr. Willow, this is my associate, Mr. McGee. McGee, may I present Miss Kathy Marcus."

"Who *is* this person?" Willow said in a voice of despair. "Good God, I had no idea you were going to bring in—"

"A place where we can talk?" Meyer said. "Just to have Kathy tell us in her own words before we get into anything else. Then we won't be taking up so much of her time."

"Take a lot," she said. "I've got a three-dollar short that's driving me up the wall."

"We'd better use one of the small conference rooms upstairs," Willow said.

Upstairs was 1910 banking, as opposed to the 1984 version in the lobby. Oak paneling, green rugs, leather libraries. The computers were hidden offstage. Park your Mercer under the elm trees and come in and talk about buying a block of Postal Telegraph.

There were six chairs around the table in the small conference room. There were two framed prints of clipper ships and a seventeen-pound glass ashtray on the polished walnut. As soon as the door was shut, I shed the ranch hat, shades, and camera.

"Enjoying your stay?" Kathy asked me with a quick wink.

"Little gal, when I come across those Everglades in that big old air-conditioned Greyhound bus, I said to the little woman, I said, Mother, we shoulda—"

Kathy guffawed, stopping me. Willow rang the big glass ashtray with his pipe in authoritarian tempo, silencing everybody. "Please! This is a very serious matter. If I have your attention, Miss Marcus, we would like to find out to what extent you are involved—"

"Whoa, friend," she said sharply, no laughter in her voice or her level stare.

"Now you will *listen* to me, Miss Marcus! I was saying—"

She got up and went to the door and smiled and said, "When you go home to the wife and kiddies tonight, Woodie, tell her that nice Miss Marcus quit the bank and went right down the street to another bank. Some loyalty, huh?"

"Come back and—"

"Woodie dear, the banks are so hard up for anybody who is worth a damn, it's pathetic. They've been hiring people here if they're ambulatory and feel warm to the touch. And I am one very damned good teller, and I have been here four years, and I am not now, nor have I ever been, *involved* in anything hanky or panky."

"Please, come back and—"

"Woodie dear, you just can't have it both ways. You can't call me Kathy and fun around with me when we're alone in an elevator and give me a friendly little grab in the ass and a chummy little arm pressure on the tit and then expect me to sit meek and mild in front of these gentlemen and take some kind of accusatory shit from you. No thanks. I'll tell them downstairs who ran me out of this bank."

"Kathy," he said.

With her hand on the knob she looked at him with narrowed eyes and said, "That's a start at least. Say the rest of it."

"I'm sorry. I didn't mean to imply—"

"Do you want me to come back and sit down, Woodie?"

"Please. I would appreciate it very much."

She came slowly back to the chair, sat, and smiled and said, "If these men had been strangers, Woodie, I would have let you go on being a jackass, and I would have cooked you later. But I'm among friends. Friends who rescued an eerie blonde from the oldest floating houseparty in the world."

"I remember already," Meyer said.

I looked at her more closely. "Delmonica Pennypacker?"

"Just a little name I made up for my vacation. Anyway, as I understand it, Woodie, you want a play-by-play account of cashing the check for Mr. Harry Broll."

Woodrow Willow was coming out of shock. He cleared

his throat and told how a Mr. Winkler, a vice president of the bank, had received a telephone request last Wednesday at closing time from Harry Broll, stating that he would be in at about eleven on Thursday to cash a check for three hundred thousand on his personal account. He wanted to make certain the bank would have cash available in hundred-dollar bills. This is not an unusual request in an area where large real estate deals are made.

Kathy took over and said, "The way our system works, everything has to go through teller records, or we're out of balance. The cashier is Herman Falck, and I suppose Mr. Winkler told Herm to have the cash on hand. Herm told me he would run it through my balance, and he said Mr. Broll would probably bring in a dispatch case for the money. That amount would fit with no trouble. We run a minimum cash balance in the drawer at all times to make the place less appealing to the knockover boys. We signal the vault for more cash or to come make a pickup when we get too fat. They come zipping in a little electric money cart.

"So at ten after eleven Herm brings these two men over to me. I put out my closed sign so that a line won't build behind them. He takes the dispatch case from the man with Mr. Broll and hands it around to me. Mr. Broll gives me the check, and Herm initials it. Then Herm goes back and brings the cash cart behind the cage. It's just a matter of packing the sixty wrapped stacks of hundreds into the case. A black plastic case, imitation lizard. I counted them out as I packed them. Five, ten, fifteen, on up to three hundred. The case was below eye-level looking from the floor of the bank. I snapped the snaps and slid it up onto the counter, and the other man took it, and they walked away."

"Had you ever seen Mr. Broll before?" I asked.

"I think so. He looked sort of familiar. Maybe I waited on him. The name seems familiar."

"How did he act?"

"Well, I guess he's really a pretty sick man. I don't think he could have managed without the other man helping him."

"In what way did he seem to you to be sick?"

"Well, he was very sweaty. His complexion was gray, and his face was wet. He kind of wheezed. Like asthma sometimes. He didn't have much to say. Usually, men joke about lots of money when they put it in or take it out. They joke with me because I'm all girl, I guess. His friend had to kind of support him walking to my window, I noticed. Mr. Broll walked slowly, a little bent over and taking small steps. His friend was very nice to him. Considerate."

"What did his friend look like?"

"Younger. Dark curly hair. Tall. Middle thirties, I'd guess. A very nice voice. Some kind of accent. Marvelous clothes. Conservative mod. But he was too pretty for my taste. Husky pretty. Great eyelashes. He called Mr. Broll 'Harry,' but Mr. Broll didn't call him anything. Let me help you, Harry. Here, let me take that, Harry. Come on, there's no hurry, Harry. Take your time, old man. It took them a long time to walk to the main doors. The fellow helped Mr. Broll and carried the dispatch case. I watched them. They didn't go right out. I guess Mr. Broll felt faint, because they stopped and sat down in that lounge area left of the main doors. It made me uneasy. You like to see three hundred thousand get to where it has to go and get locked up again. They sat side by side on the couch. I could see the fellow

leaning toward Mr. Broll and talking quietly and confiden-
tially. I saw Mr. Broll put his hand over his eyes. The other
man pulled it away and took his handkerchief and wiped
Mr. Broll's face, wiping the sweat away, I guess." She
frowned. "Maybe I shouldn't say this, but the whole scene
had a funny flavor. It seemed faggoty to me, like a wife with
a sick husband. . . . No. The other way around. A youngish
husband with kind of a fat, sick old wife he doesn't really
love but feels sort of affection and gratitude and . . . a sense
of duty to, if I don't sound flippy."

"Not flippy at all."

"I was busy, and when I looked again, they were gone. I
would guess it was about twenty minutes before noon when
they left the bank together."

Willow said, "Would you say Mr. Broll was drunk or
drugged?"

She thought it over. "No. He kept his eyes sort of squinted
up. He knew what he was doing. He just seemed . . . fragile. As if he was in terrible pain. As if he had the world's
worst bellyache and was wondering if he was going to pass
out with it. And . . . he smelled sort of sour. He was wrinkled, and he had beard stubble. I wondered if he'd been
traveling all night or he'd slept in his clothes. I suppose it
could have been the world's worst hangover."

"Thank you, Miss Marcus," Willow said. "Uh . . .
Kathy."

"That means take off, huh?"

"With our thanks, Kathy," Meyer said. "You are a bright
girl and a good observer. And if it ever becomes possible to
tell you anything about this whole matter, we will."

"Thank *you*," Kathy said. She paused at the door and said, "McGee, do you still have that wild floating pad?"

"The *Busted Flush*. Slip F-18."

"I'll come visit. If you haven't gotten married up."

"Come visit, Kathy. Bring your swim pants."

"I'll bring a bowl of Greek salad. I make one hell of a Greek salad."

When the door shut, Willow said, "Good help is so terribly hard to find and hard to keep that one has to . . . uh . . . put up with a degree of impertinence that . . . uh . . ."

"Like she said, Woodie," I told him, "it's a lot easier to get respect from the pretty ones if you don't keep grabbing them by the ass in the elevator. Right, Meyer?"

"Absolutely right. An executive can't have it both ways."

"Keep the pretty ones at a distance," I said. "Grab the dog-faced ones by the ass. Then you have a happy bank."

"A contented bank," Meyer said.

"Goddammit," Willow yelled. "Tell me what this is all about!"

Meyer said, "I'll ask you the same question I asked you before, Woodrow. Could you swear that you were absolutely, positively certain that Mary Broll was alive when you processed that loan?"

"The answer is still the same. But why are you asking the question?"

"I'll ask you another. What was Harry Broll going to use the money for?"

"To buy the SeaGate stock, to pay the balance due of three hundred thousand. Don't look at me like that. It's legal, you know. It is illegal to borrow money to buy *listed* securities."

"He'd lose a great opportunity if he didn't buy the block of stock?"

"Oh, yes! Really great."

"Would he have to have cash to buy that stock, Woodrow?"

"Of course not! A certified check would—"

"Do you think he bought it?"

"I don't know."

"Can you think of any way of finding out?"

"Don't go away."

We were left alone. Meyer sighed. I told him he was pushing Woodie around beautifully. All he did was sigh again. When Meyer gets the silents, he isn't very good company.

Twenty-one

AS MEYER DROVE conservatively back toward Lauderdale in fast traffic, he said, "We can summarize what we
know, if you think it will help."

"You do it, and I'll tell you if it helps."

"We do not care whether Harry Broll was running from
Dissat or hurrying to meet him. Immaterial. Dissat had him
from some unknown hour early Wednesday morning until
they walked into the bank Thursday at ten after eleven. By
three o'clock Wednesday afternoon Harry Broll was forced
to make the phone call to Mr. Winkler about the large cash
withdrawal. Dissat had to then sustain Broll on that depressed level where he could make his appearance at the
bank without creating suspicion, yet would have no interest
in appealing for help. Total emotional and physical defeat.
A person reduced to Harry Broll's condition is beyond feel-

ing terror. Only despair. The only part left would be the details of disposal, or if he'd already planned how to do it, to go ahead with it. If it required darkness, he would have to have a place to take Broll to wait for night, or better yet, a place to immobilize him safely so Dissat could put in an appearance elsewhere. If we are building the structure of limitation, the parameters of time and space, we need to know if Dissat appeared at the West Palm office on Wednesday, and if he did, the time spent there."

"And where he is right now," I said. "When I wonder where he is right now, I wonder if he's crouched on the floor behind us. That's what he does to me, Meyer. Sorry. He was so *pleased* with himself, so damned *delighted* when he reached out with his bare toes and turned her head so she looked at me with those empty, crazy eyes. It was a funny kind of innocent pleasure, as if he had no idea there was anything really wrong about it. He was like a little kid who'd built a kite that would fly, and he wanted me to tell him how great it was. He tried to talk tough. Movie tough. But it was like something that had to be said. An obligatory part of the ceremony. After that we were going to share something, he and I. Some special personal important relationship. Dammit, I can't say it so that you can understand how it was."

"He fits the pattern of a certain kind of damaged personality I have read about, Travis. He could be called the activated sociopath sadist. Bright, healthy, energetic, competent. Excellent in areas requiring ritual. Mathematics, accounting, engineering. Quite cold inside. Tricky. Unable to concede the humanity of people around them because, having no basis of comparison, they think all of us have their same dry and barren soul. They are loners. They can charm when they choose. Sexually stunted, inhibited, often impotent. When Mary tried to escape from him and he caught her and they fell badly and injured her seriously, that activated him. Now he knows what he wants. He wants inventive episodes like the one with Lisa. The money will be meaningful only in how many such episodes it will buy. He isn't aware of evil. Only of being caught. You have to think of him as a bored child who suddenly discovers that it is wonderful fun to go to the pet store and buy a mouse and bring it home and do things to it until it is dead. Life is no longer boring. It is full of rich and wonderful excitement. The mouse shares the experience, so he feels fond of the mouse for as long as it lasts. You could say that the child loves the mouse to the extent he can feel love."

"Jesus!"

"I know. Stroking Lisa's forehead, drying Harry's sweaty face, are imitations of emotion. We can imagine he spoke tender words to Mary because she was pleasing him, giving him release. He's not a madman in any traditional sense. He cannot feel guilt or shame. If caught, he would feel fury and indignation at the game ending too soon. He'll go to great lengths to stay free, unsuspected. His career is a lot less important to him than it used to be. My guess is he'll be gone by the deadline, the tenth, a week from today."

We rode in silence for a time. "Meyer? How did you get that Woodie Woodchuck to snap to attention?"

"By reminding him that he had informed me of the approximate value of the assets in one of his trust accounts without any authorization from the trust customer or the senior trust officer. Banks take all confidential relationships very seriously. He soon said he would be very happy to help me find out all about the three hundred thousand."

"How did he find out Harry had forfeited his option?"

"I don't know. Probably phoned a contact at SeaGate and asked what value, as collateral, Harry's hundred-thousand-share block would have. The stuff is too closely held to have an OTC quote."

"Couldn't he have borrowed against the stock he was going to get?"

"Not if he had already done so."

"Sick condominiums and a sick construction business. How about the seven hundred thousand he's supposed to get back from SeaGate?"

"If it went into land improvements at the site, then I guess he'd have to wait until the public issue money comes back to SeaGate."

"So that goes to pay off other debts, and then Harry's business quietly fades away and dies?"

"Reasonable guess."

"He had to take Harry somewhere and keep him there. Harry and Harry's car. Transportation problems, Meyer. Logistics and tactics. If he took him to wherever he lives—"

"A cluster apartment complex at West Palm on the bay shore. Rental apartments. Not likely."

"I suppose you have his phone number?"

"You asked me to check him out. Remember?"

"And your overall impression?"

"A very dull fellow, competent and humorless."

"You know the name of the cluster apartments?"

"I'd rather not say it. Palm Vista Gardens. D-2."

"The first phone booth after we get off the pike, please."

• • •

He parked at a gas station by a shiny row of vending machines under a roof made of plastic thatch, incredibly green. I phoned from the hotbox provided by Gen Tel out on the cement wasteland. I hoped Palm Vista Gardens was big enough to have a rental and administration office on the premises. It was. The lady's voice came right from the resonant bridge of her Indiana nose.

"Yes, maybe you *can* help me. Have you got any furnished one-bedroom vacancies?"

She was not a well-organized lady. She tended to ramble. She gave information and then with cries of dismay retracted it and called herself names, mostly "old fool."

She finally discovered that one of their renters, "a nice young man" who had been on the special month-to-month basis with one month in advance (an arrangement they made with the "nice young people" from that new SeaGate company) had come in on the last day of April, just last Friday, and given his notice. He said he was vacating in a week. And that would make it . . . the eighth? No. The seventh. Yes. Next Friday. They could start showing it again the following Monday if there wasn't too much to be done. That was number D-2, which meant apartment 2 in cluster D. Just stop at the office. But don't wait too long. They go very quickly to nice young people, providing they don't have any pets. Or any babies, of course. I wondered how they felt about noisy goldfish, the kind that do a lot of leaping and splashing and churning around.

I tried to blot out all rational thought with a lot of peripheral items. Goldfish. Lead-free gasoline. Diminishing aquifer. I walked to the car, realizing I had left the cheap camera on the backseat. An essential part of my tourist costume. Meyer stood beside the rental car, drinking a can of orange pop, and it suddenly seemed insane that Meyer wore no tourist disguise. Paul Dissat knew exactly who I was and where I lived. And if he had gone to Bahia Mar and poked around as such a thorough chap would, he would have learned that Meyer was associated with me in certain obscure but apparently profitable ventures. Though believing me safely drowned off Grenada's lovely beaches, he might conclude that it was a very good chance my letter of self-insurance had been sent to Meyer to stow in a safe place. And so, as a percentage play . . .

It worked on me to the point that Meyer stared at me and said, "What the hell is wrong, Trav?"

My mouth wasn't going to work. Alarm is contagious. He trotted around and got behind the wheel, whipped us out into the traffic flow with a good imitation of teenage technique. At last I managed two words. "No hurry."

I saved the rest of it for my rackety motel unit. I tried to smile at Meyer. "Pure chicken. Sorry. I just don't know what the hell is . . ." Then I felt the sudden and humiliating sting of tears in my eyes and turned quickly to blink them away before Meyer could see them.

I stood with my back to him, staring out between the slats of the battered tin blinds at the side wall of a restaurant and a row of trash cans haloed with bluebottled buzzing. I spoke too fast and chuckled where there was no need, saying, "It's the old bit of the brave and noble hunter, gliding silently through the jungle, following the track of the big black panther, and slowly beginning to realize that the panther is also a-hunting and maybe he's flattened out on top of that thick limb up ahead or behind that bush over there or in the shadow of that fallen tree, with just the tip of his thick glossy black tail moving and the shoulder muscles rippling and tightening under that black hide. I'm spooked because I kept telling myself the son of a bitch would be gone by now, but he isn't going until Friday, and—"

"Travis. Come on. Slow down."

Can't ever really fool ol' Meyer. I sat on the bed. We're all children. We invent the adult facade and don it and try to keep the buttons and the medals polished. We're all trying to give such a good imitation of being an adult that the real adults in the world won't catch on. Each of us takes up those shticks that compose the adult image we seek. I'd gone the route of lazy, ironic bravado, of amiable, unaffiliated insouciance. Tinhorn knights of a stumbling Rosinante from Rent-A-Steed, maybe with one little area of the heart so pinched, so parched, I never dared let anything really lasting happen to me. Or dared admit the flaw. Maybe in some crazy way Paul Dissat was a fun-house mirror image of me, a warped McGee with backspin, reverse English.

The adult you pretend to be convinces himself that the risk is worth the game, the game worth the risk. Tells himself the choice of lifestyle could get him killed—on the Daytona track, in the bullring, falling from the raw steel framework forty stories up, catching a rodeo hoof in the side of the head.

Adult pretenses are never a perfect fit for the child underneath, and when there is the presentiment of death, like a hard black light making panther eyes glow in the back of the cave, the cry is, "Mommy, mommy, mommy, it's so dark out there, so dark and so forever."

Cojones are such a cultural imperative, the man who feels suddenly deballed feels shame at reentering the childhood condition. Papa Hemingway will never take him fishing. George Patton will slap his face.

In all my approximately seventy-six inches of torn and mended flesh and hide, in all approximately fifteen-stone weight of meat, bone, and dismay, I sat on that damned bed and felt degraded. I was unmasked as a grotesque imitation of what I had believed myself to be.

Frowning, I tried to explain it in halting fashion to Meyer. "You talked about . . . the reflexes slowing, the warning system not working, the instincts inaccurate when . . . the only reason Harry Broll didn't kill me was because he lacked one more round in the clip. Then in Grenada I didn't even think of being careful . . . didn't sense his presence, got such a shot in the skull bone my head is still blurred. Meyer, people have been a few steps ahead of me other times. I've played pretty good catchup. This time I have this feeling that there's no way. He's going to stay out in front, and if I get too close, he'll turn around and take care of the problem. Maybe I've gotten too close already, and I have ten more minutes or ten more hours."

"Travis."

"I know. I'm scared. It's like being very very cold. I can't move well, and I can't think at all."

"So I do the thinking?"

"I wish you would. Don't go back to your boat. I have a very ugly hunch about your boat."

"We have to talk to Dennis Waterbury in absolute privacy, and I have to make contact in such a way that he will trust us to the limited extent that rich and powerful people can trust anyone."

"Can you do it?"

"I don't know. I have to try to reach some people by phone. In Montreal and Toronto and Quebec."

"Start trying."

"If I can get through to someone he knows and trusts, who can tell him I am reputable, not a shakedown artist, then we are going to give him whatever lead time we can spare before I go to the law."

"With what?"

"With enough. Woodrow Willow's contact said Broll didn't buy the stock. So there's a missing three hundred thousand and a missing Harry Broll. If they dig around the seawall at Blue Heron Lane, they'll find Mary's body. Kathy Marcus and the other bank people could pick Paul Dissat out of a lineup. Maybe it will sink the SeaGate public issue without a trace. Even if Dissat never took a penny from the Waterbury enterprises, a breath of scandal can make the accounting firm and the underwriters back off."

"So why don't we go to the law? Why do we screw around with Waterbury if we've got all this?"

"Think about it, Travis. Think about it."

I instinctively fingered the place on the back of my skull where I had been so soundly thumped. Meyer was right. SeaGate was a very large thing, and Dissat was an operating officer in the SeaGate power structure. The lower echelons of the law would never go cantering into battle on the say-so of an apparently unemployed beach bum and a semiretired and eccentric economist. It was a two-county operation with both state and federal implications. Lower echelons would take the eccentric pair into skeptical custody and sweat them both.

Suppose you go to the top level, such as approaching the United States attorney in the area and suggesting he refer the problem to the FBI for investigation because of possible violations of the criminal code insofar as banking regulations are concerned. Then the approach would be made so tentatively—due to the SeaGate clout and the dubious source of the tip—that Dissat would be alerted, and he would disappear into his large countryside or ours.

First, you sell Dennis Waterbury on the idea that his boy, Paul Dissat, has been a very very bad boy lately and any publicity given his activities can founder the SeaGate plans. You convince him and give him some facts he can quietly check. You speak to him in absolute privacy and secrecy. Then, when *he* picks up the phone and relays his unhappy suspicions to the highest level, Dissat will be pounced upon first and investigated later, giving Waterbury additional time to plug up the holes and protect the upcoming public issue from scandal.

I said, "Okay. Do you think I'll ever be able to think things out for myself any more? Or will you have to be on permanent standby?"

"I think they start you on baskets and work up to needlepoint."

"I am supposed to laugh. All right, Meyer. Ha ha ha. Make your phone calls. What if the bastard won't listen even if we can get him alone?"

"Men who are rich have times when they don't listen.

Men who are quite bright have times when they don't listen. Men who are both bright and rich *always* listen. That is how they got the money, and that is how they keep it."

"Then do we go to Canada, or does he come here?"

"He's here now. I found that out when I was learning all I could about Paul Dissat. Waterbury is in a guest cottage on a Palm Beach estate. The owners are in Maine now, but they left enough staff to take care of Waterbury. Pool, tennis courts, security system, private beach."

He started making calls. He had to push the thermostat high enough to kill the compressor before he could hear. I lay a-doze, hearing his voice come from metallic distances, sounding like the voices of grown-ups when I had been a child half-asleep in a moving car or train.

Twenty-two

HE FOUND AN OLD FRIEND at last, a Professor Danielson in Toronto, who knew Waterbury well and was willing to try to set it up. Meyer gave Danielson the motel number and unit number and asked to have Waterbury phone him as soon as convenient. If Danielson found that Waterbury was unable or unwilling to phone Meyer for a secret meeting, Danielson would phone back.

Nothing to do but wait and try to digest a roast beef sandwich which lay in my stomach like a dead armadillo. The motel television was on the cable. We turned the sound off and watched the news on the electronic printer, going by at a pace for a retarded fifth grader, white on black printing with so many typos the spelling was more like third grade than fifth.

The woes of the world inched up the screen. Droughts

and murders. Inflation and balance of payments. Drugs and demonstrations. Body counts and new juntas.

Spiro was dead wrong. The trouble with the news is that everybody knows everything too fast and too often and too many times. News has always been bad. The tiger that lives in the forest just ate your wife and kids, Joe. There are no fat grub worms under the rotten logs this year, Al. Those sickies in the village on the other side of the mountain are training hairy mammoths to stomp us flat, Pete. They nailed up two thieves and one crackpot, Mary. So devote wire service people and network people and syndication people to gathering up all the bad news they can possibly dredge and comb and scrape out of a news-tired world and have them spray it back at everybody in constant streams of electrons, and two things happen. First, we all stop listening, so they have to make it ever more horrendous to capture our attention. Secondly, we all become even more convinced that everything has gone rotten, and there is no hope at all, no hope at all. In a world of no hope the motto is *semper fidelis,* which means in translation, "Every week is screw-your-buddy week and his wife too, if he's out of town."

The phone rang, and Meyer sprang up and cut off the compressor and took the call. He made a circle of thumb and finger to tell me we had gotten through the corporate curtain. He listened for several minutes, nodded, and said, "Yes, thank you, we'll be there." Hung up.

"A Miss Caroline Stoddard, Mr. Waterbury's private secretary. We're to meet with him out at the site at SeaGate. We go through the main entrance and follow little orange arrows on sticks that will lead us to the storage and warehouse area. There are two small contracts going on now out there. Earth moving and paving. They stop work at four, and the crews leave. The area is patrolled at night, and the guard shift starts at eight at this time of year. Mr. Waterbury will meet with us at an office out there in the end of one of the warehouses behind the hurricane fencing near the vehicle park and the asphalt plant. We can find the place by looking for his car. If we meet him out there at five, we should have plenty of time for uninterrupted talk."

We got to the area a little early, so we drove down A-1-A for a little way, and when we found a gap in the sour commercial honky-tonk, Meyer pulled over. Down the beach there was a cluster of fat-tire beach buggies, some people swimming. Meyer and I were walking and talking over our plans when a chunky trail bike came growling up behind us, passed us, and cut in and stopped, and a fellow with enough black beard to stuff a small pillow glowered at us and gunned the bike engine. He looked very fit and unfriendly.

"You've got a problem?" I asked.

"You are the guys with problems. How come there are so many of you characters so cramped up you got to come creeping around to stare at naked people?"

"Where, where, where!" Meyer said, smiling. "If it's required, I'll stare. But as a rule, it's dull. If you have some graceful young girls cavorting, that is an aesthetic pleasure for a certain amount of time. Doesn't sand get into the working parts of that thing?"

Meyer is disarming. Maybe a completely frantic flip,

stoned blind, could run a knife into him. Otherwise, the belligerent simmer down quickly.

"It's sealed so it doesn't happen too bad. But you can mess it up if you try. I thought you were more guys with binoculars, like the last pair. See, if you walk down this way far enough, then you can see around the end of the buggy and see the girls."

Meyer said, "Excuse me, but I was of the impression that the current belief is that the flaunting of the natural body cures the woes of society by blowing the minds of the repressed."

"A lot of people think that way. But we're opposed to the brazen display of the body and public sexuality. We're here on a pilgrimage mission for the Church of Christ in the Highest. And we have permission to camp on this part of the beach while we're bringing the word of God to the young people in this area."

"Wouldn't it be a lot easier to cover those girls up?" I asked him.

"Four of our sisters have got the crabs, sir, and they are using the salt water and the sunshine to cure them. The drugstore stuff didn't work at all, hardly."

Meyer said, "I have worked and studied in primitive countries, and I have caught about every kind of body louse a bountiful nature provides. And I have yet to contract a case that did not respond immediately to plain old vinegar. Have your girls soak their heads, armpits, and their private parts in vinegar. It kills the crabs and kills the eggs, and the itching stops almost immediately."

"You wouldn't kid me?" the beard asked.

"It is the most useful and generally unknown information in the modern world."

"They've been going up the walls. Hey. Thanks. And God bless you guys."

He roared away. I told Meyer he was fantastic. Meyer said that my continual adulation made him uncomfortable, and it was time to see The Man.

We turned around, and where A-1-A curved west, away from the Atlantic beach, Meyer drove straight, down a road that was all crushed shell, ruts, and potholes, and marked private. Soon we came to the entrance pillars, a huge billboard telling of the fantastic city of the future that would rise upon the eleven square miles of sandy waste, where no child need cross a highway to get to school, where everything would be recycled (presumably vitiating any need for cemetery zoning), where clean industry would employ clean, smiling people, where nothing would rust, rot, or decay, where age would not wither nor custom stale the fixed, maniacal smiles on the plastic faces of the future multitude who here would dwell.

Once past the entrance pillars we were on a black velvet vehicle strip (trucks stay to right, off blacktop) which restored to the rental Ford the youth and ease it had lost during a few months, a few thousand miles of being warped, rocked, and crowded by the dozens of temporary owners.

We followed the small, plastic orange arrows and saw some yellow and green and blue arrows on yard-tall sticks marching in other directions, forming a routing code for workmen, planners, delivery people. A small sign in front of a wilderness of dwarf palmetto said starkly: SHOPPING PLAZA E 400,000 SQ. FT. ENCL. Yes, indeed. A multi-level, automated, air-controlled, musicated selling machine, where—to the violins of Mantovani and the chain gang shuffle of the housewife sandals—only those processed foods would be offered which the computer approved of as being saleable in billion-unit production runs.

We turned away from the sea and against the glare of the high western sun saw the construction headquarters, the belly and stack and hoppers of a portable asphalt plant, saw the trucks and spreaders, piles of aggregate, loader, and loading ramp. That area outside the warehouse and office compound enclosed by hurricane fencing was deserted, as if a flock of Seabees had slapped blacktop on it and been air-lifted out. There was a big, vehicle gate in the hurricane fencing, and it stood wide open. In the fenced area were some above-ground fuel tanks and pumps for the vehicles, outdoor storage of some unidentifiable crated items, a generator building, and six small prefab steel warehouses backed up against a truck loading dock. A dark green Lincoln Continental limousine was parked by the next to the last warehouse.

Meyer parked nearby, and we got out. Meyer said in a low voice, "He'll be tempted to think it's some kind of a shakedown. Give us money, and we'll keep quiet about Dissat and let the public issue go through. But Danielson says Waterbury is honest by choice, not as a matter of necessity or operating policy."

There were three crude steps up to the cross-braced plywood door. It stood a few inches ajar, the hasp folded back, a thick padlock opened, hanging from the U-bolt in the door frame.

I gave the door a couple of thumps with the underside of my fist. It made a nice booming sound in the metal structure.

"Hello?" said a pleasantly feminine contralto voice, elusively familiar. "Are you the gentlemen who phoned? Come in, please."

It was dim inside. There were no windows at the end where we entered, only at the far end. We were on an elevated area with a floor made of decking with steps leading down to the slab floor of the warehouse proper. The office was at the far end. The air was very thick and still and hot in the warehouse portion, but I could hear the whine of air-conditioning in the enclosed office at the far end.

"I'm Caroline Stoddard," she said. "So nice to see you again, Mr. McGee."

I located her off to the left, standing down on the lower level. At first I thought she was one very big secretary in some kind of slacks outfit, and I blinked again, and my eyes adjusted, and it was Paul Dissat. That odd feeling of having heard the voice before was because of the slight residual accent.

"Be very nice," he said in his normal voice, "and be *very* careful. This is a new automatic nailer. They use it to knock the forms together for footings and pilings and so on. That hose goes over there to that pressure tank, and the compressor is automatic, and the generator is on."

It seemed heavy, the way he held it. He turned it to the side and triggered it. It made a hard, explosive, phutting sound, and nails zinged off the concrete and whanged the metal wall twenty feet away. He turned it toward us again.

"I'm a bad shot," he said. "But these things spray. At more than six inches they begin to turn. They'd make a ghastly hamburger of your legs, I think. I don't know why I've always been a poor shot. I'm well coordinated otherwise. Harry was a fantastic marksman. I guess it must be a natural gift."

"Fantastic marksman?" I asked numbly.

"Didn't you know? You could throw three cans in the air, and with that silly little popgun of his he could hit each one of them twice before they hit the ground without even seeming to aim, just pointing at them by some kind of instinct."

"When he came to see me——"

"He was coming apart. I was having trouble keeping him quiet. He had to make some mock show of being terribly concerned about Mary so that later people could testify he was almost out of his mind with worry. He said you moved so quickly and startled him so badly, he nearly hit you in the foot."

"Where is Mr. Waterbury?" Meyer asked in a tired and wistful tone.

"Playing tennis, I should imagine. This is his time of day for it. Cool of the evening. When word came this morning of the request for information from Mr. Willow, I called him back and after a little hesitation he told me one McGee and one Meyer had initiated the request. Don't keep edging sideways, McGee! It was really a shock. I thought you dead. From drowning or brain damage. You pranced like a sick, ugly stork, and you went floating out at an incredible speed. You are very lucky and very hard to kill."

"Where is Mr. Waterbury?" Meyer asked.

"You are a bore," Dissat told him. "I went to his eminence and told him I had confidential information that two sharpshooters were going to try to get a private audience with him and try to frighten him into parting with money. I gave him the names. He told me to handle the problem. I handle a lot of problems for the man. When the information came in from Toronto, he had me take the call. Don't you think limousines allay all suspicions? They're so symbolic. Sit on the floor slowly and carefully, Travis. That's very good. Now, Meyer, make a wide circle around behind him and come down the steps. Fine. Walk over to that coil of wire on the floor next to the pliers and stretch out on your face with your head toward me. *Very* good. Now, Travis, you can come down and go around Meyer and kneel on the other side of him. Hold it. Now I want you to wire your friend's wrists together and then his ankles. The better job you do, the better all three of us will get along."

It was a heavy-gauge iron wire, quite soft and malleable. It was such dim light I felt I could do a fairly sloppy job. Dissat moved back to the wall, and an overhead bank of daylight fluorescent tubes winked on.

"You're doing a lot more talking, Paul," I said. "All keyed up, aren't you? All nerves?"

"Pull that strand tight. There. That's fine. Let's say I'm more talkative because you're more receptive. Would you like to know how the wave action affected Lisa's body?"

"I bet it was fascinating."

"It was. I sat and watched the whole thing. After the waves were breaking way in beyond where she was, the outgoing wash started to scoop the sand out from around her until she was almost uncovered. Finally she toppled over onto her left side. Then the waves began digging the sand out from under her, settling her lower and lower and flowing and forming around her as it began covering her. The very last thing I saw of her was her right shoulder, and it looked like a little, shiny brown bowl upside down on the smooth sand. And then that disappeared, too. I imagine that on all beaches the sea is a scavenger, burying the sad, dead things and the ugly litter every time the tide comes and goes. Now one more turn *under* the other wrist and then twist it and cut it. Good!"

I wished the pliers were heavier. I rehearsed the motions in my mind. Whip the arm up and hurl the pliers at his face, falling forward at the same time to give the throw more velocity and also shield Meyer from the expected hail of nails. I could scramble forward and take the nails in the back and get to his ankles and yank his feet out from under him, provided no nail went head-deep into the spine. And provided he didn't swing the muzzle down fast enough to drive a close pattern into my skull.

I hesitated, thinking how badly I had missed Harry with the ashtray, and while I hesitated, Dissat moved, making plier-throwing a much worse risk.

He shifted the heavy nailer, swinging the pneumatic hose out of the way, much as a singer manipulates the mike cable. In the bright fluorescence he looked almost theatrically handsome. He was like a color still shot for those strange ads Canadian Club used to use. (I never knew how challenging it would be to hold two men captive with an automatic nailing device until I tried it.)

"Talkative?" he said. "Perhaps. Relief, I suppose. I've made a decision and simplified the future. Harry's money and mine make enough, you know. I've sent it to safe places. You two are the last loose ends. I'm taking sick leave. Actually, I'm retiring. Maintaining two identities compounds the risk factor. I told you in Grenada what I learned about myself from Mary Broll and poor Lisa. Now I shall have a chance to devote all my time to exploring it further. Very thoroughly. Very carefully. Mostly it's a matter of selecting people who might logically disappear of their own accord. I suppose the challenge excites me. So I talk a great deal, don't I? There's nothing I can reveal you can't guess, so it's not a help to you, is it? We shall explore the matter of the letter you sent from Grenada. As a matter of form. It isn't really important whether I learn about it or not, so I don't have to be awfully careful, do I? To keep everything tidy, I might leave with a traveling companion. A certain Mrs. Booker. Betsy. Would you know about her? Never mind. His ankles are finished? Walk backward on your knees. Further. Further. Right there. Sit down there, please, and wire your own ankles together, leaving a length of wire between them, the same length as the nylon cord that day on the little beach."

One uses any small frail idea. From handling the thick, soft wire I guessed that if one bent it back and forth enough times, it would snap. So I took a couple of turns around my ankles, tight enough to keep the wire from turning on my ankle. I made the binding turns, squeezed the wire knots with the plier jaws, nipped away what was left. With luck, management, and timing the wire might part at the squeezed place after enough steps.

He moved to stand over Meyer. He bent over and held the business end of the nailer almost touching the base of Meyer's spine. "I have this on single fire, McGee. Or single nail. If you can wire your own wrists nicely, I'll be so pleased with you, I'll give up the pleasure of finding out just how he'd react to one nail right here. Use ingenuity, McGee. Do a nice job. After Grenada, I take no chances with you."

I did a nice job. I was even able to nip off the extra wire by wedging the pliers between my forearm and the flooring. By holding my wrists together, exerting pressure, I could make it look as if there was no slack at all. Cheap little tricks never do any good at all, except to give the trickster false hope when he needs it.

Dissat came lithely over, bent, and inspected, kicked the pliers away with the edge of his foot. He grunted with satisfaction and walked over and put the nailer down beside the pressure tank, then swung and flexed his arms. "It got much too heavy," he said. He picked up a short, thick piece of metal. I thought it was steel pipe with a dull, gleaming finish, but as he walked toward Meyer, flipping it and catching it, I guessed from the way he handled it that it had to be very light metal, probably aluminum bar stock. It spun and smacked neatly into the palm of his hand each time.

"I don't even know what we use this for," he said. "There's a lot of it in the last warehouse. I've been taking an inventory personally, to check on pilferage of materials, small tools, and so on. That's where I kept Harry, in that warehouse. This piece just happens to have perfect weight and balance. I picked it up by accident the first time. After that, every time I picked it up, old Harry would start rolling his eyes like a horse in the bullring."

He bent suddenly and took a quick swing, very wristy, and hit Meyer on the back of the right leg, just above the knee. It made an impact sound halfway between smack and thud. Meyer bucked his heavy frame completely off the floor and roared.

"See?" Paul said. "Heavier stock would crush bone and tissue, and lighter stuff would merely sting. I experimented with Harry and went a little too far. I whacked him across his big belly once too often and possibly ruptured something in there, God knows what. For a time neither of us thought he could walk into the bank for the money."

"I'll trade Meyer for all you want to know about the letter."

He looked at me owlishly. "*All* of Meyer? Alive and free? That's naive, you know. Meyer is dead, and you are dead. There's no choice now. I *could* trade you, say, the last fifteen minutes of Meyer's life for information about the letter. He would approve a deal like that when the time comes. But what would be the point? I'm not that interested in your letter, really. I learned a little bit from Mary and more from Lisa and a little more from Harry. Now I can check what I learned and learn a little more. Why should I deprive myself?"

"Why indeed?" Meyer said in a husky voice.

"I like you both," Paul said. "I really do. That's part of it, of course. Remember, Travis, how Lisa became . . . just a thing, an object? It moved and made sounds, but Lisa was gone. I made the same mistake with Harry but not until the very end. The problem is to keep the person's actual identity and awareness functioning right to the end. Now we have to get Meyer out of here. Get up and go bring that hand truck, Travis, please."

I got the truck, and at Paul's request I bent and clumsily wedged and tugged and lifted my old friend onto the bed of the truck. Meyer ended up on his right side. He squinted up at me and said, "I have this terrible pun I can't seem to get out of my head, like one of those songs you can't get rid of. Let's hope his craft is ebbing."

"How is your leg?" I asked him.

"Relatively shapely, I think, but considered too hairy by some."

"Are you trying to be amusing?" Paul asked.

Meyer said in his public speaking voice, "We often notice in clinical studies that sado-sociopathic faggots have a very limited sense of humor."

Dissat moved to the side of the truck, took aim, and clubbed Meyer right on the point of the shoulder, and said, "Make more jokes, please."

Meyer, having exhaled explosively through clenched teeth, said, "I hope I didn't give the wrong impression, Dissat."

"Are you frightened, Meyer?" Paul asked politely.

"I have a lump of ice in my belly you wouldn't believe," Meyer said.

Instructed by Paul, I rolled the hand truck along the warehouse flooring, turned it, and backed laboriously up a ramp, pulling it up. He unlatched a big metal door with overhead wheels and rolled it aside. The white sunlight had turned yellowish outside as the world moved toward evening, but it was still bright enough to sting the eyes. I wheeled the truck along the loading dock and down a steeper ramp where it almost got away from me.

I pushed the truck along the concrete roadway, the steel wheels grating and clinking. I became aware that with each stride I could feel less resistance to bending in the wire joining my ankles, and I was afraid it would snap before I wanted it to. I took shorter steps and changed my stride, feet wider apart to put less strain on the wire. We went through the big gates in the fence and over toward the asphalt plant. Dissat told me to stop. He put a foot against Meyer's back and rolled him off the hand truck. We were in a truck loading area with a big overhead hopper. The concrete was scabbed thick, black, and uneven with dried spills of asphalt tar. Paul motioned me away from the hand truck and pushed it back out of the way. Above us was the hopper and a square, bulky tank that stood high on girder legs.

"Do you see that great big wad of wasted asphalt over there, Travis? Meyer is facing the wrong way to see it. Vandalism is always a problem. Last Thursday night some hippies apparently came over from the beach, and for no reason at all they dropped at least two tons out of the holding tank. That's the big, square tank overhead. It's insulated. Just before the shift ends, they run what's left in the plant into the holding tank. It's hot enough to stay liquid all night in this climate, and in the morning while the plant is being fired up and loaded, the trucks draw from the holding tank. But last Friday morning they couldn't drive the trucks under the hopper until they got a small bulldozer over here to blade that solidified hunk of warm asphalt away from where I'm standing. It's all cooled now, of course. And our old friend,

Harry Broll, is curled right in the middle of that black wad, snug as nutmeat in the shell."

I remembered being taken on a hunt when I was a child and how my uncle had packed partridge in clay and put the crude balls into the hot coals until they baked hard. When he had cracked them open, the feathers and skin had stuck to the clay, leaving the steaming meat. Acid came up into my throat and stayed, then went slowly back down.

I swallowed and said, "And the patrol checks here tonight and finds more vandalism?"

"You belabor the obvious, McGee. They'll have to blade your hydrocarbon tomb, big enough for two, over next to Harry's. It's hotter now, of course, in the holding tank than it will be by morning." He moved over to the side. "This is the lever the foreman uses. It's a manual system. If I move it to the side . . ."

He swung the lever over and pulled it back at once. A black glob about the size of your average Thanksgiving turkey came down the chute, banged the hanging baffle plate open, and fell—swopp—onto the stained concrete, making an ugly black pancake about four feet across, very thin at the perimeter, humped thick in the middle. A couple of dangling black strings fell into the pancake from overhead. A tendril of blue smoke arose from the pancake. Meyer made a very weary sound. Pain, anger, resignation. The pancake had formed too close to him, splattering a hot black thread across his chin, cheek, and ear. In the silence I heard the faraway flute call of a meadowlark and then the thunder rumble of a jet. I smelled that sweet, thick, childhood scent of hot tar.

When Meyer spoke, his voice was so controlled it revealed how close he was to breaking. "I can certify. It comes out hot."

"Hardly any aggregate in it," Paul said. "It cools and hardens quickly. Travis, please turn Meyer around and put his feet in the middle of that circular spill, will you?"

I do not know what started the changes that were going on inside me. They had started before the meadowlark, but they seemed related somehow to the meadowlark. You used to be able to drive through Texas, and there would be meadowlarks so thick along the way, perched singing on so many fenceposts, that at times you could drive through the constant sound of them like sweet and molten silver. Now the land has been silenced. The larks eat bugs, feed bugs to nestlings. The bugs are gone, and the meadowlarks are gone, and the world is strange, becoming more strange, a world spawning Paul Dissats instead of larks.

So somehow there is less risk, because losing such a world means losing less. I knew my head was still bad. It was like a car engine that badly needs tuning. Tromp the gas and it chokes, falters, and dies. It has to be babied up to speed. I had a remote curiosity about how my head would work with enough stress going on. Curiosity was changing to an odd prickling pleasure that seemed to grow high and hot, building and bulging itself up out of the belly into the shoulders and neck and chest.

I knew that feeling. I had almost forgotten it. It had happened before, but only when I had turned the last card and knew the hand was lost, the game was lost, the lights were fading. I had been working my wrists steadily within the small slack I had given myself, bending a tiny piece of connecting wire back and forth, and the bending was suddenly easier as the wire began to part.

The hard, anticipatory joy comes not from thinking there is any real chance but from knowing you can use it all without really giving that final damn about winning or losing. By happenstance, he'd made a bad choice of wire. And maybe the twisted child was so eager to squash his mice, he might give one of them a chance to bite him.

The wrist wire broke as I put my hands on Meyer to move him. "Can you roll?" I asked in a voice too low for Paul to hear. Meyer nodded. "Roll on signal, to your left, fast and far."

"What are you saying!" Paul Dissat demanded. "Don't you *dare* say things I can't hear!"

"Careful, darling," I told him. "You're going into a towering snit. Let's not have any girlish tantrums."

He quieted immediately. He picked up his chunk of aluminum. "That won't do you any good, and it isn't very bright of you to even try it. You disappoint me when you misjudge me. You take some of the pleasure out of being with you again." I looked beyond him and then looked back at him very quickly. I couldn't be obvious about it.

The instant he turned I broke the ankle wire with the first swinging stride. He heard me and spun back, but by the time he raised the aluminum club, I was inside the arc of it. I yelled to Meyer to roll clear.

My head went partly bad. I knew I had turned him back into a kind of corner where the girder legs of the holding tank were cross-braced. I was in gray murk, expending huge efforts. It was a stage. Somebody was working the strings of the big doll, making it bounce and flap. At times its doll chin bounced on my shoulder. It flailed and flapped its saw-dust arms. I stood flatfooted, knees slightly bent, swaying from left to right and back with the cadence of effort, get-ting calves, thighs, rump, back, and shoulder into each hook, trying to power the fist through the sawdust and into the gristle and membrane beyond.

Pretty doll with the graceful, powerful, hairless legs, with the long lashes, red mouth, and hero profile. Sawdust creaked out of its throat, and Raggedy Andy shoebutton eyes swung loose on the slackening threads.

Soon a blow would burst it, and it would die as only a doll can die, in torn fabric and disrepair. I had never killed a doll-thing with my hands before.

Somebody was shouting my name. There was urgency in the voice. I slowed and stopped, and the gray lifted the way a steamed windshield clears when the defroster is turned on. I backed away and saw Paul Dissat slumped against a crossbrace, one arm hooked over it. There was not a mark on his face.

I backed away. I imagine that what happened next hap-pened because he did not realize what punishment to the body will do to the legs. He was conscious. I imagine that from belly to heart he felt as if he had been twisted in half.

The shapely, powerful legs with their long muscle struc-ture had carried him through the slalom gates down the long tricky slopes. They had kept their spring and bounce through the long sets of tennis. So perhaps he believed that all he had to do was force himself up onto those legs and run away on them.

He tried.

When his weight came onto them, they went slack and rubbery. He fought for balance. He was like a drunk in a comedy routine. He flailed with both arms, and his left arm hit the load lever, and he staggered helplessly toward the thick, gouting torrent of asphalt from the overhead hopper. He tried to claw and fight back away from it, screaming as I once heard a horse scream, yet with an upward sliding note that went out of audible range, like a dog whistle. But it entrapped, ensnared those superb and nearly useless legs and brought him down in sticky agony. I ran to try to grab him, yank him out of that black, smoking jelly but got a steaming smear of it across the back of my hand and forearm. I turned then and did what I should have done in the first place, went for the lever and swung it back to the closed position. The last sight I had before I turned, was of Dissat buried halfway up his rib cage, hands braced against the concrete slab, elbows locked, head up, eyes half out of the sockets, mouth agape, cords standing out in his throat, as the black stuff piled higher behind him, higher than his head.

I yanked the lever back and spun, and he was gone. A part of the blackness seemed to bulge slightly and sag back. The last strings of it solidified and fell. It was heaped as high as my waist and as big as a grand piano.

I remembered Meyer and looked over and saw him. He had wiggled into a sitting position, his back against a girder. I took a staggering step and caught myself.

"Pliers," Meyer said. "Hang on, Travis. For God's sake, hang on."

Pliers. I knew there wasn't time for pliers. The gray was

coming in from every side, misting the windshield as before. I found my way toward him, fell, then crawled, and reached his wrists. I bent the wire, turning it, freeing it. I saw a sharp end bite into the ball of my thumb, saw blood run, felt nothing. Just one more turn and then he could . . .

Twenty-three

I WAS NOT ENTIRELY ASLEEP and not yet awake, and I could not remember ever having been so completely, perfectly, deliciously relaxed. The girl voices brought me further across the line into being awake.

Rupe had said how very sweet their voices were, how touching, how heartbreaking, aboard the *Belle*. Their harmony was simple, their voices true and small.

"What a friend we have in Jeeeeee-zusss. All our sins and griefs to baaaaaaaare."

I wondered why the extraordinary crew of the *Hell's Belle* should select a number like that. Yet there was the tidy warmth of Teddie's thigh under the nape of my neck, a sweet, firm fit. Fabric over the thigh. I opened my eyes, and it was night. Light came slanting and touched the girl faces, touching their long, hanging hair. I realized I was on a blanket, and there was the unmistakable feel and consistency of dry sand under the blanket. Teddie's face was in shadow. I lifted a lazy, contented arm and put my hand over the young breast under thin fabric so close above my face. It had a sweet, rubbery firmness.

She took my wrist and pushed my hand down and said, "No, brother." They had stopped singing the words of the song. They were humming the melody. "He has awakened," the girl said. It was not Teddie's voice. They stopped singing.

A man's voice said, "How do you feel, brother?"

I raised my head. There were five or six of them in a glow of firelight. Bearded, biblical men wrapped in coarse cloth. I had been hurled out of my historical time and my place.

I sat up too quickly. I felt faint and bent forward to lower my head down between my knees.

A hand touched my shoulder. Meyer said, "I was trying to get you to a doctor and ran off into the sand. This one here is their healer, and he—"

"I was a third year medical student when I heard the call. I'm the healer for the tribe on this pilgrimage mission."

I straightened and looked into a young bearded face. He nodded and took my pulse and nodded again. "We got that tar off your arm and hand with a solvent, brother, and treated your burn and dressed it."

My arm was wrapped with gauze. There was a bandage on my thumb. I turned my head and saw the beach buggies and several campers. A baby was crying in one of the campers.

I lay back very carefully. The thigh was there, cozy as before. The face leaned over me and looked down. "I will comfort you, brother, but no more grabbing me, huh?"

"No more, sister. I thought I was somewhere else with someone else. A . . . different group of girls."

"On a pilgrimage, too?"

"In a certain sense of the word, yes."

"There is only one sense, brother, when you give your heart and your soul and your worldly goods and all the days of your years to the service of almighty God."

"Did your . . . healer put vinegar on my burns?"

She giggled. "That's me you smell, brother. Blessed providence sent you and your friend to us this afternoon before I flipped right out of my tree. If it isn't sacrilege, my sisters and I are enjoying a peace that passeth understanding ever since."

I tried sitting up again, and there was no dizziness. One of the sisters brought me a cup of hot clam broth. She wore a garment like an aba, made out of some kind of homespun. She too smelled of vinegar. There was a crude cross around her neck with green stones worked into it. The automatic slide projector in my head showed me a slide entitled "The Last Known Sight of Paul Dissat in This World." A small gold cross hung free around his straining throat.

After I drank the broth, I tried standing, and it worked reasonably well. They were not paying any special attention to me or to Meyer. We were welcome to be with them. Feel free to ignore and be ignored. Listen to the sweet singing, taste the broth, and praise the Lord.

I found the vinegar girl and gave her back her cup with thanks. Meyer and I moved away from the fire and from the lights in the campers.

"I panicked," Meyer said. "I got the rest of the wire off me and threw you in the damned car and drove like a maniac."

"Where is the car?"

"Up there on the shoulder. It was in deep. They pulled it out with a beach buggy."

"What about that limousine?"

"Good question. Joshua and I went back in there on his trail bike. The keys to it were on the desk in the office. We put the trail bike into the trunk. I locked everything in sight, and we were out of there before seven thirty. I took the long way around, and we left it at the West Palm airport, keys in the ashtray. Call it a Dissat solution. By the way, I made a contribution to the pilgrimage mission collection plate in both our names."

"That's nice."

"One of the wrapped stacks of hundreds from the Southern National. Initialed. Unbroken. There were four stacks in a brown paper bag on the desk in the warehouse office."

"What did Joshua say?"

"Thanks."

"No questions about the kind of help you asked of him?"

"Just one. He said that before he took the name of Joshua, he had clouted cars to feed his habit. He said all he wanted to know was whether, if we had committed a sin, we repented of it. I said that even though I didn't think of it as a sin, I was going to pray for forgiveness. That's when he nodded and said thanks and riffled the stack with his thumb and shoved it into the saddlebag on the trail bike. I walked out of the airport parking lot, and he drove the bike out and waited for me down the road from the airport. Long way around coming back here, too. I had the idea you'd be dead when I got here."

"Meyer?"

"Yes?"

"Get me home. Get me back to the *Flush*. Please."

"Let's say goodnight to the tribe."

I did a lot of sleeping. I was getting to be very good at it. I could get up at noon, shower, work up a big breakfast, and be ready for my nap at three. The gray fog rolled way back into the furthest corners of my mind. People left me alone. Meyer made certain of that. He passed the word. McGee has pulled the hole in after him. And he bites.

Meyer would come over during that part of each day when I was likely to be up and about.

We'd walk over and swim. We would come back and play chess. I did not want to be among people. Not yet. So he would cook, or I would cook, or he would go out and bring something back.

The longer we delayed the decision, the easier it was to make. The random parts fell together in a pattern we could find no reason to contradict. Harry Broll had grabbed his three-hundred-thousand loan in cash and fled with Lisa, the girlfriend he had promised to give up. Except for some irate creditors nobody was looking for him diligently. Harry's wife had been reported missing in the Windward Islands, presumed drowned while swimming alone. Paul Dissat was missing too, possibly by drowning, but in his case it would more likely be suicide, emotional depression, and anxiety over some kind of disease of the blood. He had requested sick leave.

Jillian had been astoundingly sweet and helpful and had even lived up to her promise to ask no questions. She had flown down to Grenada and stayed a few days and with the knowing assistance of an attorney friend had obtained my packet from the hotel safe and my other possessions from their storage room.

The favor was, of course, Jilly's concession to apology, to regret. When she and her new friend got back from Grenada, she came over with him to give me back my belongings. They had a drink with us, and they did not stay long. Meyer arrived before they left.

"I keep forgetting his name," Meyer said later.

"Foster Cramond. Still a close personal friend of both his ex-wives."

"Rich ex-wives."

"Of course."

"Likable," Meyer said judiciously. "Good manners. No harm in him. Good at games, what? Court tennis, polo, sailing. Splendid reflexes. Did you notice the fast draw with that solid gold lighter? Twelfth of a second. Interesting phenomenon when they looked at each other."

"What? Oh, you mean the visible steam that came out of her ears? And the way he went from a sixteen collar to an eighteen? Yes. I noticed."

"Travis, what was your reaction when you met her new friend?"

"Relief at not running into some big fuss about breaking my word to visit her for a week. And . . . some indignation, I guess. In all honesty, some indignation."

"And you wished you could change your mind again?"

I let his question hang in the air for a long time, for three moves, one involving tightening my defense against his queen's bishop. I found a response that created a new problem for him. While he was studying it, I leaned back.

"About changing my mind. No. My instincts hadn't turned bad when Harry came here. He had no intention of shooting me. So let's suppose I'm slower by a half a step or a full step. Maybe I'm old enough and wise enough to move into positions where I don't need the speed. The only thing I know is that I am going to run out of luck in the future, just as I have in the past. And when I run out, I am going to have to make myself some luck. I know that what counts is the feeling I get when I make my own luck. The way I feel then is totally alive. In every dimension. In every possible way. It wouldn't have to be Jillian. I could lay back, watch the traffic, select a rich lady, and retire myself to stud. But that would be half-life. I have an addiction. I'm hooked on the smell, taste, and feel of the nearness of death and on the way I feel when I make my move to keep it from happening. If I *knew* I could keep it from happening, there'd be no taste to it at all."

Meyer gave that a lot of thought, and then he gave the game a lot of thought. Finally he said, "When in doubt, castle." He moved his king into the short corner, the rook standing guard. "Travis, I am very very glad that you were able to make us some luck. I am glad to be here. But . . ."

"But?"

"Something else is wrong with you."

"I dream some rotten things. I've got my memory almost all straightened out. Picked up nearly all the cards off the floor and put them back in the right order. But I have real rotten dreams. Last night I was buying a shirt. The girl said it was made in the islands, and they weren't sized correctly

and I should try it on. When I put it on and came out, I realized that it was exactly the same print that Lisa had worn
that first night I knew her. A dashiki. As I started to tell the
girl that I didn't want it, she came up to me quickly, and she
reached out, and she snapped something onto the front of
the shirt. It made a clack. It was a big, round, white thing,
too heavy for the front of a shirt. I turned it around, and I
saw that the sound had been the lower jaw of a skull being
closed with the fabric caught between the teeth. It was a
very white, polished, delicate skull, and at first it looked
feral, some predator's skull. Then I knew it was Lisa's skull.
I tried to get the girl to take it off, but she said it went with
that particular shirt. No other shirt. Just that one. And I
woke up."

"Good Christ," Meyer whispered softly.

"But usually I don't dream at all."

"Be thankful, Travis. Is something else wrong?"

"Yes."

"Do you have the words for it yet?"

"I think it's getting to the point where there will be
words for it. When there are words, I'll try them on you."

"Are you going to check me with that knight? Go ahead.
See what happens if you do."

On the following Sunday afternoon, a Sunday late in May,
Meyer and I were over on the beach. When the wind died,
it got uncomfortably hot in the sun, so we moved to a bench
in the shade. I watched two lovely ladies approaching along
the beach, consciously keeping shoulders back and tummies
in as they strode along, laughing and talking. Elegant lass-

ies. Total strangers. They were walking across the edge of my life and right back out of it, and I would never know them or touch them nor two million nor ten million of their graceful sisters.

"Maybe I can put that problem into words now. But it's just a try. Maybe you can be patient?"

"How often do you see me impatient?"

"This starts with a word Rupe Darby used down in Grenada. A phrase, not a word. It designates a condition. Womaned out. He meant it in the physical sense. Total sexual depletion to the point where you think you never want to see another woman. I think I'm womaned out in a different way. All my love life is pre-Grenada, and that was a lifetime ago."

"So. Womaned out but not in a physical sense."

"God, no. Those two who just went by created the intended reaction. And I keep remembering how neat and warm the thigh of the little Jesus singer felt under the nape of my neck. Physical capacity is just dandy. No, Meyer. I feel foundered and wind broke in some other dimension of myself. I feel sick of myself, as if the prospect of me in action would turn me off, way off."

"How?"

"Everything I thought I believed about making love to a woman sounds very stale. I hear myself talking to too many of them. There has to be affection, dear. Respect for each other. We must not hurt each other or anyone else, darling. There has to be giving on both sides and taking on both sides, honeybunch. Oh Meyer, God help me, it all sounds like a glossy sales talk. I was kidding them, and I was kidding myself. Look. I was holding out a package deal. And on the bottom of the package in small print was the guaran-goddamn-tee. Mary Dillon picked up the package. I didn't force it on her. I just left it around where she'd see it. She picked it up, enjoyed the product, and then married Harry Broll, and now she's buried in a washout behind a seawall under transitmix concrete. So something is wrong with the small print or the service contract or the damned sales force, Meyer. I just can't . . . I can't stand the thought of ever again hearing my own sincere, manly, loving, crap-eating voice saying those stale words about how I won't ever hurt you, baby, I just want to screw you and make you a more sincere and emotionally healthy woman."

"Travis, Travis, Travis."

"I know. But that's what's wrong."

"Maybe there is some new kind of industrial waste in the air we breathe."

"Fractionated honesty?"

"Don't suffer all over me, McGee. You are a good man. There is no man alive who is not partially jackass. When we detect some area of jackassery within ourselves, we feel discontent. Our image suffers."

"What should I do?"

"How do I know what you should do? Don't make me an uncle. Go get lost in the Out Islands and fish for a couple months. Go hire onto a tug and work yourself into a stupor. Take five thousand of what was in that brown bag and lease the *Hell's Belle* all by yourself for ten days. Take cold showers. Study Hindustani."

"Why are you getting sore?"

He bounded off the bench, whirled, bent over, yelled into my face, "Who's getting sore? I'm not getting sore!"

And he ran down to the water, bouncing hairily along, and plopped in and swam out.

Everyone was not acting like himself. Maybe there *was* some new kind of guck in the air lately.

By the time we had finished our swim, Meyer had gotten over his unusual tizzy. We walked slowly back across the bridge, and as we neared the *Flush,* I could see a figure aboard her in the shade of the sundeck overhang, sitting on the shallow little after-deck.

I did not recognize her until we were within thirty feet. She lay asleep in the deck chair with a tidy, boneless look of a resting cat. There was a big red suitcase beside the chair and a matching red train case, both well scuffed by travel. She wore a little denim dress with white stitching. Her white sandals were on the deck under the chair. Her sleeping arm clamped her white purse against her.

Suddenly her eyes opened wide. There was no sleep-stunned transition. She leapt back into life and up onto her feet in the same instant, all smiling vitality. "Hey! McGee! It's me. Jeannie. Jeannie Dolan. I should have looked over on the beach, huh?"

I introduced them. Meyer said he had heard nice things about her. He seemed to approve of the lively mop of red-brown hair and the quick glinting of the gray-green eyes.

I unlocked the *Flush,* and we went in. She said, "Leave my stuff right there, unless you've got thieves. Hey, can I look around? Say, this is a great kind of boat, Trav! Look, is the timing bad? Am I in the way or anything? If you guys have something all lined up . . ."

"Nothing," Meyer said. "Nothing at all."

"Wow, what a great kitchen."

"Galley," I said.

She looked at me blankly. "Galley? They row those with big oars. And a man walking around with a whip. Do you row this thing, for God's sake?"

"Okay, Jeannie. It's a kitchen," I said.

"Does it have engines in it? I mean, it will cruise around and so forth?"

"And so forth," Meyer said, looking happier.

"Wow, would I ever like to go someplace on a boat like this."

"Where's your friend?" I asked her.

"Betsy? We got tossed out of that Casa de Playa by the bank that took over. Not we, just me. Because she was gone by then. She went back to cleaning teeth. For a widower dentist in North Miami."

"Vodka tonic for you?" I asked her.

"Exactly right! It's wonderful when people remember things, isn't it? What I'm going to do, I'm on my way back to Columbus. No, not back to Charlie, that creep. But I called my old job, and I can make enough money so I can save enough to fly to the Dominican Republic and get a quickie divorce, instead of beating my brains out down here."

"Won't you sit down, Jeannie?" I asked her.

"I'm too nervous and jumpy, dear. Whenever I impose on people, I get like this. I've got the bus schedule and all, and then I thought, oh, what the hell, I wanted to see that McGee guy again and never did. A girl sometimes has to be brassy or settle for nothing, right?"

I looked at Meyer. He was wearing a very strange expression. I handed Jeannie her drink and said, "Sometimes a girl gets brassy at just exactly the right time, and she gets invited on a private cruise. What would you say to that?"

"Aboard this wonderful ship! Wow! I'd say yes so fast—"

"HOLD IT!" Meyer roared, startling her. He trotted over to her and with raised finger backed her over to a chair. She sat down on command, staring up at him with her mouth open.

"I am going to ask you some very personal questions, Mrs. Dolan."

"What's the *matter* with you, huh?"

"Have you been in a lot of emotional turmoil lately?"

"Me? Turmoil? Like what?"

"Are you at a crisis point in your life?"

"Crisis? I'm just trying to get myself a plain, ordinary, divorce-type divorce."

"Mrs. Dolan, do you feel like a pathetic little bird with a busted wing who has fluttered aboard, looking for patience, understanding, and gentleness and love which will make you well and whole again?"

She looked at me with wide, round eyes. "Does he get like this a lot, Travis?"

"Pay attention!" Meyer ordered. "How do you relate to your analyst?"

"Analyst? Shrink? What do I need one for? Chee! You need one, maybe."

"Are you in love?" he asked.

"This minute? Hmmm. I guess not. But I sort of usually am. And pretty often, I guess. I'm not a real serious kind of person. I'm just sort of dumb and happy."

"One more question, and I must ask you both this one."

"You answer him, honey," Jeannie said to me.

"Would either of you two happy people mind too much if I spend the next few weeks in Seneca Falls, New York?"

"Speaking for the two of us, Meyer, I can't think of a serious objection, really."

He trotted to the doorway to the rear deck and opened it. He picked up the two pieces of red luggage and set them inside the door, gave us a maniacal smile, and slammed the door and was gone.

Jeannie stood up and sipped frowningly at her drink. Then she looked at me. "McGee?"

"Yes, dear."

"Everybody I know is acting weirder all the time. Have you noticed that too?"

"Yes, I have. Meyer isn't often like that."

"It's pretty weird and pushy for me to barge in on you like this. I'm not like this, really."

"It does have engines."

"That's nice. But do you feel like you've been maneuvered into something you'd just as soon not do, huh?"

"The more I think about it, the better I like it."

She put her drink down and came over and gave me one quick, thorough, and enthusiastic kiss. "There! Now it's just a case of getting acquainted, huh? Want to start by helping me unpack?"

We carried the luggage back to the master stateroom. She asked me what Meyer had meant about her having a broken wing. I said he was one of the last of the great romantics. I said there used to be two. But now there was just the one left. The hairy one.

Read on for an excerpt from *The Scarlet Ruse*.

One

AFTER SEVEN YEARS of bickering and fussing, the Fort Lauderdamndale city fathers, on a hot Tuesday in late August, killed off a life style and turned me into a vagrant.

"Permanent habitation aboard all watercraft within the city limits is prohibited."

And that ordinance included everything and everybody from the Alabama Tiger aboard his plush *'Bama Gal*, running the world's longest floating houseparty, all the way down to the shackiest little old pontoon cottage snugged into the backwater mangroves.

It included Meyer, the hairy economist, living comfortably aboard his dumpy little cruiser, *The John Maynard Keynes*, low in the water with the weight of financial tomes and journals in five languages and chess texts and problems in seven.

It included me and my stately and substantial old barge-type houseboat, the *Busted Flush*. The edict caught me off balance. I had not thought I was so thoroughly imbedded in any particular environment that being detached would be traumatic. Travis McGee is not hooked by things or by places, I told myself.

But, by God, there had been a lot of golden days, a lot of laughter and happy girls. Moonrise and hard rains. Swift fish and wide beaches. Some gentle tears and some damned good luck.

Maybe that is what made the gut hollow, an old superstition about luck. Long long long ago I stepped on a round stone in darkness and fell heavily at the instant that automatic weapons' fire yellow-stitched the night where I had been standing six feet four inches tall and frangible. I had two souvenirs from that fall—an elbow abrasion and the round stone. I still had the half-pound stone after the elbow healed. I kept it in the side pocket of the twill pants. Then they leapfrogged two battalions of us forward by night to take pressure off some of our people who'd dug in on the wrong hill.

Our airplane driver didn't care for the attention he was getting and kept his air speed on the high side as he dumped our group. I came to the end of the static line with one hell of a snap, and there was such a sharp pain in my ankle I thought I'd earned another Heart. I pulled the shrouds around, landed on shale, favoring the right leg, rolled and unbuckled, unslung the piece, and listened to night silence before I felt my ankle. No ripped leather or wetness. Pain lessening. Then I missed the round rock. When the chute popped, the rock had popped the pocket stitches, and it had gone down the pant leg, rapping the ankle bone on the way out, hurting right through the oiled leather of the jump boots. And I felt at that moment a terrible anxiety. "My rock is lost. My luck is lost. Some bastard is sighting in on me right now."

Later I realized that I had made some bad moves during those next five days before they pulled us all back.

This was the same feeling. I'd clambered up onto the sundeck of the *Flush* so many mornings at first light and had looked out at my world from the vantage point of Slip F-18 and known who I was. True, the great panorama of the sky had been dwindled over the years by the highrise invasions. But it was my place. I'd taken the *Flush* out a hundred times and brought her back and tucked her, creaking and sighing, against the piers, home safe. Safe among her people and mine.

I guess there weren't enough of us, all told. The City Commissioners authorized a survey and found out there were sixteen hundred people living on boats within the city limits. That isn't much of a voting block in a place the size of Lauderdale. And boat people are not likely to act in unison anyway.

We'd all been pretending it would be voted down, but they made it unanimous.

So all day Wednesday, little groups formed, re-formed, moved around, broke up, joined up again aboard the watercraft at Bahia Mar.

Meyer lectured an embittered audience aboard the *'Bama Gal*, standing on the cockpit deck amid a decorative litter of young ladies, quaffing Dos Equis, spilling a dapple of suds onto his black chest pelt.

"They say we have added to the population density. Let

us examine that charge. Ten years ago perhaps a thousand of us lived aboard cruisers and houseboats. Now there are six hundred additional. During those ten years, ladies and gentlemen, how many so-called living units have appeared in this area? Highrise, town houses, tract houses, mobile homes? They were constructed and trucked in and slapped together and inhabited without thought or heed to the necessary water supply, sewage disposal, schools, roads, police and fire protection. All services are now marginal."

"Fiffy thousand more shore people, maybe, huh?" said Geraldine, mistress of the old *Broomstick*.

"They say we have created sewage disposal problems," Meyer intoned. "Doubtless a few of the live-aboard people are dumb and dirty, emptying slop buckets into the tide. But for the majority of us, we have holding tanks, we use shoreside facilities, we want clean water because we live on the water. Thousands upon thousands of transient cruisers and yachts and houseboats stop at the area marinas every year. Hundreds of millions of dollars' worth of marine hardware, paying a high ticket for docking privileges and bringing ashore a lot of out-of-town spending money. And we all know, we have all seen, that it is the transient watercraft which cause a sewage disposal problem. They do not live here. They take the easiest way out. They do not give a damn. But will the City Commissioners pass a law saying transients cannot stay aboard transient boats? Never! Those transients are keeping this corner of Florida green, my friends."

He was applauded. Yay! We would march on City Hall. They would see the error of their ways.

But Johnny Dow put the whole thing in perspective. He

cleared his throat and spat downwind, turned away from
the rail and said, "*Ad valorem*, goddamnit!"

"Speak American," said one of the Tiger's play-girls.

"They hate us. Them politicals. You know what they
make their money on. They come from the law and real
estate and selling lots and houses. *Ad valorem*. We not putting dime one in their pockets. They drivin' past seeing
folks live pretty free, not needing them one damn bit, and
they get scalded. We're supposed to have property lines and
bushes and chinch bugs and home improvement loans. Jealous. They all nailed down with a lot of crap they don't like
and can't get loose of. So here we are. Easy target. Chouse
us the hell out of town forever and they don't have to see us
or think about us. Figure us for some kind of parasite.
Scroom, ever' damn ass-tight one of them. Can't win this
one, Meyer. We're too dense, and we make sewage. Easy
target. Neaten up the city. Sweep out the trash. *Ad valorem*."
He spat again, with good elevation and good distance, and
stumped across the deck and down the little gangway and
off into the blinding brightness of noontime.

Meyer nodded approvingly. "Scroom," he murmured.
The end of an era.

We walked together back to the *Flush* and went aboard.
We sat in the lounge, frowning and sighing.

Meyer said, "I saw Irv. He said something can be worked
out."

"Something can always be worked out. Sure. If a man
wants to live aboard a boat, something can be worked out.
If he can pay the ticket. A man could buy a condominium
apartment right over there in that big hunk of ugly and
make it his legal and mailing address and stay there one

night a month and aboard all the other nights. Can something be worked out for all the people who get hit by the new law?"

"Hardly."

"Then it isn't going to be the same, old friend. And do we want any part of it, even if I could afford the ticket?"

"You short again?"

"Don't look at me like that."

"You in the confetti business? You make little green paper airplanes?"

"I have had six months of my retirement in this installment, fella."

He beamed. "You know, you look rested. Good shape too. Better and better shape this last month, right?"

"Getting ready to go to work, which I seem to remember telling you."

"You *did*! *You did!* I remember. That was when I asked you if you would help an old and dear friend and you said no thanks."

"Meyer, damnit, I—"

"I respect your decision. I don't know what will happen to Fedderman. It's just too bad."

I stared at him with fond exasperation. A week ago he had tried to explain Hirsh Fedderman's unusual problem to me, and I had told him that it was an area I knew absolutely nothing about.

Meyer said, "We have thirty days of grace before we have to move away, boat and baggage. I just thought it would be a good thing to occupy your mind. And I told Hirsh I knew somebody who maybe could help out."

"You got a little ahead of yourself, didn't you?"

He sighed. "So I have to make amends. I'll see what I can do by myself."

"Stop trying to manipulate me."

"What are you talking about?"

"Take a deep breath and say it. If it's what you want, take a deep breath and say it."

"What should I say?"

"Take a wild guess."

"Well . . . Travis, would you please come with me to Miami and listen to my old friend Hirsh Fedderman and decide if you want to take on a salvage job?"

"Because you ask me so nicely, yes."

"But then why was it no before?"

"Because I had something else shaping up."

"And it fell through?"

"Yesterday. So today I need Fedderman, maybe."

"He is a nervous ruin. He's waiting for the roof to fall in on him. If it would be okay, how about this afternoon? I can phone him?"

Two

FEDDERMAN ASKED US not to arrive until quarter after five, when both the female clerks in his tiny shop would be gone for the day. I put Miss Agnes, my Rolls-Royce pickup, in a parking lot two blocks from his store. He was in mainland Miami, a dozen blocks from Biscayne and about three doors from the corner of Southwest Eleventh Street.

There was a dusty display window, with a steel grill padlocked across it. Gold leaf, peeling, on plate glass, said ornately "FEDDERMAN STAMP AND COIN COMPANY." Below that was printed "RARITIES."

Meyer tried the door, and it was locked. He knocked and peered into the shadowy interior and said, "He's coming."

I heard the sound of a bolt and a chain, and then a bell dingled when he opened the door and smiled out and up at us. He was a crickety little man, quick of movement, quick to smile, bald rimmed with white, a tan, seamed face, crisp white shirt, salmon-pink slacks.

Meyer introduced us. Fedderman smiled and bobbed and shook hands with both hands. He locked the door and led us back past dim display cases to the small office in the rear. There was bright fluorescence in the office and in the narrow stock room beyond the office. Fedderman sat behind his desk. He smiled and sighed. "Why should I feel better?" he asked. "I don't know if anybody can do anything. The whole thing is impossible, believe me. It couldn't happen. It happened. I can't eat. I can't sleep. I can't sit still or stand still since I found out. Mr. McGee, whatever happens, I am glad Meyer brought you to hear this crazy story. Here is—"

I interrupted him. "Mr. Fedderman, I try to recover items of value which have been lost and which cannot be recovered by any other means. If I decide to help you, I will risk my time and expenses. If I make a recovery of all or part of what you have lost, we take my expenses off the top and split the remainder down the middle."

He nodded, looking thoughtful. "Maybe it wouldn't fit perfect, because what is lost isn't mine. I understand. Let me tell you."

"Go slow because I don't know a thing about stamps and coins."

He smiled. "So I'll give you a shock treatment." He took a desk-top projector with built-in viewing screen from a shelf and put it on his desk and plugged it in. He opened a desk drawer and took out a metal box of transparencies and fitted it into the projector. He turned off the light and projected the first slide onto the twelve-by-fifteen-inch ground-glass viewing area.

A block of four stamps filled the screen. They were deep blue. They showed an old-timey portrait of George Washington. The denomination was ninety cents.

"This was printed in 1875," Fedderman said. "It is perhaps the finest block of four known, and one of the very few blocks known. Superb condition, crisp deep color, full original gum. It catalogs at over twelve thousand dollars, but it will bring thousands more at auction."

Click. The next was a pair of stamps, one above the other. A four-cent stamp. Blue. It pictured three old ships under sail, over the legend "Fleet of Columbus."

"The *only* known vertical pair of the famous error of blue. Only one sheet was printed in blue instead of ultramarine. In ultramarine this pair would be worth . . . twenty-five dollars. This pair catalogs at nine thousand three hundred and will bring fifteen at auction. The top stamp has one pulled perf and a slight gum disturbance. The bottom stamp has never been hinged, and it is superb. Quite flawless."

Click. Click. Click. A couple of crude bears holding up an emblem, with "Saint Louis" printed across the top of the stamps and "Post Office" printed across the bottom. A block of six brownish, crude-looking five-cent stamps showing Ben Franklin. There were no rows of little holes for tearing them apart. A twenty-four-cent stamp printed in red and blue, showing an old airplane, a biplane, flying upside down. And about a dozen others, while Fedderman talked very large numbers.

He finished the slide show and turned the bright overhead lights back on. He creaked back in his swivel chair.

"Crash course, Mr. McGee. I've showed you nineteen

items. I've bought them for a client over the past fifteen years. Right now there is another twenty thousand to spend. I am looking for the right piece. Another classic. Another famous piece."

"Why does he want them?" I asked.

Fedderman's smile was small and sad. "What has he put into these pieces over fifteen years? A hundred and eighty-five thousand. Plus my fee. What do I charge for my time, my advice, all my knowledge and experience and contacts? Ten percent. So let's say he has two hundred and three thousand, five hundred dollars in these funny little pieces of paper? I could make two phone calls, maybe only one, and get him three hundred and fifty thousand. Or if I spent a year liquidating, feeding them into the right auctions, negotiating the auction house percentage, he could come out with a half million."

Meyer said, "As the purchasing power of currencies of the world erodes, Travis, all the unique and the limited-quantity items in the world go up. Waterfront land. Rare books and paintings. Heirloom silver. Rare postage stamps."

"Classic postage stamps," Fedderman said, "have certain advantages over that stuff. Portability. One small envelope with a stiffener to prevent bending, with glassine interleafs for the mint copies, you can walk around with a half million dollars. These classics, you can sell them in the capital cities of the world, cash money, no questions. Well, some questions for these items because all the old timers like me, we know the history, which collections they've been in over the years—Hines, West, Brookman, Weil. We know when they changed hands and for how much. For each item here there is a certificate from the Philatelic Foundation saying it is genuine. The disadvantage is they are fragile. They've got to be perfect. A little crease, a little wrinkle, it would break your heart how much comes off the price. These, they never get touched with a naked finger. Stamp tongs if they ever have to be touched. They are in a safety deposit box."

Meyer encouraged Hirsh to tell me how he operated. It was intriguing and simple. He and any new client would take out a lock box set up to require both signatures and the presence of both parties before it could be opened. He used the First Atlantic Bank and Trust Company, four blocks from his store. When he made an acquisition, he and the client would go to the bank and put it in the box. The reason was obvious—as soon as Fedderman explained it to me. He made a formal legal agreement with each client. If at any time the client wanted to get out from under, Hirsh Fedderman would pay him a sum equal to the total investment plus five percent per year on the principal amount invested. Or, if the client desired, he could take over the investment collection himself, at which point the agreement became void.

"It's just to make them feel safe is all," Fedderman said. "They don't know me. They don't know if the stamps are real or forgeries. I started it this way a long time ago. I've never closed one out the way it says there in the agreement. But some have been closed out, sure. There was one closed out six years ago. About fifty thousand he had in it. I got together with the executor, and we auctioned the whole thing through Robert Siegel Auction Galleries, and a very happy widow got a hundred and forty thousand."

"They can get big money that easily?" I asked.

Fedderman looked at me with kindly contempt. "Mr. McGee, any year maybe twenty-five millions, maybe fifty millions go through the auction houses all over the world. Maybe more. Who knows? Compared to the stock exchanges, very small potatoes. But if the merchandise was available, the stamp auctions would be twice as big. Three times. That is because shrewd men know what has happened to classic merchandise during forty years of inflation. They'll buy all they can find. You put money in a Swiss bank, next year it's worth five percent less. The same money in a rarity, it *has* to be five percent more because the money is worth less, and the demand adds more percent. So in true rarities these days, the increment, it's fifteen to twenty percent per year."

"How many clients do you have right now?"

"Only six. This one and five more. Average. Sometimes ten, sometimes three."

"How much do you invest in a given year?"

He shrugged. "Last year, over five hundred thousand."

About the Author

JOHN D. MACDONALD was an American novelist and short-story writer. His works include the Travis McGee series and the novel *The Executioners,* which was adapted into the film *Cape Fear.* In 1962 MacDonald was named a Grand Master of the Mystery Writers of America; in 1980 he won a National Book Award. In print he delighted in smashing the bad guys, deflating the pompous, and exposing the venal. In life he was a truly empathetic man; his friends, family, and colleagues found him to be loyal, generous, and practical. In business he was fastidiously ethical. About being a writer, he once expressed with gleeful astonishment, "They pay me to do this! They don't realize, I would pay them." He spent the later part of his life in Florida with his wife and son. He died in 1986.